THE PERFECT CANDIDATE

A 13th Boy Mystery
Book 1 of Finding Cindy
(Revised Edition)

Michael Owen Luke

ISBN: 978-0994078131

Published by The Write Luke, P.O. Box 684, Pinawa, MB,
R0E1L0, Canada. This edition published June 2018

The following books in the Finding Cindy saga are also available:

The Morning Light Conspiracy, Book 2 of Finding Cindy

The Murder House, Book 3 Part 1 of Finding Cindy

Finding Cindy, Book 4: The Final Chapter.

Also by Michael Owen Luke, writing as M. O. Luke:

Some Great Enterprise, a Science Fiction Novel

Great SF Stories You've Never Read

For Stephanie, and Jimmy and Betty.

For the stories that are out there, floating just out of reach, or, maybe, sometimes, when the moon is right and the wind appropriate, close enough so you can hear them breath, daring you to grasp them, pull them down, carefully, prudently, making sure their colour doesn't fade, and fix them to the page, so all can enjoy their bright sparkle and mysterious life.

Prologue

May 1965

His friend had told him of her travel plans, how she would be coming down this narrow stretch of highway early this morning, driving alone. Now he lay in wait beside the road, in the first line of trees, watching. He was excited thinking of how carefully he had prepared for this moment. He had selected the tree patiently, eyeing them until he found one that was thick enough and long enough for his purpose yet of a size that he could manage using only saw and chains.

He had loved her once, of course he had, with all his heart and soul, but then she had betrayed him and now she must pay, there was no doubt in his mind about that, no hesitation at all over what he was planning to do. As he waited for her headlights to show up in the dark, he thought back again to how he had got everything ready for her, how carefully he had arranged his deadly trap.

The day he felled the tree he dropped his tools off in the weeds beside the road then parked the red 1946 Dodge Power Wagon a mile away, down a dirt side road that quickly petered out. He had walked back down the twisting, narrow highway to the work site like someone out for a walk. That time of year there was little traffic and few to wonder what he was doing in the middle of nowhere, but he was cautious even so. He meant to murder someone and he meant to get away with it.

After he'd cut the pine to length and trimmed the branches, he struggled to put the length of chain on, working it under the log. Only on his third attempt was he able to make a gap under the trunk big enough that he could drag the chain under it. He wrapped the chain twice around the log and then locked it in place by hammering in spikes through the links. Then he'd brought the Power Wagon round, driving it down through the ditch and then turning and backing into the beginning of the forest, finally securing the free end of the chain to the rear of the truck. He used the Dodge to pull the log slowly along the side of the road until he had positioned it close to where he needed it. He manoeuvred it carefully with the hardy vehicle so that it was perpendicular to the road and sufficiently hidden in the weeds fringing it that no one could possibly notice it. It was just beneath the brow of a hill that twisted up towards the top and then slid right and down, then left. Afterwards he used a rake along the shoulder where the log had been dragged, erasing the marks it had made.

It was growing dark by the time he finished. He put the tools into the truck and then drove the Dodge home. He was excited by what he was about to do and worried only that his friend's information might be wrong.

At 4 in the morning he got carefully out of bed, put on his clothes including a jacket and heavy work gloves, and slipped out into the early morning. He started the truck and drove slowly into the dark of the forest along the lonely road until he came to the spot he had chosen. For a moment he panicked when he failed to spot the log with his flashlight. But he moved the truck so that the headlights shone down into the ditch and there it was. There was no hint of sunrise yet, the sky still black, the stars impossibly sharp overhead. It was too early in the season for insects, but frogs were making a racket nearby.

He backed the Dodge into the ditch on the other side of the road, then paid out the cable from the winch across the tarmac and fastened it to the chain attached to the log. He winched the log into position across the road, blocking both narrow lanes, took one last look at it then unshackled it. He drove the Dodge well down the road and into the side track, shut it down, and walked back towards the log. He took up a position in the fringes of the forest where he could see the road but not be spotted.

Now, as he watched, he thought of how it would be. She would have a second perhaps at the most to notice it, to understand, as she came over the brow of the hill. He wanted her to have that time, time enough to know what was going to happen but insufficient to avoid her fate. Perhaps she would think about what she had done, or perhaps not, but in either case she would be dead. Yes, yes he had loved her once, loved her as deeply as life itself, but no longer. Now he wanted her only dead.

High overhead he heard honking, the birds themselves invisible. Nothing else moved. Now in the distance there was the soft glow of headlights, disappearing, intensifying, then disappearing again as the vehicle moved round curves, into dips and up inclines. Gradually they brightened, getting nearer and he heard the first sound of tires and engine noise. He crouched down now. He felt a surge of gratitude towards his friend. He had been very helpful and urged him to act, to seize his chance. He felt a thrill go through him as he thought of her sitting in her car, clutching the steering wheel, coming closer and closer, unaware of how soon she would be made to pay for what she had done. The headlights were bright now as the car neared the final bend and then dimmed as she mounted the hill. Then they were intense as the vehicle came down the final slope and around the last twist in the road.

1

THE INVITATION

To those who knew him as a cop, Harry seemed a good guy, a respected public servant who did his job well and who was reassuring to have around. I had a rather different opinion of him of course. To be honest, I hardly knew the man at all, despite his involvement in three of the most momentous years of my life, and I actually met him, face to face, only twice. Yet I knew something about him that nobody else did: that he was a murderer. Not that he ever touched either of his two victims himself, apart from what he did initially, to start it all off. No, he was a murderer by proxy, using trickery and manipulation to get others to do his dirty work. Forty years ago, it was his best friend. In the summer of 2005 it was me.

Of course I hadn't any intention of doing anything that would lead to someone's death, but Harry had seen how it all might unfold, had planned it out carefully, then set it up, wound me up and pointed me in the right direction. Unknowingly I had acted exactly as he had hoped I would, and I loathed him for his clever malice. So, as I looked down onto the closed lid of Harry's coffin, deep in the ground, I had every reason to despise the man for his patient hatred and cold cunning. Yet, because of what he had done for me, his reward I suppose for my doing what he wanted me to, I knew that I owed him a debt that I could never repay. And Harry being Harry, there was of course a message, this one delivered by his lawyer, who was also at the funeral. And I thought how appropriate it was that it should end with a message, because of course that was how it all began.

2005, May

Subject: GE Locomotive
Date: Sun, 22 May 2005 00:49:59 CST
From: <YDKMAABIKY@hottestmail.com>
To: Colin.therman@sympatico.ca
Dear Mr. Therman;
On Friday June 10, CP 8536, a GE AC4400 CW, will be
waiting for you at 12:00 noon where the track crosses the trail
to Bear Lake. This is a one-time opportunity to ride the rails for
a short distance in the cab of a modern diesel locomotive. The
engine will wait for precisely thirty minutes, after which it will
leave. This opportunity will not be repeated. Should you wish
to take advantage of this once in a lifetime offer, rest assured
that you incur no obligation as a result and no fee will be
charged for this chance to experience the sights and sounds
from the cab of this exciting locomotive. Accept this invitation,
or regret it forever.
June 10, 12:00 noon, Bear Lake Trail.
391 4425

I didn't know it at the time but this was Harry's opening move.
Of course, I was unaware it was a move, opening or otherwise,
that there would be many more to come, or that Harry even
existed. All I did know was that I had an email in front of me
that was intriguing but also ominous. The intriguing part is
easy: I'm a train fan after all, so it would be hard to find
anything more enticing than this offer of a ride in the cab of a
locomotive. But that was also the ominous part because I knew
damn well that CP doesn't allow members of the public to take
rides in their freight trains. And that meant that the email was
either a hoax, which raised a whole set of disturbing questions,
or, if real, that whoever sent it had gone to a great deal of

trouble, and had considerable clout. But why go to all that trouble for me? And why was the email anonymous? The sender knew who I was but wouldn't tell me who he or she was. Why make an offer he must have known I would find very enticing but be coy about his name? Why hide? What did he want from me in return, I wondered. He assured me that there was no obligation but I didn't believe it. He wanted something, presumably something he couldn't come right out and ask me for. Instead he wanted to build up a debt on my part, so that I might have no choice but to return the favour in some way.

There were other things wrong with the email as well. The final sentence was alarming: accept or regret forever! That was pretty heavy! Finally, what the hell was the meaning of that seven digit number at the end. I thought at first it was a telephone number, perhaps a clever way for the sender to identify himself, but although I used every area code I could think of with it, I got the same response each time, telling me that the number could not be reached as dialled and asking me to check the number and try again, in that trying so hard to be patient, long suffering voice the telephone company uses. I wish I had kept at it, I really do, but at the time it didn't seem all that important, and I let it go.

I knew there was really only one way of finding out if the invitation was for real or not and that would be to go along to the trail on June 10, but I was sufficiently unsure of myself to want a second opinion. That's why I phoned my lawyer and invited her to lunch at Jennifers. I know that sounds pretentious, as if I were some big-shot corporate guy with lawyers at my beck and call, but nothing could be further from the truth. I'm just an ordinary guy with a modest consulting company I run out of my house. Now and then I need contract wording checked over and I've found Alex – Alexandria Yeou is her full name – to be fast and effective.

If it's a sin to lust after your lawyer then I guess I'm a sinner. Even worse, I'm happily married – and not to the lawyer - which makes me even more of a sinner I suppose. But then I never did believe in sin, or sinners for that matter. Evil now, deep corrosive evil, well that's another matter entirely, one that, unknown to me at the time, I was to become deeply familiar with over the course of the year.

Of course people don't believe in evil any more, think it's a thing of the past or something that happens only in far off distant places, like the killing fields of Cambodia or the genocide of Darfur. Evil is so sharp edged, unequivocal, black and white. Today we prefer nuances and underlying causes. But evil brushes by us every day. As you will see, it's a matter merely of paying attention.

Evil, or sin for that matter, were the furthest things from my mind that day as I parked in front of the restaurant and got out of the car. There's a story behind Jennifers that proves that the right business idea and the right kind of energy can work wonders and make a success even literally on the foundation of a whole series of failures. Ice cream bar, burger joint, video arcade place, all had been tried and shortly failed. The businesses had been doomed to short, tourist length summer seasons, and had never made enough money to interest anyone for very long. Then along came Chef Josef with his European ideas, his imaginative decorative touches and innovative menu concept and before you could catch your breath it was a success, rebuilt, expanded, booming, with a patio for summer use, and a formula of simple meals, bargain priced, with exotic touches.

Chef Josef met me at the door and told me that Alex was already seated. We chatted briefly about the past season and then he showed me to our table, set for two in a cozy nook tucked around to the side.

Alex is by any one's standards an attractive woman, only average height, but with a curvy body and a striking face with long, dark hair that most of the time she keeps in a pony tail. The challenge with Alex is to have an innocent conversation. She's very clever, she's very business like, and she's sexy as hell. She's the kind of woman who makes your skin tingle when she enters the room and does something that makes it difficult to breath. She envelops you in an invisible mist of fairy dust. To make it worse, she's a flirt, physically and verbally, so it's not too surprising that people come to the wrong conclusion. Business lunch, yea right, roll of the eyes, nod, nod, wink, wink.

Alex looked up with those intoxicating green eyes of hers as I sat down, smiled, and put her hand briefly on mine. "I've ordered," she said. "Goulash, the special, a glass of Cabernet."

"I do like a woman who knows my mind," I told her.

She smiled modestly. "What's to figure? Men's minds are so ... simple!"

"Alex, you know I trust you.."

"Oh, if only there was more sizzle in our relationship than that! I was hoping for something a little more romantic than trust," she hinted. She looked at me in an inviting way as if to suggest I was an idiot for not letting things venture beyond mere trust.

But I had little patience today for games with sexual overtones. I think she did it with me just to stay in practice, knowing she was perfectly safe, but today I just wanted to show her the e-mail and get her opinion. Still, when she leaned forward and looked intensely at me the effect was arousing and I won't pretend that a few erotic thoughts didn't cross my mind.

"You've got that penis look," she said, with satisfaction.

"The goulash is excellent," I responded, with what I thought was stunning self control.

"Ooh, I'd love to give that lovely wife of yours something to worry about, but I can see it's not going to be today! So what is it that forced you to the unusual gesture of paying for my lunch?"

"I got this yesterday." I handed her a printout of the email.

Alex read it over carefully then set the message down on the table and looked up at me. "But why does it need a lawyer?" she asked.

I smiled at her. "It's a wonderful invitation," I responded, "but you know CP Rail doesn't allow members of the public to ride in their locomotives."

"Ah. So you think it's a hoax?"

"I hope not, but it could be. Either that or a very interesting offer indeed! And I can't help wondering, why me? Why make that offer to me?"

"Well, whoever sent it obviously knows something about you – that you like trains," Alex said.

I wondered what else they knew about me, how much sniffing around they'd done.

"Usually when someone asks you to do something in complicated ways, it's not a good sign," she continued. "Probably means you'd never do it if you were asked straight out. A trick in other words, or worse. So this guy wants to lure you out to someplace fairly isolated...."

"And what? Bump me off?"

"Who knows! That's the point! Why stick your head into a noose voluntarily? But anyhow, as I was saying, if it's good stuff they just ask straight out. No junk about giving them your credit card number so they can charge the duty on your valuable prize. Bottom line – forget it. But since it's a GE locomotive, well I guess you're going to go, right, and this whole expensive lunch is just a waste of money on your part, or did you get me out here just to have another look at my sexy body?"

"Well, there is that. Always worth the cost of a meal!"

"Oooh, gallantry! But just think of how much more you could have!"

"If what – if I followed your advice?"

"Some day," she said, "some day you'll look back and regret all these missed chances you had."

I smiled at her. "The thing is, Alex, I want you to go with me."

She laughed and shook her head.

"You have to come," I said. "After all, I need someone to keep a level head!"

She shrugged, then sighed, as if knowing it was pointless to continue to argue with me, but that she had to be true to her profession. "And why did he choose you I wonder? He didn't select you just because he can hook you with trains. There's some other reason he chose you. He wants you in a position where you have to do a favour for him, and he can't or won't just come out and ask you. Nope, he has to play games and snare you with whatever it takes to hook you and he's found trains. And the questions are: why did he choose you, and what does he want?"

"Maybe he heard how I got my hiking boots back," I suggested

"Hiking boots?"

"I never told you about the hiking boots?"

She just looked at me patiently.

"They were stolen from my car one day while it was parked beside the road to the solid waste site. I was out blueberry picking and these two idiots broke the window, pulled the trunk release and took off with the hiking boots, that's all they took – all that was there. I liked those boots, they'd been up

Mount Washington, up Mount Katadin, all along the White Mountains, were nicely broken in, Vibram soles, old fashioned ones, real leather everywhere, red laces. And you see I saw who did it, well saw the vehicle, recognized the blue and white half ton with its split rear window, the old fashioned kind."

I finished my meal, the waiter took away the plate and then brought the deserts. Today it was Nanaimo bars. I prefer the little puff pastry things they have sometimes.

"After I got the glass replaced, I cruised around town until I saw the truck and then I just followed them home. So now I knew where to go."

"You didn't trespass to get them back!"

"They were my boots! Of course I did. I waited until after midnight and walked into their garage – the back door was unlocked - turned on the light and they were just hanging there on a hook, brazen as could be, like a trophy displayed. Ass holes! So I put an old pair of sneakers I'd got from the dump in their place and walked off with my own property."

"Jesus, Colin, that was stupid!"

"Don't agree. They're lucky I didn't smash a window on their truck to go along with taking my boots back. So what I figure is maybe whoever it is that sent that email heard about it and concluded I was someone he needed."

Alex laughed. "Somehow, Colin, I don't think so. And in any case, if he wants you to do something, why not ask? And I suspect he's not after getting some boots back."

"I would really like you to come with me. What are you doing on June 10"

"Why did you invite me to lunch if you are so set on disregarding my advice, that's what I want to know?"

"Isn't that standard procedure with clients? Seriously, I hoped you could talk me out of it, but it seems your powers of persuasion are less potent than I suspected."

"You're just too thick headed to respond properly."

"That must be it."

"June 10th" I prompted.

"I hate to disappoint you, but on June 10th I've got to go to some god forsaken hiking trail in the bush with some lug who wants to go for a ride on a train engine."

"Ah! Must be some lug."

She smiled, thanked me for the lunch, said ta, ta, gave Josef a wave, and sent ripples of lust through the dining room as she strode out to her car, got in and drove away.

I sat looking at the email and thought about what she'd said. Was I really stupid to want to go to the rendezvous? She obviously thought so, but I just couldn't see the harm in it, didn't see what I had to lose. If it was a practical joke, well so what? I looked at the number at the bottom again. What was that? It had to be significant yet it wasn't a telephone number, at least unless it was scrambled in some way. I had a feeling the sender didn't intend it to be difficult or challenging. No, he wanted to hide his meaning just a little, to heighten its impact when I figured it out. So what could it be? Not a telephone number, then what? Perhaps it was a code of some kind, but if so, what? Stop playing fucking games! I thought to myself, but my annoyance did nothing to solve the mystery.

I paid for the meals and got into the car. Outside it was sunny and cheerful, but I was angry now. Angry at being manipulated like this, angry that the sender wouldn't tell me straight out what he wanted, angry that he was being clever. I knew that with or without Alex I would show up at the Bear Lake trail at the appointed time – it just seemed the right thing to do and there was more to it than satisfying my desire to ride in a locomotive: I wanted to find out what the sender was up to, who he was and why he was doing this. Alex was right to worry about the motives behind it, what the consequences might be, but at that point I wasn't too concerned. I didn't know that it would be the first step in a long chain that would eventually take me where I didn't want to be and that someone would die because of it. She worried that there would be a price to pay and that it would be a big one. As it turned out, she was right about that but even she didn't realize how big the price would be.

2

A LONG WAY FROM ERIE

It was June and farm rigs were moving on the highway, the fields were freshly ploughed black and those high, big-wheeled fertilizer machines were bouncing along, like huge tall spiders. Farming always fascinates me, the activity, the changes in the fields, the equipment, but I never wanted to do it. In gardening, after a promising start with roses, my green thumb had abandoned me and I eventually surrendered to the marauding white tail deer and hunkered down to just growing grass and weedy grass at that, badly enough to irritate my neighbours.

I stopped at Dorothy Lake and walked along my favourite strip of sand. The water was high behind the Seven Sisters dam after spring run off and most of the beach was underwater. Geese indignantly and loudly protested my presence but moved off into the water and honked their way some distance off shore. I dipped my hand into the lake. As I expected, it was still numbingly cold. The long flat stretch of water, barely ruffled by a slight breeze, extended half a mile or so to a few small unpopulated islands beyond which lay the opposite shore. I was the only person on the beach, a situation that would persist until school ended and then the city crowds would start to bring their noise, their boats, their juke boxes, their crowds, their garbage. What I often thought of as my beach and my picnic table would soon no longer be mine.

After looking around once more, I got back in the car and resumed my journey.

The road through Whiteshell Provincial Park is narrow and twisty. In the summer, it's shared not only by the usual vehicular traffic but joggers, bicyclists, people with dogs, hikers, slow moving RVs, trucks towing boats, and occasionally a bicycle outing, complete with safety cars front and back. This early in June, however, there were few other vehicles on the road and nothing else except deer to watch out for. I always enjoyed driving here, such a pleasant change from the click the cruise control on and hold the steering wheel straight for the next hour of the major roads. It was a joy to power nimbly and sure footedly around corners and up twisty bends. In the Whiteshell the land lies at the transition between shield and prairie and bogs alternate with sudden rock outcroppings.

Alex arrived in her own car just moments after I parked in the dirt area just off the tarmac and got out of the car. She was wearing a long tan leather coat, grey slacks and hikers, and her dark hair was tied in a long pony tail. It was 11:50. There were a couple of decrepit looking picnic tables, two wooden outhouses marked men and women and a sign.

The sign said Bear Lake hiking trail. Round trip 2.5 km. Supposedly the spot had been a favourite place to stop long ago when this highway was the main route across the country. I could imagine the old vehicles chugging along the twisty narrow road and stopping to picnic on a hot summer afternoon. Today the Trans Canada Highway lies further south, a straight, level, smooth, four-lane corridor leading east and west.

"Stay here for a second" I said, and set off down the narrow ruts that led through the trees beside the sign. Just before I came to where the trail twisted left and allowed a view of the tracks I could hear an engine throbbing gently and a moment or two later could smell the sweet smell of the exhaust. I turned back and retraced my steps to the car.

"It's there all right," I told Alex. "Stay here and give me an hour. If you haven't heard from me by then, call the cops!"

"I was hoping it was a stupid joke," she said. "Colin, don't get on it or anything dumb like that." She looked at me sternly. "Look it at, OK, talk to the driver, but don't get on board."

"Honey, if they let me on that thing, I'm going to get on it. Don't fret!"

Not fretting isn't her style. You'd think as a lawyer she'd have given it up long ago, but she relapsed into resigned silence and got back in her car, locked the doors and glared at me.

I set off at a run this time, back down the narrow rutted trail to the road bed. They'd taken the second set of tracks up a few years back in a move I didn't understand – more traffic, fewer tracks wasn't an equation that made any sense to me - but the gravel bed on which the second set of rails had rested was still there. As I cleared the last line of trees, I saw the diesel sitting there, gleaming in its CP maroon paint scheme, the golden beaver herald bright in the morning sun. CP 8536. The nose door was open.

I'd never been this close to a working engine before, well not since I'd stood beside a steam engine as a child, a long past ago. The locomotive looked immense, standing there, throbbing. I could feel the slow beat of its engine through my feet. Was it the size of such machines that attracted me, their power, or just the idea of something than ran on rails, no steering needed, that could go as far as the track stretched?

Somehow I'd never thought the email would turn out to be real. I'd felt compelled to come along, it's true, yet I'd always doubted that it would amount to anything, yet here was the engine, waiting for me. It didn't make a whole lot of sense, but it was no dream. And I realized again that there was probably going to be a lot more to this business than just going for a ride in a locomotive, that there was danger here and things I wouldn't want to do.

I went up to the locomotive and touched the metal of the wide safety cab. It trembled gently beneath my hand, transmitting a faint suggestion of the immense engine working not far away. Even the ground beneath me seemed to echo softly to the slow beat of the 16 huge cylinders of the engine and the whirl of the cooling fans.

The General Electric AC4400 CW locomotive weighs 250 tons, is seventy six feet long and puts out four thousand four hundred horsepower. A single unit costs about 2 million dollars. This one was a long way from the Erie Pennsylvania plant where it was built. And it was definitely not the sort of working machine the general public was invited to board. Which is why I was surprised it was there, waiting for me, as promised in the e-mail. Why a locomotive, I wondered. Why me? Why now? And how was it arranged? Those were just the beginning of the whys that were to accumulate until finally, months later, the answers came, one by one.

I looked around a final time then pulled myself up onto the platform, and walked through the door and up the few steps into the cab. Inside it was quiet and still, with no sense of the brute strength idling not far away.

The engineer turned in his seat and handed over a brown envelope.

"Mr. Therman, I presume," he said. "I'm Arnie."

"Hi," I said breathlessly and reached out to shake his hand. For a moment I just stood taking it all in, the view through the twin windows ahead, the functional but comfortable seats, the control stand.

"Ever been in one of these before?" Arnie asked me.

I shook my head. "I love trains, though," I said, feeling I ought to let the man know I cared. "And this is my favourite locomotive."

"She's sweet all right," the engineer said. "Steady, powerful, real sweet. The engine beats slow but she beats strong as hell. This thing can lug a coal train single handed so long as we don't go upgrade any. And the AC just doesn't quit, never stalls and runs forever."

Sweet wasn't quite what I was thinking. I felt a strong urge to close the nose door and just head down the rails forever, never touch the real world again, well not outside the cab of this machine, ride it to the end of the world and on beyond.

I tore open the envelope and extracted the single piece of paper from it.

> Dear Mr. Therman. Glad you could join us. Assuming you got here on time, you've got about an hour before CP wants its engine back. I hope you enjoy the ride. Where you go is up to you, although it's mainly a question of going forward or going backward, but of course you're looking for something else now, the second step of this little adventure of ours. I'm sure you didn't expect to find out why I invited you here just like that! Don't think I should give you many clues though except to say it's visible from the track oh and to point out that the engine you're on at least isn't German.

I looked at my watch. It was ten after, so I assumed that meant I still had fifty minutes left. Presumably I was supposed to ask the engineer to take me somewhere. Being on tracks sort of limited the possibilities but what was I supposed to suggest? Well, fifty-fifty odds always struck me as pretty good and somehow I didn't think whoever was arranging this was trying to make the stuff hard, at least not yet. The train was pointing ahead so ahead I would go, back towards Whitemouth.

"Straight ahead," I said, pointing, and then, unable to help myself, "Engage!"

"Hate to tell you, but this thing doesn't do warp speed," Arnie said. "Like to take her yourself?

"Damn right!"

"Just notch that throttle there up a little. No danger of bogie shake with this load!"

I stood looking through the big windshield at the single track stretching ahead then curving gently right. The big diesel motor behind me sent a rhythmic muted throb through the insulation and isolation damping of the cab. Gingerly I moved the throttle to the right. The engine bellowed and the loco began to move smoothly forward. Into the unknown – well, I knew what was down the track, but not what I was looking for down the track. So far – trees, and telephone poles dragging their cables, up and down up and down all along the line.

"Must see a lot of trees on this job," I remarked.

The engineer laughed. "You'd be surprised what you see from a train. Trees, farms, water. People don't expect trains sometimes and you catch them doing weird things. Most of the time though you don't see many people down a track like this, away from the road much of the time."

The trees glided slowly past. I hoped whatever I was looking for wasn't small and inconspicuous, wasn't hidden away shyly among tree trunks because the wide right of way meant the trees were a long way away. What could be hidden down a railroad track? Why down a railroad track? Had to be something reasonably large to make it visible from a locomotive cab.

I upped the throttle, sending a brief plume of black smoke out of the stack.

"Don't get too confident up there," the engineer laughed at me.

There was a signal ahead. It was green. And beyond it a sign post, a dirt clearing, and a siding with a line of empty gondolas. It was hardly a busy scene, but already compared to the trees it seemed a relief. There was an old half ton parked at an angle half into the grass into which the gravel area petered out. I throttled back again and we went through it at a leisurely pace, almost ghosting through, the big pistons barely moving, the wheels turning slowly in the trucks, the six electric motors hardly working.

I was sure I must have missed it, whatever *it* was. The old truck? The empty wagons? The shed by the tracks? But none of them had triggered anything, certainly nothing about German. But just what did that mean exactly? And was it really a clue, or a red herring of some kind, a private joke perhaps?

More trees, a curve to the left, the rails gleaming briefly as the angle of the sun fell just right. There was a microwave tower jutting up spike like from the trees maybe a mile away, up ahead. Hydro had come down here and buried optical cable, their orange markers jutting up just off the ballast like strange bright trophies signalling its presence underground. Freight trains thousands of tons heavy, some over a mile long came down this line each day, moving east and west, while less than a hundred feet away a torrent of signals flashed silently and weightlessly at light speed in the same directions, with no noise, no shake, no rumble and growl, no diesel smoke, no thundering rails, no ties moving up and down with the hammering pressure of hundreds of loaded wheels. The old and the new economies were squeezed together here, sharing almost the same space, exploiting this thin corridor through trees and swamps, underbrush and rocks, a thin, engineered line through the natural chaos and untidiness of nature.

The engineer reached forward and sounded the horn, two long, one short, one long. We passed another signal, also green, and another track-side building, painted silver, festooned with doors. And a sign, Telford, marking another untidy sprawl of gravel. And an unmarked dirt crossing meandering somewhere into the trees. And a silver Audi, shimmering in the sun. I looked at it, looked away then suddenly back again. German, I thought. The train isn't German, but that car certainly is! Did something move just off to the left? I looked and thought I saw another vehicle, withdrawing, just a movement through the obscurity of trees but couldn't be sure.

"I think," I said, "this is where I get off."

The engineer throttled down and applied brakes with a short hiss of air, bringing the engine to a smooth, gentle halt.

"Thanks for the ride!" I said, "It's been a real thrill." I shook the engineer's hand, then climbed back down the steps, through the nose door and down from the front of the train.

The engineer blew the horn once and rumbled off. When the engine had gone, I turned and approached the car carefully. What was I supposed to do – break into it or what?

Its silver metallic paint work gleaming and polished, not a speck of dirt on it, the Audi A4 was foreign to the scene. This had to be what I was supposed to be doing! No one would just drive a car like this out here and abandon it. Yet at any moment I expected the arrival of a suspicious owner, nervous at my sniffing around the car like this.

First the locomotive I like, and now the car I like. It was far too neat and contrived not to be deliberate. What if I touched the car and the alarm went off. Who was to hear?

I walked all around the car. It was a 2.0 A-4, with 16 inch wheels. Nobody came out of the woods or down the dirt road to climb in it and drive off. And how was I supposed to get in?

Tentatively, nervously, I tried the door. To my astonishment it opened. I looked inside the vehicle, but there was no sign of personal things, no briefcase, no litter, no Kleenex box near the arm rest, or CDs scattered about. No one came running up demanding to know what I thought I was doing. I hesitated, then slid into the driver's seat and closed the door with a thunk. The keys dangled invitingly from the ignition. God damn it, I thought, he's arranged this too! I turned the ignition and the engine fired and the instruments came to life. Full I saw, and hardly any miles. The thing was practically brand new. And still no one came running out to protest.

It was becoming clearer and clearer that this was what I was supposed to do. I opened the glove compartment, hoping to find some clue to the identity of whoever it was that had arranged all this. I took out a leasing form. My jaw dropped when I read it. I was now the proud owner of a three-year, paid up leased vehicle. I couldn't make out the signature on the documents but there was a name printed on the form: Tim Surtowski. The name meant nothing to me. Whoever Tim was, he was no one I knew. A three-year lease just like that, a gift, for nothing, just for being here, for taking a train ride! What the hell was going on? Why was he doing this? What did he expect in return? Maybe I should just get out and walk away, hike back to Hansen Creek and the Bear Lake trail – it wasn't that far. Alex would probably come looking for me soon anyway and pick me up. Just get out and abandon this madness now, but even as I thought it I knew I wouldn't just walk away from this. Already I was hooked, intrigued by the audacity and imagination of whoever had arranged all this and curious to find out why. And I wanted to drive the damn car! I'd always hankered after one of these machines, looked enviously at any I saw on the road, admired them in parking lots and now this was mine, for a while at least, at no cost to me. No cost? I smiled ruefully. The fact is I didn't know yet what the cost was going to be, but I was pretty damn sure that there would be a cost involved, a price tag, even though it had been discretely removed. But one day it was going to be presented, and then what was I going to do?

There were other things in the glove compartment as well. An owner's manual, instructions on calling for roadside service, included in the lease, registration papers all made out, paid for, in my name but unsigned, and two 3.5 x 5 inch colour photographs of a weird brick building, taken from two slightly different perspectives.

Time to get out of here! I adjusted the black leather seats, fiddled with the steering wheel and mirrors, put the car in gear, gave the horn a brief toot and drove back towards the road.

This deep into the park the highway was rough, narrow and twisty, edged abruptly with wicked looking ditches on either side that I had no desire to get familiar with. But the car handled like a dream, quiet and steady on the pitching pavement and I felt as if I was on a grand adventure suddenly, in control.

I sped through the curves, over the narrow bridge across Hansen creek and was slowing down, ready to turn left into the Bear Lake parking area where I'd left Alex and my own car. There was a police cruiser there drawn up alongside our cars and instinctively I lifted my foot from the brake and pressed down on the gas again and sped past and around the bend and out of sight. A few hundred feet further on I made an awkward back and forth u-turn and drove past the parking area again, looking away. Alex wouldn't recognize the car, but she'd recognize me. I drove around the bend that put the parking area out of sight and turned left just before the bridge onto the dirt road that led briefly up to the starting point for the Francis Lake canoe route.

I got out of the car, locked it and walked back to Alex and the cruiser.

"Ah, there you are!" Alex said. "This is Corporal Simard. I asked him to keep an eye on us – just in case."

The corporal was tall and looked like someone you wouldn't want to get on the wrong side of. Big head, I thought.

Where do they find people with such big heads? His face was rough and pitted too, but smiling, obviously untroubled.

"Hi," he said, holding out his hand. He was in his thirties I estimated, and in good shape. His hand was firm and warm but dry.

"Corporal." I shook his hand and turned back to Alex. "Well, I had my train ride. I still don't know why, but it was certainly interesting. It's quite something riding one of those big beasts, up there in the cab. Pretty comfortable, too."

"How did you get back here?" Simard asked.

"Hitched a ride" I told him. "Engineer let me off at a clearing and I just stuck out my thumb."

"Hmm," he said, as if he knew I was lying. He gave me a level stare, started to say something else and then shrugged. "You should take up driving the trains, if you're so interested in them," the Corporal suggested.

I laughed and shook my head. "I don't think so. I'm pretty old for that now and training is pretty exacting I hear." I grinned to draw attention to the pun, but nobody bit. "Takes quite a while to learn to handle one of those things pulling a load. Anyhow, thanks for coming by Corporal but things are pretty much under control. I don't quite know what Alex thought was going to happen, but,"... I shrugged, "nothing has!"

"Make sure it stays that way," Simard said. "Got to get going. Nice seeing you Alex. Take care. You too Mr. Therman."

"Thanks John." Alex went with him to the car and waved as he drove off further into the park.

"What are you hiding Colin?" Alex demanded. "Pretty dumb move just showing up as if you materialized out of the trees! He knows you're up to something and he's going to turn around and come back again so let's just cool it," she said. "Tell me what's going on but don't get animated."

We sat down at the picnic table. The day was chilly suddenly, clouds covering the sun, and a breeze that was still laced with ice sprang up. "I've got a shiny silver Audi A-4 hidden up the road," I told her. "The engineer gave me this." I handed her the note I'd got in the locomotive. "The car was waiting there in a clearing, unlocked, keys in the ignition and my name on the papers with a paid-up three-year lease. When I saw it, I figured that was what the clue in the note was supposed to point me to."

Alex whistled.

Corporal Simard went by again. He tapped his horn. We waved.

"He knows," Alex said

"Sorry?"

"He can smell someone hiding something a mile away. He knows you were fobbing him off."

"I don't care what he thinks he knows. I don't want the police looking into why does a Mr. Colin Therman suddenly get offered fancy train rides, with CP Rail providing one of their newest engines, all spanking cleaned up for the occasion, and not only that but a brand-new Audi thrown in for good measure. What, they are going to wonder, has Mr. Therman been up to? And what are he and this high priced, busy as a bee lawyer doing hanging around in the middle of nowhere not exactly racking up billing hours?"

"But you're innocent. Whoops, what have I said! I mean you haven't done anything – we've even got paid up park passes so he can't report us to the park wardens!"

"Doesn't matter. It's not a good thing to have the police sniffing around. I wouldn't be surprised if he hasn't taken a little drive down the road where I stashed the car and is running the plates."

"I say it's a good thing if there is danger out there, danger you don't know about."

"Back to that are we. There's no danger, Alex! When are you going to get that through your PLH."

"PLH? That wouldn't be pretty little head, would it? Well it hadn't better be, or you can sock it you jerk. You lured me all the way into the wilderness then for what, if not to keep you out of trouble, hmm? Maybe it was to get you into trouble! Can't say that reassures me. Your name on a three-year lease? Can't say it reassures me at all. Why would anyone do that? There's probably a tracking device on the vehicle, just so whoever he is can keep close tabs on us."

"Well so what?" I said. "He probably already knows exactly who we are, where we live, our telephone numbers, our e-mail accounts and so forth. So what else is he going to learn?"

"But Colin, what is this guy trying to do? Why is he doing it? What's his motive? And why are you just doing whatever he wants, like a lamb, sure, yep, OK, right away? It's not smart Colin!"

"Since when has smart got anything to do with it? I'm enjoying this!" As I said it, I realized it was true. I *was* enjoying myself now. My earlier apprehension had lifted and now it did indeed seem like an adventure. "You need to loosen up." I told her.

"People don't hire loosened up lawyers, Colin! I'm not supposed to be loosened up. I'm supposed to be smart and suspicious and it's about time you were too, or you are going to get yourself in trouble. And I mean more trouble than the slight problem we've got now with three vehicles and two drivers."

"Let's see," I said. "I can solve that with a little calculus I think. Amazing how differential equations come in handy."

"Look, Colin. Why the hell did you drag me away from paying clients, feed me lunch, then lure me out into the middle of nowhere, force me to cool my heels surrounded by boring trees and go through the enormous excitement of having you ignore every single sensible word I say! What's the point?"

"The point, dear Alex is this. I want someone to know what is going on, every little thing about what is going on, just in case something does turn around and bite me. Someone who knows. Maybe there is a hook buried in this bait, a big nasty sharp one, just as you suspect, who knows, but if so I'm going to nibble carefully around it, if I can. And just in case something goes wrong, I have you! Besides I need someone to sweet talk the cops, stuff like that!"

"And what's to stop whatever may bite you from biting me as well?" She had her hands on her hips now and was looking very stern indeed.

"Apart from the fact that you're smart and suspicious whereas I'm gullible and unquestioning? Nothing, I suppose, it's just that it's a little harder to deal with two than one, that's all."

"Not to mention my being gorgeous and intelligent and people don't like mucking about with gorgeous intelligent people."

"Well, sure, there's that too," I agreed.

She sighed. "But you can't keep the car."

I laughed at her, much to her indignation.

She looked at me and said, "But it's hopeless talking to you about that, isn't it?"

I nodded my head.

The classic three-car two-driver problem is one that even Einstein didn't solve, so after agreeing that my use of differential calculus probably wasn't going to solve it either, we resorted to the traditional solution. Each of us drove our own car home, she drove me back out to the place I'd parked the Audi, she drove home alone, and I got into the Audi and beat my record home, with luckily no sign of Corporal John Simard. It was a big carbon footprint solution I suppose, but it got the job done.

3

THE STRANGE BRICK BUILDING

June had brightened. The trees were fully in leaf, the grass bright green and winter seemed suddenly a distant memory, like a bad dream that fades and fades as the day goes on. The wind had lost its teeth of ice and softened and mellowed. Now it held promise instead of threat.

Despite my statement about wanting Alex to know everything about what was going on, I hadn't yet shown her the photographs I'd found in the glove compartment of the Audi and I wasn't sure if I ever would. Maybe, I thought, this part of the job would be a solo effort. So I drove out that June afternoon on an exploration mission, with the sun high overhead. There was a thin blue sky with a few wisps of cloud way up, contrail weather, several of them knifing their sharp straight lines like alien intruders silently high. In a few fields hay had already been turned into giant wheels and tractors chugged about organizing them into ranks and rows, and encasing them in plastic, like giant sausages.

I figured I'd seen the building in the photographs before somewhere just off the highway leading to Winnipeg, looking abandoned and mysterious, so I drove slowly keeping an eye out to the right across the trees and fields. The Audi was a dream, silent and smooth, the driver's seat firm and comfortable, the cabin with its full range of instruments and impeccable design, fit and finish, exhilarating to be in.

Why the sudden switch from things with wheels, I wondered. Steel wheels, rubber wheels and now no wheels. What was the progression there? What was this guy after?

Alex was right to worry at that question. There had to be a reason, something not obvious – a reason why it had to involve me, a reason why he couldn't or wouldn't just do whatever it was he wanted doing himself. When would he let me know? How much more of this adventure game would he play before he finally got serious and let me know what he wanted? Was he testing me, seeing how far I would go, sizing me up as he put me through these trials and temptations? But there really hadn't been anything very difficult so far, nothing terribly taxing, so what was it all about?

I shrugged, pulled over onto the shoulder and poured myself a cup of my special half decaf from my steel Thermos. I sat by the side of the road drinking the coffee and mulling over the conundrum I was facing. It was pretty clear he wanted me to break into the building shown in the photographs – I didn't imagine it would conveniently be open for me or that I would be able to talk myself into it, or that it would simply have a sign outside telling me whatever clue it was all about. And the question was, was I going to? Would I break the law to follow this, the next step? Would that be the end of the chase, with alarms whooping and cops arriving to drag me off to jail, Corporal Simard's suspicions corroborated? But that made no sense. Why pay for a three-year vehicle lease only to lure me into the clutches of the law a few days later? No, I didn't think it would be a trap, but I still wasn't sure if I would do it or not, if that's what it turned out I was supposed to do.

I drove the Audi back onto the highway and then I saw it, tiny in the distance but unmistakable. I pulled off onto a dirt road that seemed to lead in the right direction, drove down it and found the building on the left hand side. I pulled over onto the grass at the side of the road, shut off the engine and got out of the car. I looked around. The building was really only a few hundred yards from the highway but the traffic was mostly shielded by some trees. Further up the road and across on the right was a cluster of buildings, including a dilapidated house. A dog barked distantly.

Not many buildings hereabouts are brick and fewer yet yellow brick. And it sat right next to power lines. It was three storeys high with a two-storey annex, exactly as shown in the photos I found in the Audi. At the front there was a tall steel overhead door, with a faint track leading to it from the road across which ran a wide gate preventing access. The side next to the power lines bristled with wooden triangular supports and at the top big wooden boxes jutted out over them. Boarded up openings were distributed around three sides of the building but along the side opposite the hydro lines were three glass windows set high off the ground, too far up to allow anyone to look into them. The building was pitch black inside.

What was it I wondered. A generator building for early days power supply? A small factory of sorts located conveniently close to power lines? And why did it seem to be looked after? Although it didn't appear to be used, it clearly wasn't abandoned either. What went on inside it? Was this the mystery I was supposed to solve – to find some nefarious activity and squeal to the police about it thus keeping whoever was behind it out of the news? But then why not just a simple anonymous tip to the cops? Why get me involved and go to the trouble of arranging a train and three-year lease? There had to be more to it than that I figured. Perhaps it was a test: if I would break in here then perhaps I would do anything and the mystery man would finally show up and explain what it was he wanted me to do. Or maybe it was just a game, a giant joke of some kind, nothing more than that. I shook my head. I was like a mouse in a maze and I didn't really have much choice except to keep on.

I walked around the building eyeing it like a tourist admiring a piece of architecture. There were no signs, no slogans, no graffiti, no marks of any kind. Its function must have had something to do with the power lines, I reasoned. Perhaps it was an old generator station of some kind, now no longer used. But the grass around the building was neatly cut so it hadn't been abandoned although it didn't seem to be in use at all. No noises came from within the building, no smoke issued from the narrow brick chimney that ran up the side of the main part of the building. Once stuff had been moved in or out of here, hoists and pulleys had been used, but no more. That was all done now, washed away with the big power damns throttling the rivers and harnessing their floods and torrents.

There was no obvious easy way in that I could see except through the front door and for that you'd need a key or to smash your way in. Not that I have any expertise in such matters. Breaking into my own house one time when I lost my key had been challenge enough. The back of the building would be the best, away from the road, screened almost completely, but there were no windows boarded up or otherwise there.

"There's something you didn't tell me," Alex said when I called her and before I could get a word in. "So now you are going to confess your sins, throw yourself on my mercy and ask me to lunch at Jennifer's again so you can inveigle me further into this ridiculous nonsense."

"That's almost as bad as ordering my food for me," I said.

"Oh, you are so transparent, Colin. Our mysterious puzzle setter can see right through you and so can I."

"Maybe he's a high-priced lawyer too."

"But not as sexy."

"No one could be as sexy."

"Ooh!"

"We'll have to go in on the side facing the highway," I told Alex after I showed her the pictures. "The other side would be easier but anyone looking from that house would spot us easily."

"Go in? What are you talking about? And what's with this us nonsense?" Alex was wearing a red sweater with a zip neckline and black slacks, both rather provocatively form fitting. When she leaned forward, the zip dangled there and I wondered what she would do if I reached over and pulled it down. I mentally slapped my hand and fought back the impulse.

"Well of course us," I said, when I had recovered my composure. "You're not going to back out now are you?"

"Don't tell me, please don't tell me you're thinking of breaking into that building, Colin!"

I laughed. "Of course I am! How else are we going to find out the clues inside?"

"Clues? Inside? Did it occur to you that this place is probably under surveillance right now and that all of this grand adventure with a diesel locomotive and a fancy car is probably just to lure you into throwing away all vestiges of common sense and catch you in the act of committing a crime?"

"Breaking into an abandoned building? What kind of crime is that! Pretty minor if you ask me."

"Thank God no one *is* asking you! As for me, well I think I'm going to pretend we never had this conversation so that I will not have to perjure myself when I'm on the witness stand, or trying to avoid going down with you as an accomplice! No, my Lord, never seen the idiot in my life. I'll say one thing for him though M'Lord, he's a shifty looking one though isn't he."

"Alex!"

"Don't Alex me, Colin. OK so far it's been pretty harmless, yes I agree. An amusing little ride, and a nice shiny car, but breaking into that place, nope, not for me, and if you have any brains, which I seriously doubt, it won't be for you, either."

"Alex, you're the one who's not thinking. Look he's already left a pretty good paper trail. CP has a record, the leasing company has a record and I've got these photographs. I mean even if I do get caught I'm not likely to go to jail, you know that. A fine maybe, a suspended sentence. OK I don't want even that, but the point is it doesn't make sense to set it up that way deliberately. If the grand puppet master here wanted some harm to come to me, he could have done that already. If he wanted to kidnap me he's already had plenty of opportunities. Kill me, ditto. No, he wants me to do something for him, something useful and he's working me to the point where I can't say no."

"That's what I've been telling you all along and now it's your idea!"

"That's what leadership is all about! And speaking of leadership, you don't happen to know anyone who might be able to provide some expertise for this jaunt do you?"

"You don't know how to do it, do you?"

"Nope. Haven't a clue," I admitted. "But I figure you must know someone who could give us some pointers."

"Sure," she said. "Me with my extensive contacts in the criminal network!"

He was a little man called Joe, shifty eyed, with long arms and big hands. He was in his fifties I'd guess and looked as if he'd done some time, for some reason, or maybe that was just a guess on my part. His hair was thin and fading fast and he was dressed in denim, head to foot, with a denim baseball cap for good measure.

We took him out to the mysterious building in the Audi. Any excuse to go out in that car was a good one. I put the shift into the multitronic mode and trod on it. The Audi leapt forward with a muted growl.

When we reached the yellow brick building, I did a u-turn, and parked well down from the building.

"Mr. Therman is writing a book," Alex told him, "and in this book he has to break into this building for some reason I won't go into. How would you do it if you were doing it?"

"A book is it?" He looked at me and shook his head. "Sure, whatever! First thing is, I wouldn't do it," the man said. "I'd choose some place with more money inside. This place ain't got any."

"It's not about money," she said.

"Everything's about money, honey!" he said.

He spent half an hour walking around, tapping the walls, measuring window heights, pulling at the big metal door, and looking up. Once or twice a car drove by, enveloping us in its dust and the crunchy roar of the tires on gravel, but mostly what we heard was the steady distant whir of traffic on the highway and the periodic bark of the dog in the house nearby.

He was a little furtive man who would look guilty no matter what he was doing. He kept his grubby, navy blue baseball cap low over his forehead so his eyes were barely visible. He moved his arms constantly as if he was about to launch into some expressive statement requiring lots of body English and gestures, each of these broken off in mid go, so that his arms and hands moved in a twitchy kind of dance.

His eyes roved but always without making eye contact, cast down, around you but never at you. Yet when he was looking over the building his eyes were alive and thorough.

"That's the best place - the north wall," he commented. "Windows are low, but you can't do it there 'cause it's visible from the house up the street. Yea, probably not a good idea. Safest, you know, would be the back, but there's nothing there, no way to get in. The front – forget about it. That's impossible. The door is way too big and obvious and probably pretty secure. What I would do – get up onto the annex roof from the back and break in through the windows on the south side of the main building. The only trick is what's inside. Do you end up two stories up there with no way to get down. I think you should take a chance. Probably there's something inside to walk on, a catwalk or something like that. The good thing of it is, no one will see you up there – a car can drive right by and nobody's gonna notice you!"

He was beginning to sound enthusiastic, as if he'd like a shot at it himself.

"Maybe we should hire you," I suggested. He looked at me then, just for an instant, and I knew suddenly that he no longer had the nerve for such things. He knew what to do, had done it all before but something, sometime, had cured him of the doing of it.

He shook his head violently. "Nah, nah," he muttered. "Advice is what I sell these days, just advice. You wanna do it, you gotta do it yourselves."

"It's just a book," I said reassuringly. "Just a book. All pretend and no reality."

"How would you get up to the roof, if you actually wanted to do it?" Alex asked.

The back of the building was a featureless solid wall of brick, two stories high with a thin edging around the rim of the roof. It looked huge, towering, an unscalable mass of brickwork. You'd need a 30-foot ladder to scale it, and how could we possibly carry it there and set it up unseen we wondered out loud.

Joe laughed at us for the first time. Snickered would be a more accurate description of his action. Snickered and rolled his eyes. "People don't notice stuff," he said. "You can set things up under their noses and they have no clue. If you look official, you're invisible! All you'd hafta do here is bring the ladder on top of your car or a truck at night and park down the road, lights off. Wait till you can see no one's coming, OK. Drive up with your lights off, get out, take out the ladder, put it on the ground, take the truck back down the road. Walk up, pick up the ladder, two of you, take it round the back and set it up. It's a cinch. If anyone sees you you're just carrying a ladder in a truck – who's gonna think anything about that!"

"All it takes is boldness!"

"Yea," Joe agreed. "You just gotta do it, without all this thinking about it, all this yakkity, yak, nattery natter stuff. Hard for folks is writing books I suppose!"

We thanked Joe for his advice and said we'd mention him in the book. "Keep me outta your book," he said with alarm. "It'll just encourage the wrong people to think the wrong things about me!"

"A contribution to your favourite charity," I commented as I gave him a $100 bill.

"Smart ass!" he observed accurately.

We drove him back to where he wanted to be let off and then continued back home.

"Seems to have a pretty poor opinion of lawyers," I said as we drove.

Alex looked puzzled.

"Yakkity, yak, nattery natter comments!"

"Well that's that," Alex said. "You can take your stupid cheap ring back and stick it you know where!"

"Why Alex, I seem to have offended you. I do apologize."

"And also can the movie quotes, already!"

We drove to a nearby beach to walk and talk. It was still early in the season and the tourists hadn't yet arrived, which meant it was quiet and peaceful. There was a middle-aged man flying a Frisbee against the wind, tossing it and catching it, over and over. We stood for a while watching him as he flung the disk high against the wind and caught it as it came sailing back towards him. The wind was fairly strong blowing off the water and the Frisbee flew high and far. Boats hadn't had their breakfast yet and no one was screaming around in a water jet. Even the birds seemed to have agreed it was quiet hour.

"He's good," I said. I'd seen him before at this beach flying his discs and he was always impressive. We took off our shoes and socks and started walking barefoot along the thin strip of sand along the shore.

"Got it all figured out now have you?" Alex began.

I snorted. "If I had it all figured out I wouldn't be thinking of breaking into you know where!"

"We're both of us crazy," she said. "Stark raving mad."

"Just a label," I said dismissively. "Sometime soon this guy has to declare himself. He can't keep on leading us around by the nose forever with no clue why he wants us to do this."

"Very insightful," Alex said sarcastically.

"You'd make a great wife," I said.

"Oh, Colin," she said and nestled against me. I could feel the curve of her breast through her blouse. It was a nice feeling.

"Yep," I continued. "Got the sarcasm down pat I'd say."

She growled.

"I'm going to do this, you know that don't you?"

She nodded.

"And that's with you or without you."

"You need me for the ladder."

"If I have to I'll wrestle with it myself. I'm strong enough to do it."

"We could end up in jail. You know that, don't you? We could end up dead even, if things go badly wrong. I mean that building is used still. There are lights over the door, electric wiring running into the place, lawn carefully cut. It's certainly not abandoned."

We sat down on a table looking out over the water. It had grown warm, the first real heat outside I'd felt for a long long time. The surface of the lake was ruffled and ducks were dipping up and down in the action. As we watched a couple of them took off with great splashing of wing tips and then they were airborne and veering towards the islands. Far out a windsurfer had silently appeared scudding across the water at high speed.

"Look," I argued. "I know I shouldn't do it. I know it's wrong. But I have to."

"That's why he gave you the train ride and the car," she said. "He's judged his man well. If he'd started with this, well it would end right here, that would be it. But now you're committed, you're feeling good about it."

"There are two clues in that building and I'm betting they're big ones."

"Two? How do you know there are two? How do you know there are any at all?"

I smiled. "He gave me two photos, right? There it is, a building with four very different sides and he gave me two pictures – of the same side. The photos were taken at slightly different angles, just enough difference to make it obvious they weren't two copies of the same shot, but not enough to be of any use for casing the place or figuring out how to break in. So I assume it means we should look for two clues."

She nodded. "So now the trail bifurcates."

"That what you learn at lawyer school, smart ass talk like bifurcates? Sounds like something the Catholic church would be against."

"Most churches," she said. "He's telling you it's not about the building."

"Right! Two pictures of the north side taken from different angles. It has to mean two clues inside along that wall. "

"Ah!"

"In other words, a warning not to leave after we've found one clue. Stick around and look for another."

"We, yes." Alex said and shrugged.

The man had switched to a smaller disk now, a flattish yellow one he sent skimming way out over the water, then catching it as it came screaming back at him in the wind. A gull twisted suddenly to avoid being hit as it stooged over the water near the shore.

"Pick a moonless night," Alex said.

"Flashlights, work boots, heavy clothes, gloves, satchel, tape, rubber mallet, axe, rope, hacksaw."

"And hope like hell there's no alarm system."

"I didn't spot any signs. No point having an alarm system unless you tell people about it. The point is to deter, not to catch!" I said. "And we rent a truck to do it and throw our boots away afterwards."

"What about the ladder? We can't just leave it. The police would track it to where we bought it, get our names and addresses from the credit card file and hello handcuffs. You know, Colin, this is scary. We have only to forget one little thing and we're screwed."

"Yes, but look, Alex. What are the cops going to find when they investigate the scene? A broken window high up and nothing stolen! Nothing taken, no significant damage done. What's to investigate? They'll just figure someone threw a rock at the window. They've got more important things to worry about than that!"

"Feel like going for a swim?" I asked her, changing the subject.

She smiled, dazzling the whole beach for a moment. "In these clothes? Nope! And skinny dipping, well maybe one night Colin dear we should do it but not now, not in broad daylight! Besides, I must get back to the office."

"Yes, sorry." I'd had a vivid image of what I imagined her body would be like if we did go skinny dipping and I was embarrassed.

"Oh, it's a delight to be with you, Colin dear, it's just that I do have to earn my keep."

"He's got nice buns!" she said as we moved back to the car, looking at the man flying his discs.

The guy was in his fifties I estimated, but he was in good shape, and showing it, having stripped down to his bikini trunks.

"Wonder what he does in the winter to keep in shape." I said.

4

BREAKING IN

From the stage of the moon it was clear we'd have to wait a week to get into the building. I phoned the Avis President's Club number and booked a car to be ready in two days for a West Jet flight from Toronto. On the day I drove the Audi to the airport, parked it in the Park and Ride, took the shuttle bus to the airport, walked to the Avis counter and told them my name. They looked at my driver's license, handed me the documents and the keys and a fawn Toyota Camry was mine.

After the Audi, the Camry was dull and numb, way too characterless to be interesting, but it was smooth and quiet enough. I picked up the essentials - flashlights, tape, hacksaw and so forth, ticking the items off on the list I'd made, using three different home renovation/hardware stores, and using cash not credit card at each. I bought sturdy work boots for myself and Alex at a nearby Marks Work Wearhouse.

Inside the car I transferred all the items except the shoes and flashlights into a backpack, got out of the car and stashed it in the trunk. Then I drove to the Park and Ride, parked the Camry, locked it and then walked over to the Audi, paid the parking ticket at the gate and drove home. I figured none of that car shuffle stuff would fool anyone who knew I was guilty, but I thought it might stop anyone thinking I possibly might be.

Driving home in the Audi through the Agassi forest, which seemed to be turning into the Agassi sand and gravel pit despite its supposedly protected status, I asked myself mentally just what the hell I thought I was doing. There was no traffic on the road and the fir trees were flitting past the car endlessly, the landscape penetrated here and there by small creeks, and the occasional granite outcropping.

Was I really contemplating climbing onto a two-storey roof at night in the dark, breaking a big glass window, climbing down into an unknown industrial interior, looking around for something I'd recognize when I saw it but not before presumably, climbing back up, onto the roof and down the ladder, then disposing of that somehow? And if so, for what? No wonder Alex thought I was nuts. I *was* nuts! But then why was she so eager to help me? Why didn't she tell me she drew the line at break and enter? Was she in some way as hooked on this as I was, as eager to find out what was going on as I had become?

Oh, come on, I told myself. Stop pretending. I was hooked instantly: the e-mail and the train were all it took. In fact I still had an enormous anxiety that there wouldn't be a point to this thing, that the person behind it would just keep pushing me into doing stupid things like breaking into buildings on and on until it just petered out or I finally decided enough, that's it, no more. That was definitely a possibility, but I didn't believe it. I was sure he would get to the point, that there was a reason for all this adventuring. The train ride and the car hadn't come cheap, so I figured there was some serious purpose here. Otherwise it would be a waste of his time and mine. And that damn 7-digit number kept bothering me. It had to be significant and I was pretty sure I was supposed to have cracked it long ago.

A couple of deer flitted across the road, their tails held whitely erect, then vanished into the trees on the other side. I shivered suddenly. I don't know why but the deer had spooked me, coming suddenly from nowhere, and I had a sense of something dangerous nearby, a sense that the so-called adventure I was on would end badly.

After a while the feeling ebbed and I grew more cheerful. I wondered suddenly if it was possible Alex was in it just because of me! Did she fancy me so much she'd do almost anything for me? I grinned thinking to myself, come on, who was I kidding! A gorgeous woman like that must have plenty of guys to choose from, perhaps none with quite my magnetism and flair, sure, but still. But even accepting that I have some appeal, that someone as gorgeous as Alex would do something that ordinarily she wouldn't touch with a ten-foot pole just because of me was preposterous, and to think it was arrogant, insufferably vain and stupid.

Come on you idiot, I told myself. Most of the time she's just playing games, keeping her hand in, practicing in a safe environment. Yet she'd crossed the big barrier the guy behind this had put up without even commenting on it, I realized suddenly. The train and the car had been easy, fun, no danger. The building was suddenly a huge step change, requiring planning, and care, and involving danger and risk. There was no immediate positive outcome to it, like the train ride and the free car. It was a risk for no apparent gain, like a test of some kind, as if he were saying, after this, things get serious. Whatever clues were in there must be important, would surely start to zero in on why he was playing all these games, or so I hoped.

Maybe I am fool, I thought to myself, speeding down the road, but I don't think there's any danger in that building, other than falling off a ladder or something like that. There'd be no alarm, simply because whoever was behind this wasn't aiming to get us into trouble. What he was doing was testing our resolve, our ability to tackle something outside our experience, yet within our abilities, which disabling alarms certainly wasn't. He was aiming to stretch us, not snap us. So the only risks were an accident on the job or someone seeing us, and the building was about as remote and lonely as it could be and still be accessible at all.

On the day we'd chosen it was warm and bright. Alex borrowed her cousin's truck – a man who farmed nearby – and his long aluminum ladder, and in the evening drove into the city. I went into the city separately, parked my Audi at the airport this time and took the shuttle to the Park and Ride where I picked up the Camry and drove back to where she was waiting at a Subway restaurant. Then she drove to the yellow brick building while I tagged after her in the Camry. The evening had been long and lingering. The sun loitered on the horizon, blood red. Long shadows stretched out across the fields.

We stopped just off the highway facing down the dirt road that led to the building, turned off the lights and took stock. The dirt road ran straight for several miles and it would easily be possible to see from headlights if anyone was coming down it. The only risks were a sudden vehicle exit from the house just beyond the building, or someone turning onto the road behind us. Even then, by the time we got to the building we'd be able to see anyone turning onto the road behind us in time to abort the idea of dropping off the ladder, and could just keep driving down the road.

"Shit we're actually going to do this," Alex said. She was dressed head to toe in black, her hair tied tightly in a bun, with a dark watch cap over it.

"You just need shoe polish on your face and you'd be perfect," I told her.

"Grrr, why am I doing this, that's what I want to know?"

"Because you love me!" I told her.

"Yea, right," she said, "Dream on McTavish."

"Let's get the show on the road," I said.

"Whoa! Where do you come up with those original lines!" She checked the mirror, looked up the now dark road, and started up, lights off. We drove slowly up to the building, all the while alert for lights suddenly showing up ahead or behind us, but it remained solidly dark, with only a faint glimmer in the sky to mark where the sun had finally gone down.

We stopped just short of where the building loomed beside the road, got out, lifted the ladder from the truck bed and carried it across the grass and behind the building, where we put it flat on the ground. We ran back to the truck, got in and carefully reversed down the road towards the Camry. I got into the car and again followed her, this time back to her cousin's place, where she parked the truck just shy of the long narrow track leading down to the farm, got into the Camry and we drove back to the building.

Again we parked down the road, turned off the lights and engine, waited and watched. Cars whizzed by on the highway and once a truck came down the dirt road and turned onto the highway. The lights shone from the nearby house. At 11 they went out. We waited another half hour. The night was clear, the sky etched with stars, but dark, the moon safely tucked away out of sight. We put on the gloves and boots, grabbed a flashlight each and got out of the car. I opened the trunk and took out the backpack with the other equipment we needed and then we set out down the road.

The gravel crunched loudly under our boots. While we walked along the road we were vulnerable to any vehicle that came along. Anyone walking down the road surely would seem strange, especially as it was now approaching midnight. Our plan was to turn around and appear to be walking back to the car if anyone came along. There was no place to hide, so we'd just have to brazen it out if anyone did come by. The last thing we wanted was a neighbourhood watch group after us. Amateurs chasing amateurs would be a nightmare.

As we crunched along the side of the road, we kept imagining lights in the distance but the road remained dark, and the house up ahead obligingly inactive, with no lights showing. Even the dog remained silent.

We moved behind the building with relief, lifted the ladder, extended it to its full length and set it up against the wall. Despite being made of aluminum the damn thing was heavy. Looking up, it seemed a mile high, a dangerous, impossible height to scale. "You go up first while I hold the ladder," I whispered. "Then you hold it at the top and I'll come up after you."

Alex went up slowly, carefully, hanging on to the sides of the ladder with both hands, planting her feet firmly. At the top, she got off, knelt down to hold the ladder and signalled to me with her flashlight.

I started to climb. It was a long way up but the ladder was steady and although I felt clumsy in the new heavy boots and work gloves, I made it up easily and onto the roof. I went up to one of the windows and shone my flashlight through it. It was dark and dirty and I couldn't make out anything inside. Carefully, as best I could with shaky hands and fast beating heart, I applied tape to the rearmost window and then swung my axe at the glass. It shattered with a loud smash. I knocked out the shards remaining near the bottom and sides and then froze. A pair of lights had turned onto the road from the highway and was speeding down the road towards us.

"Down," I whispered frantically. Suddenly I thought that with our luck it would be someone who would steal our car and leave us stranded here, or come around, discover the ladder and take it down, leaving us up on the roof. Lying flat on the dirty, wet roof we couldn't see the lights or the car, but the noise of its passage was clear enough, as it travelled towards us and then suddenly slowed. I heard the dog bark and voices.

Christ, they've spotted something and woken up the house, I thought. I lifted my head carefully above the level of the roof. Up the road, the house was now lit up, and I could see tail lights near the front. Then the car went dark, I heard doors open and shut, and the dog went silent again.

"We may not be able to go home after all!" I whispered to Alex.

"Christ this is not a Gladiator moment, Colin!"

"People coming home," I explained. They'd have seen the car and wondered maybe about it, I knew. People living around here would notice anything new or different, would be sensitive to the slightest change. If the cops came round asking questions they'd tell them about the car, which I guess is why it was rented. Still, we'd have to hope they didn't get the license plate number. I'd obscured it with mud as best I could, alert to that danger, but that was no guarantee. I saw now that we should have parked it just off the highway rather than pointing down the road. That way they'd be more likely just to think the car had run out of gas, or the engine had given trouble. Pointing down the road here was much more suspicious.

Having people newly home at the house could be a problem if we had to make any more noise breaking in. I just hoped I wouldn't have to cut through metal bars at the window. They'd be bound to hear it at the house and maybe put two and two together.

We stayed flat against the roof for another half hour. The house had gone dark again by then, so I carefully shone the flashlight at the open space in the window. There were bars there but I thought them easily wide enough to let us squeeze through without having to cut, which made me wonder what the point of them was. I shone the light down into the interior, looking for a way to get inside. There was a metal catwalk just below the window running all along this side of the building.

I had a sudden urge to scramble back down the ladder, get in the car and get the hell away from here. Was it fear of this task, or terror at what I might end up involved in that prompted that, I wondered. Shut up, nerves, I told myself, but the thought that this might be a trap kept niggling at me.

"Maybe you should stay outside," I suggested. "That way you can let me know if anyone is coming, and maybe get away yourself if there's real trouble. Get in the Camry and get the hell out of here."

Alex shook her head. "We're in this together," she said. "I'll stay outside but I'm not running away!"

I clambered carefully over the sill, and felt for the grating below me. It seemed much further down than it had looked from the outside, but eventually, at a considerable stretch, I felt something under my feet and fumbled fully over the window ledge and down onto the metal surface. Getting back through the window was going to be challenging, but I'd worry about that later. I shone the beam of the flashlight low along the grating. It ran along the back of the building and then there seemed to be a set of metal stairs descending down to the main floor. I walked carefully along the grating, hoping it was secure and not rusting away, and then down the stairs. If anyone came along now I was screwed, that was for sure.

It was decidedly gloomy inside but there was just enough ambient light for me to make out that the floor below was littered with stuff. I shone my flashlight around looking for something – anything – that might resemble a clue.

Along one wall was a control panel or the remains of one, a broken chair and a wooden table, leaning acutely to one side where the legs had been splintered . What was I looking for, that was the question. Something small, something portable, something light, but what exactly? Obviously there could be nothing on the table, not with it set at that sharp angle. I was moving the beam of the light further into the room when I when I thought suddenly, not ON the table. As I swung the beam back I caught a glimpse of something suddenly that made me shine the flashlight fully at the table. Faintly, shadowed by the overhanging surface of the table top, I made out what looked like a drawer front. It was small, shallow, and set deeply under the table. There was no knob on the front, but by reaching deep under the table and behind, I managed to ease the drawer out a few inches and then gingerly tease out the single piece of paper contained in it. The paper was blank except for a large rectangular space outlined in thick dark border and within the space this: L210065780/RT. Was this really a clue I wondered, or just a bit of paper left lying around with a code number on it. The fact is, I couldn't know for sure, but I had a feeling it was significant, so I folded the paper and put it safely in my right trouser pocket. One down one to go, but supposing I was wrong? Supposing there was no particular significance to their being two photographs, that there were two just to draw my attention to the building, as if to show that it is important, not to indicate two clues?

Muzzling the flashlight and pointing it downward to avoid lighting up the place suspiciously, I tried to take stock of the rest of the building. Huge presences loomed around me, shrouded in plastic wrappings, and jumbles of unknown objects, tools, barrels, wiring lay scattered around. Whoever ran this place wasn't too worried about neat housekeeping, I thought.

Where the large metal door was, the floor was clear and just off to one side there was an office marked off in partition walls, open at the top, but with a door. I approached it carefully, stepping around the debris. I tried the door, and to my surprise found it unlocked. I opened it and stepped into the small room. Inside was a desk with a computer, phone and fax machine. In a corner was a battered, metal, four-drawer filing cabinet on top of which sat a coffee maker. There were a couple of chairs and a bookcase with half a dozen engineering manuals lying there. For a mad moment I felt the urge to switch on the light. Near the computer were scattered several sheets of paper and an e-sized blueprint, half unfolded.

I sorted through the paperwork. Two pieces were work orders of some kind, another a memo about time keeping and overtime, stock in trade of administrative officers. One held my attention for a while before I decided it had nothing to do with me. Drawers again, I wondered? Indeed there were two large drawers to the left. I slid the top one open and stared helplessly at the contents. Row upon row of files. I shut it and opened the second but it was equally mysterious and unhelpful.

Come on, think I urged myself. As I shut the drawer again I must have jostled the keyboard because the computer screen lit up suddenly and there blinking at me was an invitation to enter a password. I took the sheet I'd extracted from the broken table and looked at it. This is where the alarm bells go off I suppose I thought fatalistically as I slowly, carefully entered the letters and numbers inside the box on that sheet. When I finished I hit enter and waited, holding my breath. The hard drive light flickered and then I was staring at a short list of two files, Colinfile1, and Colinfile2. I felt eerily as if I had indeed just stepped into the spider's web, like a video I had once seen of a mouse curious about and bumbling into a round hole in which lurked a tarantula, about to have a juicy meal. I double clicked on the first file and hit the printer button. It was a single sheet with a kind of riddle on it, obviously another quest-inducing instruction set of some kind. It appeared the guy wasn't through playing games yet, damn it.

While the printer was printing the page, I clicked on the second file and brought up another list of sorts about trees. Yea, sure I thought. I hit the printer button again and waited until the second single sheet had emerged. I turned off the computer then and made my way carefully back to the metal stairs at the rear of the building. Now that I'd got what I came for, or hoped I had, I was overcome by fear that we'd be discovered at any moment and I moved faster than I should have in the cluttered, murky interior of the building.

I managed the loud metal steps all right and moved rapidly along the metal walkway at the back wall of the building. I suppose I must have tripped on something lying on the grating because I fell against the handrail to my left and felt it give, lean out and fall away. I had half fallen onto the flooring, my right leg lying against the metal, my left arm still stretched out holding onto a very insubstantial railing. Something had fallen banging from my backpack over the edge. My flashlight had also fallen from my right hand onto the grating and gone out. For a moment I held my breath, fearing at any moment that the whole floor would give way. Then I gingerly began to transfer weight to my leg and from my arm, leaning over to the right as carefully as I could. I put my right hand down and clutched at the flooring. I could just get a purchase on it and I pulled myself away from the dangerous unguarded edge inch by inch until at last I was against the wall on the right, feeling its solid presence with relief. I felt around on the floor and eventually located the flashlight and to my relief found that it was still working. I was breathing hard by this time and my sweat was prickling my head under my cap. Break a limb here and my goose was cooked that was certain.

Whatever had fallen from my backpack would have to stay, as I had no intention of going back down onto the main floor and looking for it. Perhaps that would prove to be the critical clue with which the police would track me down. I'd be sitting calmly in my living room one day when the cruiser would draw up in the driveway and there'd be a knock on the door. Still, if that was all they had, nothing else, I would simply say I lost it, misplaced it, something like that and dare them to make something of it. They might have their suspicions but it would take more than that to tie me to this scene, or so I hoped.

Getting back to my feet I inched along the grating, leaning against the wall now for comfort. One foot in front of the other, I drew closer to the other wall and then stepped around it towards the window where I'd entered. This now loomed feet above me, at a seemingly impossible height. Getting down had been difficult enough, getting back up was going to be even more difficult. Reaching up with my hands I grabbed the bottom of two of the bars and pulled myself up as far as I could and then sought purchase with my knees. Alex saw me struggling and grabbed my jacket and pulled outwards. For a moment I felt myself teetering there and knew that if I fell backwards I would probably go over the edge of the grating and almost undoubtedly end up badly hurt. Desperately I got one hand on the other side of the grating and used it to lever myself forward. At last I felt my centre of gravity shift towards the outside and I stepped through the bars onto the roof.

"I thought something had happened!" Alex said. "Coast is clear, but a car came by five minutes ago – it may have seen your light flashing inside. It slowed but then kept on going."

"OK then, let's go!" I said and we felt our way down the ladder to the ground. Oh, it felt good to be outside again. Now we had to dispose of the ladder. No good leaving it here. With any luck, the broken window wouldn't be discovered for days, making it that much harder to collect clues.

"Into the woods." I said.

We carried the long heavy aluminum ladder into the trees behind the building. Once there in the dark night it proved extraordinarily difficult to make any progress. Moving a large straight 30-foot long object through dense random forest is no easy task. Still we finally found a place a few trees in where we could lay it flat. We set it down and then spent two minutes scooping up earth and leaves and branches and whatever we could find that was loose to cover it, roughly at least. With any luck, they would never think of looking here and it would eventually become naturally overgrown. I shone my light briefly to check that it was reasonably well covered. It was then that the dog barked.

"Let's go!" I said.

We moved stealthily back towards the highway keeping just inside the line of trees, before it finally ran out and we had to move into an open area and then back towards the road.

"Nice to get a bit of fresh air," I said cheerfully as we strode back down the gravel road. "Lovely evening, officer, don't you agree! Just out for a bit of a stroll!"

Alex snorted then poked me in the ribs.

Everything ahead of us was dark. Nothing moved anywhere. It was 2 o'clock and the world seemed to have shut down.

The interior light came on as we got into the Camry, but there was no help for that. In a moment I had started up, reversed to the highway and we were gone.

"I dropped something inside," I warned her. "Haven't checked what it was yet."

"I thought you were suave and sophisticated."

"Sure, but clumsy."

She looked at me and then asked, "What did you find?" As I drove I told her about the pages and how I had found them. "I haven't looked at them yet, but they appear to be more clues."

"He's got us on a treadmill, Colin," she said with exasperation. "A bloody treadmill, jerking to his commands, faster, faster, round and round. And I've got my suspicions he knows exactly what we're doing and when we're doing it. If I had time and money for this case, I'd monitor what's going on around us. Set up video cameras around wherever we are and look for repeat vehicles, stuff like that."

"You think he's tracking us?"

"I'm certain he is, and I'm also sure the Audi's got a device on it somewhere."

Like her now, I was beginning to be worried about this guy, whoever he was. The car, OK, that just took money, but arranging for the CP locomotive and leaving clues in the computer waiting for me to break into the building spoke of the ability to do things most of us can't. But that made it even more mysterious why he even needed me at all. What do I have that he needs? I suppose I should have guessed it would have something to do with death and disappearances but the fact is I didn't, not then at any rate.

"How can he get in and out of a building like that to set up the computer?" I asked out loud. "He doesn't have to break in. He must have a key, or know someone who does and can keep his mouth shut. Or maybe he's a Hydro employee."

"Maybe he's a chameleon, becoming whatever he needs to be to do whatever it is he's up to." Alex said.

"What he's up to is leading us around by the nose." I had driven back to her cousin's place and stopped the car beside hers.

"What's Linda going to say when you get home this time of the morning?" Alex asked.

I smiled. "I'll just tell her I was out adventuring with a beautiful, stacked lawyer."

"Oh I like the stacked part! I'll take that as a sign you like me and would like to take this relationship further if you could." She turned and kissed me on the cheek. "But, time for my beauty rest," she said. "Cases, clients waiting for me tomorrow. Give me a call when you've figured out what's next. No, pop over for coffee. I'll be going mad, but don't worry about it. A little more madness won't make much difference."

I said good night, and spent the next two hours driving into the city, leaving the rental car in the rental lot, dropping the keys in the night drop box, picking up the Audi and driving home. I eased into the house quietly, slid off my clothes – amazing how much noise taking off jeans, sweatshirt, underwear and socks makes – and got gently into bed. Linda made a noise, turned over but didn't wake.

"Out with that big breasted harlot?" Linda asked me the next morning, smiling sweetly in that way of hers.

"You know I like my women sleek and sexy," I responded.

"Women?"

"Yep, you and your clone! You didn't know about your clone?"

"Hmm," she said archly. "Speaking of clones, yours is quite skilful, I must say." Her eyes sparkled saucily, with that little hint of cruel mysteriousness that always sends a shiver down my spine, and explains why even highly attractive people like Alex don't really have a chance. "Not exactly a clone so much as an improved model, I think. Tweaked substantially in all the right places."

"So long as it's only tweaked!" I said, feeling just a trifle jealous.

After breakfast I drove to Alex' legal firm, a small storefront place in a short strip of businesses. You could see the clients – well there were two of them - wondering 'Who's he?' as I breezed into Alex's office with just a wave at Marcy fielding phone calls. Alex was on the phone when I entered but pointed to the sofa across from the small conference table. She was wearing a navy blazer over a blue blouse, decorated with white daisies, and a rather short grey skirt. The blouse was open at least two buttons and when she leaned forward she showed a couple of inches of cleavage. Her hair was in a ponytail, secured with a simple band. She was wearing glasses and looked frighteningly severe, but desperately delicious as they say.

Watching a competent woman dealing efficiently with work was strangely arousing. I looked down, unwilling to let my thoughts carry on along this line. For some reason, Linda's words about the tweaked clone, although teasing, had left me feeling a little inadequate, perhaps even a tad guilty, and I was annoyed with myself for falling into her deliberate trap, her precision button pushing. Clever women use every advantage they can get, I thought, not for the first, or last time, and Linda was nothing if not clever.

Alex finished with her phone call, ignored its immediate ring when she set it down and came over to the table.

"You look none the worse for wear," I said.

She shrugged. "Five hours sleep is about all I need. Time's too precious to waste on that anyway. What you got?"

I handed her the two sheets that I printed off last night in the office of that spooky building. She looked at them for a minute without saying anything and then put them down on the table. It was a beautiful piece of polished oak, gleaming as the sun reflected off it.

"More riddles, more tricks," I said somewhat wearily.

"First one sounds promising, though," she pointed out. "This 'then you will know' stuff sounds like an end at last."

"Probably just means we'll know the next clue!"

"Pessimist!"

Alex swung her ponytail and looked seriously at me. "What does Linda know about all this?"

I laughed. "Linda knows all," I said. "She always does. I tell her everything that goes on – well pretty much everything. She knows I'm working with you on this, that you've taken the bait."

"Does she know we broke into that building?"

"Oh, Alex, Alex. What is this? Why do you want to know how much she knows? Sometimes she's smart enough not to ask too many questions, shies away from the difficult ones. Then sometimes she bangs head on into them – depends. She understands men sometimes do stupid things on the spur of the moment. Doesn't mean she'd forgive them, but she knows it happens and that it doesn't necessarily mean much."

Alex looked at me in puzzlement. "What was all that about?" she asked. "I take it that she doesn't know."

I shook my head. I put the printouts down on the desk and we looked at them.

Colinfile1

> What was above,
> Runs now below.
> Think where you started,
> And then go.
> Find the connection,
> Don't be too slow.
> Look for the number,
> And then you will know!

Colinfile2

General: Choose the first occurrence
Keep it clean. Ironwood. Under the lid

N Jack Pine
   Oak & Ash
   Jack Pine
   Jack Pine
   Blank
   Blank

W Oak & Ash
   Ironwood
   Green Ash/Black Ash
   Bur Oak
   Blank
   Blank

"I think he's one step ahead of us the whole time. You don't imagine those files were sitting there waiting for you for days and days do you?" she asked. "I suspect he's out there a lot of the time, watching us, parked in some inconspicuous vehicle, blending in among all the others."

After her little outburst, she turned back to the pages again. "What's all this tree crap?" N, W sounds like GPS coordinates to me. But what do trees have to do with latitude and longitude?"

"Ironwood!" I said.

She looked at me quizzically. The sun had come into the room at an angle and glanced off her cheekbones, illuminating her face and I realized all over again how disturbingly attractive she was. The curves of her eyebrows, her nose, her lips and cheeks flowed into each other in intoxicating ways, like a mathematician's sense of the ideal. She'd mesmerize legal opponents and juries easily I understood.

She caught me staring and smiled.

"You're used to it, aren't you?" I demanded.

"Not from you, Colin dear. Not from you!"

"Ironwood," I said again.

"You're repeating yourself!"

"Mean anything to you?"

"Name of a tree – perhaps hard to cut. Other than that, nothing."

"It's also the name of a trail that runs along the edge of the shoreline in Pinawa then connects up to the Trans Canada Trail."

"Put on my hiking boots, is that what you're saying?"

I grinned. "If you want, although it's an easy trail, sneakers are fine."

"You won't catch me in here in sneakers any time soon," she sneered. "In any case, though, Colin I'm too busy right now. Why don't you check it out and let me know what you find."

"While you figure out what the riddle means?"

"Something like that."

5

THE IRONWOOD CLUES

Most towns plan improperly and fritter away their best land to the highest bidder. Pinawa - someone should have got a medal for it but never has done - is an exception to this rule, having made the entire shoreline parkland that everyone can enjoy. The Ironwood trail that curves along this shoreline bordering the Winnipeg River provides easy access to a hiker's paradise.

I parked near the giant sundial, which I've personally never much cared for, almost a heresy in the town, took a brochure from the kiosk at the trail head and started down the path. The warmth of the day before had fled and the wind had ice in its teeth once more as it blew off the water, reminding me that the river had been mostly ice covered only a month before and breathing frosty breath from the open parts where water moved fast. But the sun was bright in the sky, birds were about and the undulating shoreline gave magical vistas downstream. Across the river, Porcupine, Hind, and Carter islands formed a false far shore.

The trail was an easy dirt track that wound up small slopes and between trees. It was pleasant out but there was nothing obvious that answered the question of why I was there. It was the little granite marker on the ground with the number 8 on it that triggered a mental twitch. I took out the brochure I'd grabbed earlier and opened it. There were twenty-four interest points marked on the trail, each described in the brochure and with a number inscribed on one of those little stone markers. Somehow these were supposed to provide a clue, a vital, meaningful something, but to me they were just numbers on grey rock. I turned to number 8 and read, "Paper birch....grows in a variety of conditions...used by aboriginal people for making canoes and containers." And so forth. Very helpful I thought.

Use the first occurrence the printout had said. What did that mean? Then I noticed that number ten was also about paper birch so supposedly I was supposed to use number 8 not number ten. But the printout hadn't said anything about paper birch, only jack pine, oak and ash and so forth. Jack Pine was point 4 I saw so I walked further down the trail looking for its marker.

Geese were honking persistently, fussing about something invisible to my eyes. Near the shore, the water swirled, hinting at fast currents. At number 6 there was a public dock and canoes on racks nearby. Dock and cattails the pamphlet said. Cattails wasn't one of the clues but Jack Pine occurred three times, suggesting it was very important. I sat in the bench stuck into the ground overlooking the dock and looked out at the shining water. It was a magical day if cool. I looked carefully around me for something, anything that would trigger an 'ah ha!' but there was only the quiet scene and the trail stretching on.

Through the trees behind me was the river road with hardly any traffic apart from the occasional cyclist and a person or two walking their dog. If anyone was watching me, as Alex suggested they might be, they would have a hard time doing it here. There were too few people about for me not to notice someone who was persistently around. And a car driving by or parked by the road would be obvious. Yet there was a car I saw, just along a little further. For some reason I'd brought binoculars and I trained them on the vehicle now. It was a grey Cavalier, a few years old, a dime a dozen around here. I looked to see if I could read the plate but it was obscured with mud. Hmm, I thought, thinking of how I'd smeared mud on the plates of the Camry, that that was suspicious in itself. There didn't appear to be anyone in the car. Should I indicate I was suspicious of it, I wondered, or pretend I hadn't cottoned on? For the moment I decided to pretend I didn't think anything of it, and I continued on up the trail.

Number 5 was Ironwood itself, a gnarled, twisted tree that I didn't find particularly interesting. And then came number 4, Jack Pine, the most northern of pines apparently, with hard curved cones that require heat to release their seeds. The marker was almost buried in last year's old, dry leaves. I was damned if I could see anything significant about it. There was no sign posted giving me the answer, nothing shouting Eureka at me, just the trail, trees, the river and that damned parked car. I would wipe off the mud, I thought, just stroll up nonchalantly, reach down and wipe it, then take note of the number on the plate. If the person who drove was watching me it wasn't obvious to me where he was. I turned all around and looked intently at my surroundings but so far as I could tell I was alone.

Jack Pine was number 4, Oak and Ash was number 9. What else did the message say? Jack Pine repeated twice more! What was that about? There were certainly enough bur oak around, hardly needed numbered posts to advertise them! Bur Oak was number 2 but the message said Oak and Ash. Ash was number 1, but two kinds, Oak and Ash, were number 9. Did the numbers mean anything? If so the message was 4944. But what were these blanks? They had to mean something or why bother? What was a blank? A gap, nothing. Zero! Was that it? 494400. North 494400.

I turned with mounting excitement. Alex had been right – it was a position co-ordinate! The car was gone! I'd seen nobody, noticed nothing. Great detective I was, hot on the trail of something and so caught up in the pamphlet I'd missed whoever it was getting back to the car, starting it up and moving off. Had the driver seen my eureka moment and known that I'd figured it out? I may have missed it this time, but I'd be on the watch from now on for a grey Cavalier with mud-obscured plates.

I looked back at the trail guide. Oak and Ash again, so number 9, and Ironwood was number 5. But what about Green Ash/Black Ash? The pamphlet said number 1 marked two kinds of ash: Green Ash and its close relative Black Ash. So Green Ash/Black Ash was number 1. As for Bur Oak, it was number 2. That gave West 9512 and then 00 for the two blanks. If that was it, all I had to do now was look up the coordinates in a directory and I would know where to go next.

I got out my cell phone and called Arthur, a friend of mine who operates an information service I've used a few times. I told him the numbers and he told me to wait while he looked them up. I could hear him working on his computer and then he said West Hawk.

"Does that make sense?" he asked. I laughed and said that it did indeed. "At least it's not Timbucktoo!" I thanked him and rang off.

West Hawk! Well, I guess it made sense all right. It was still hanging together. West Hawk is a lake on the eastern edge of Whiteshell Provincial Park, a tourist resort, just north of the Trans Canada highway. It was certainly doable, a bit far but within range of amateurs poking around. So then, now for the other piece of the latest puzzle.

I started walking back along the trail towards where I'd parked the car. A two-person shell came gliding along the river, propelled by two women working, resting, working, resting, their oars moving in a ballet of skill and coordination, the only sounds the slight creak of oarlocks and the splash of blade tips hitting the water.

Then I remembered the additional clue that had been printed on the first computer file. "Keep it clean. Ironwood. Under the lid." I'd been to Ironwood already and noticed nothing there, but I retraced my steps to the marker and looked around again. There was a trash receptacle there, one of those round ones with a hinged, push-in covered slot in the lid. "Keep it clean" – well I guess this was it. And "under the lid". I pushed the cover open and gingerly felt around under the lid with my hand as far as I could reach. There was something there! It felt like a piece of thin plastic covered with masking or duct tape. I scraped at the edges and managed to lift a corner, then peel it away.

When I examined it in the light I saw that it was a plastic envelope that had been stuck down with the tape and contained some paper. I pulled at the plastic until it tore, tugged out the contents and unfolded a single sheet of computer paper.

Tracking the Riddle?

Rails cross roads, and roads cross rails.
Do roads cross roads? And rails?

Changing places
Above and below

Not far to go. Use an old road.
Where have you been?

Drive in the car
Then not very far

I went back to the bench, sat down again and thought about this new riddle. The whole business was beginning to seem endless, with clues leading to more clues but no end, no solution, in sight. It was like pulling on a long string that you pull on and pull on and it just keeps coming out, seemingly endless. I hadn't expected it to be like this – an endless chase with no obvious end point. Still, this surely had to lead somewhere, eventually, but clearly not just yet. I felt that the West Hawk lead was an important one but what did this new riddle mean exactly? In some ways this was a worse than the one in the printout had been. So, let's get to it, I told myself.

Two statements followed by two questions. Do roads cross roads? Of course they do, and just as surely roads also cross rails. But what about this rails cross rails question? Do they? I suppose they do, or can do. There was no reason why they shouldn't or couldn't. Was that the idea? Was he telling me about someplace where rails cross rails, an intersection of sorts? But then the above and below stuff, what did that mean? Was it like a highway overpass, one rail passing over the other? And if so where the hell did that happen? Not far it says, get there by car, well almost and use an old road. I shrugged. The obvious answer was to drive along near one of the rail lines and look for where it crossed another. But I'd been along the road beside the tracks often enough to know that there was no such place visible. Still, the note says not very far but perhaps not very far was just far enough not to be able to see it from the road. So how then to find it? And when is this guy going to come to the point?

I looked out over the water and felt anything but serene. The person behind all this was beginning to try my patience. Perhaps Alex' new notion that it was just a game for the sake of it was on the mark. Perhaps, I thought, he's out there snickering at me for stupidly following his clues around like a dog following his master and fetching the stick over and over again. I decided I would give this only a few more days and would then quit if nothing had become clear by then. Saturday would be the deadline, I decided and I got up and walked home.

On Thursday, Alex was still too tied up at the office to come with me, so I set off into the park alone in the Audi to try to figure out the over/under thing. It was a wonderful car, a sheer joy to drive, and for a while I forgot about anything much except the pleasure of shifting and steering. The leather interior smelled intoxicating and the seats and driving position were ideal, supportive and comfortable. It was getting noticeably busier on the roads now, the owners of cabins, restaurants and gas stations readying their businesses for the coming onslaught, hoping for good weather. As well, farming was reaching a peak and a steady stream of hay wheels were being carted along in slow, wide, lumbering wagons behind tractors. Just north of the park entrance a giant 4-wheel-drive tractor was pulling what looked like a mile-wide seeder, huge, menacing and powerful.

At Dorothy Lake I parked, took my coffee thermos from the car and sat at my favourite picnic table. For a while I scanned the road, alert for a grey Cavalier with muddy plates but saw nothing that resembled the vehicle that might have been watching me at the Ironwood trail. Alex was sure the man behind the email and clues was watching us, that he knew exactly what we're doing, how we're doing it and when we're doing it, but I wasn't altogether convinced. Finally I turned and looked out over the lake. It was almost primordially quiet, meaning that only natural noises sounded: the wind, the waves against the shore. In a few more days the tourists would swarm here as if they owned the place, dragging the city with them to flail the place with it before retreating back to their noisy lairs. For the moment, however, as it would be again in September after school started, the place was mine alone. The wind was blowing off the land, chasing patterns across the surface of the lake, blowing them into being and then scattering them again, ephemeral patterns, born quickly and just as quickly extinguished. Watching them form and dissipate made me feel transitory too.

Two geese had already decided this was the spot for them and when I got up to walk on the sand they indignantly made for the water, seeming to regard me very much as I regard tourists. They bobbed on the water for a while, moving sedately away from the shore and then at an unseen, unheard signal flapped into a long take-off, as if showing me who was master in their effortless transition from land, to water to air. Far overhead a soundless contrail appeared, etching a white line against the blue sky, tipped with a moving silver bird, its wings and engines barely visible. There was nothing primordial about that, although it was as magical in its way as the sun and the stars.

A hundred years ago the river here ran untamed, unconstrained, a wilder beast than now, urgent, savage at times and in places, full of pools and rapids, roaring and running its way north to the big lake there. I imagined the contours of the original river hidden and drowned now by the higher levels created by the hydro damns. There would have been no beach here then, no park, no roads, no place to sit and think, but the river would have been there through the trees, running wild and free. I would have given a lot to be able to see it, I realized. It seemed strange to think of it as still there, under all this placid water, the original idea of the river, drowned but still present, buried alive in a way.

I thought about why I had been chosen. Was it random; had to be someone so was me? Perhaps, but I didn't really believe it was random, a mere accident. That couldn't explain why the locomotive had been provided. That had been aimed directly at me, or at least someone like me, deeply interested in trains. So I'd been chosen for a reason but for the life of me I couldn't figure out what it might be. And so far nothing in the clues pointed in any direction. Surely soon they must come to some point, instead of this endless chasing after the next pointless mystery. Of course it was fun in a way, a real adventure game involving me and a mysterious hidden person. So far I was just going along for the ride, driven by my curiosity, but I knew that Alex was right about there being some danger here. Nobody would set up something like this just for fun. There was obviously a purpose here and it wouldn't necessarily by a good one. This was leading somewhere and I understood that I probably wouldn't be happy when I got there. I would definitely have to watch my step.

I thought about driving directly to West Hawk and starting to check into things there but there was still this other clue to solve. So far, whoever was behind this had been methodical. Every clue had a purpose, driving me relentlessly to the next step in the puzzle. Now I knew I was supposed to go West Hawk but I didn't as yet know why. I could only hope that the rails cross rails thing would lead me to the reason.

The rail clue seemed an easy thing to solve in a way, as if the author was bending over backwards to avoid stumping us, giving us a clue he really wanted us to get. He'd stumped me with that original seven-digit number on the first email but since then I'd been able to figure him out. First he gave us the rhyme in the computer in the building, and then a second set of clues in the lid of the garbage can beside the Ironwood trail. The double treatment surely meant it was important and that he didn't want us to miss it. Tracks cross tracks was the answer but what did that mean? I felt I knew the area well but I knew of no such place. Thinking about it wasn't going to solve it, however. Instead I would chase tracks and see what I could find. The Canadian Pacific line ran all along Highway 44 so far as I knew so I would follow it and see what I could discover. Perhaps there was something there that I had never noticed before. If the tracks did cross, one would have to be above and one below as the riddle said. But where was such a thing?

Reluctantly I said goodbye to the beach, got back into the Audi, started it and drove deeper into the park, chasing the CP line. The day had suddenly turned misty, as if vapour was rising from the ground, obscuring the trees in a dull vague muzzle. At Whitemouth, the signals came down and a CP freight slowly pulled across the crossing belching exhaust, cooling fans whirring, a hundred cars of a mixed consist, almost a thousand wheels rolling down the track. After it had passed, I powered down the highway, watching the rails, visible through the trees, always parallel to the road. I soon outdistanced the train and for a while floated along hardly thinking, enjoying a sense of freedom where I could go wherever I wanted and drive forever. After a while I realized that the track was gone. As I had sped along it had moved north, or the road had veered south and road and track no longer paralleled each other. I kept on driving however, because I knew that the CP line certainly ran along the road for miles and miles further east.

Vaguely a dim idea of what was going on was coming to me. I was never good at spatial visualization, or 3D reckoning, however, so if our mysterious poser of conundrums sought such skills he'd certainly picked the wrong person in me. I rounded a curve and then the road moved into a gentle left bank, sweeping over the Canadian National track which appeared suddenly, spearing up from the south. There it was beneath me. I braked on the straight section of road after the overpass and pulled the Audi over onto the dirt shoulder. The CN track was heading north, where the CP track already was. I already knew that further east the CP track became visible again and that there was no further sign of CN trackage, so clearly between here and there the two tracks must meet! It was simple, inescapable, yet in all the years of living and driving around here I had never twigged, never put together the pieces of the puzzle lying right under my nose! Still where exactly did they meet? I knew of no place visible from the road, no location where a bridge carried one set of steel rail over another.

I started up the Audi again. There had been a reference to old road. There was an abandoned section of the old highway to my right, just visible as a peculiar stretch of isolated crumbling asphalt. There were others around too, here and there I knew. I'd seen them but never paid much attention to them before.

I drove east, peering to the left looking for signs. There! A section of disintegrating surface off to the left. Gingerly I drove the car onto it and continued on a couple of hundred feet beyond until the road ended suddenly in a pond. It was a section of the old highway that used to run here all right but it was nowhere near railroad track. I shut off the engine and got out of the car. There were dozens of otter paws lying around, a grizzly testimony to trapping activity. The sun was now invisible through the mist. I could hear birds singing all around me and frogs croaking from the pond. Then distantly I heard the rumble of diesel engines straining to pull steel wheels on steel rail!

I pushed through the trees and up, down and around rock outcroppings and tree trunks, watching out for poison ivy as I went. There was a faint deer trail snaking around the rocks and fallen logs and I followed it. Up ahead there seemed to be a clearing of some sort. After five minutes of struggling through the vegetation I came to the edge of a wide cut into the ground, sliced through solid granite. At the bottom lay a set of rails. These seemed to run roughly east west so presumably were CP rails. I scrambled down the side of the cut and onto the grey ballast. The track curved both right and left preventing me from seeing any distance. I moved left, towards where the CN rail had speared north, treading carefully over the rough gravel surface. The train sound blasted suddenly at me from around the corner and the long line of the consist snaked into view, smudged by diesel exhaust, the triple headlights spearing distantly at me along the length of roadbed. And there, up ahead, about where the train ran was a bridge. Rail crossing rail I presumed.

I waved as the train ground past, the engines beating angrily at five thousand tons of inertia, the wheels clinking and crashing over the rail welds. Amazing things trains, I thought as the mile-long consist pulled past and away from me.

Gradually the noise receded until there was just me and the tracks. I walked further until I came to the steel bridge over the CP line, and climbed up onto it and looked around. Signs warned of dire peril from CN police for trespassing. Yea right I thought. Cops hiding behind every tree no doubt! Nothing caught my eye. I crossed over to the other side and down the embankment and under the bridge. The entire underside and the retaining walls were covered with graffiti, along with signs of those who had been here before me, and statements about who loved whom. Hmm. Trouble was I had no idea what I was looking for here. Oh sure, I knew it was a clue or a message of some kind that I had come for, but how would I recognize it? Look for a number and then I will know, was what the riddle in the building had said. So I was looking for a number, not a picture or message. Suddenly I thought of the number in the email, a number I hadn't figured out but hadn't seriously tried to either. But numbers were important and so far everything that had been thrust at me as a clue was important. Why hadn't I tried to tackle that number more seriously? What was it? 3914425, that was it. I knew it wasn't a telephone number, but something much simpler, a code of some kind. Had I been supposed to figure it out earlier I wondered?

But I was suddenly sick of this, as if a virus that had been infecting me had suddenly been eradicated and removed from my body all at once. Up to now it had been a lark: a ride on a loco, a new car, even breaking into the hydro building had been an adventure. I had a wonderful flirty woman working with me and it had been fun. Now I began suddenly to wonder about it. Why? What was this all about? Was anyone watching me? Where could they possibly hide here if they were? There were only the two sets of rail, the bridge, with no road in sight, no buildings of any kind, absolutely nothing. I looked slowly around as if testing this hypothesis. Was there really no place to hide? In truth someone could be up a tree and I would never see them unless they moved or wore a stupid bright colour. Otherwise a person would be invisible and I would never see them and they could have binoculars trained on me easily. But why would they do that? To check that I'd got the clue? Why would they do that? But why wouldn't they? Surely they'd want to know something about what we were doing, how far we'd got.

I thought of that car at the Ironwood Trail, the vehicle that had been there one moment and then suddenly was gone. I'd never seen it again, or one like it, but even if I did it was too common a make and colour to be of any significance. How would they keep track of us? The car might be one way. They could have several cars. They might have a tracer on the Audi. I shrugged. Alex worried more about that sort of thing than I did.

She was the professional who wanted to set up a perimeter watch using cameras and a computer. Until now, I'd just shrugged that off as so much unnecessary paranoia. Who cared if someone watched us! We were dancing to their tune anyway, following the trail they'd laid in the forest, the little bits of coloured tape tied to tree branches, the careful pile of stones to make sure we didn't lose our way.

Alone in that cutting under the steel bridge, however, I suddenly wanted an end to this. That's it, I thought; I won't wait until Saturday, I'll just go home and do nothing else, just ignore it, keep the Audi and see what happens, pretending none of this chasing around after clues had happened. Yet I couldn't just leave here without trying to figure out why I had come. What was I looking for? Some numbers apparently.

At first the walls looked an indecipherable, uninterpretable sameness of rude, pointless, stupid scrawling. So and so was here. Somebody wanted to fuck somebody else. And strange symbols that meant nothing to innocent me. Was a crude, mammary heavy figure meant to be a sexy woman, or a threatening female figure, or an ancient fertility sign? And a box, heavily outlined in black with letter and numbers, what was that? Immediately I realized it was an accession number for a professional online database! In an instant my mood changed again. This would finally tell me something. An accession number meant an article of some kind and that meant information, not just another clue or riddle in an endless chain of them.

In a way, having the most significant clue to date hidden away in this place which really wasn't hidden, said something important about the person who had planned all this. He was counting on me to be able to work it all out, and to be persistent enough to want to, but he wasn't setting riddles for the sake of showing me how clever he was. The clues weren't obscure enough or brilliant enough for that. The object wasn't to stump me but to get me to a point where I could do something. I was sure of that now. Just around the corner, the purpose of all this was about to be revealed, or so I sensed. Now that the mystery was out of the riddle it all seemed so clear and obvious. But working backwards, reverse engineering the lines didn't step by step make it become progressively puzzling. Instead the clarity and the obviousness remained. He knew I would solve it because he knew I had all the pieces of the puzzle already. All I had to do was to think about them.

Once again I looked around to see if I could spot any observation. There was nothing. A slight wind blew under the high metal work supporting the CN track overhead, tall enough for double stack containers to pass. Black flies were beginning to be a nuisance and some swallows were darting under the steel beams and swooping near to the concrete abutments. I'd had the information I needed all along. I itemized the facts with my fingers.

First, I knew that the road from the south entrance into the park from the highway crossed both sets of tracks. I'd crossed them often enough, first the CP, then the CN. Second, I knew that just west of the south entrance the CN tracks veered under the highway and then disappeared south, never to come near the highway again. And third, I knew that the CP track pretty much paralleled the highway all the way west to Whitemouth. All the information was there, had I thought about it, to figure out that within the space of a few miles the CN tracks went from being below CP to being above them. Obviously they crossed – they had to. And, also obviously, they crossed somewhere that wasn't visible from the road or I would have noticed it long ago. And finally, that crossing had to be somewhere not far away because all the tracks were close. In fact the crossing was two minutes walk in the woods, nearby and yet just far enough to be on the moon as far as I had been concerned.

6

THE REASON WHY

Now **I knew** that we had to go to West Hawk and the number I'd copied from the stone abutment would, I hoped, tell me why. I made a call to Arthur, my information friend on my cell phone.

"A? It's Colin. Look I need you to look up a number. Maybe Dialog, I'm not sure. And if there's full text available for the item, get it and email it to me. Of course it's urgent, but it shouldn't take you a second."

A for Arthur told me he'd heard that joke too many times for it to be funny any more. "It's like the five-minute fix up job around the house," he said. "There ain't no such animal!"

I told him to do his best and then gave him the number. He promised to get back to me as soon as possible.

Arthur's a whiz with online information retrieval and has enough of a business at it that he can afford to subscribe to all the best professional systems. I knew that if I was right about the number he'd find the article it referred to pretty easily.

There was little point in my hanging around the junction of the two railway lines anymore, so I headed back the way I had come and drove the Audi home. Alex would be eager to hear what I'd found but I'd wait until I heard from Arthur before calling her.

"Been out chasing choo choos?" Linda asked. She was putting down the mat ready to do yoga.

"Examining ancient hieroglyphs more like it actually," I said, "or arcane symbols of the graphitic kind."

She raised an eyebrow and looked at me as a cat might a bird. I smiled. "Later, dear."

With the discovery of the database reference number my mood about abandoning all this stupid chasing around after clues had changed abruptly. I was sure now that we would soon know what it was all about. But in my bones, I should have known, ought to have figured out long ago, what sort of task I was involved in and why I had been selected. I realized that in a searing instant when A's email arrived, with its cruel answers.

Reward Offered

By Christopher Arnold
Miner and News
May 14, 1965

The parents of Stephanie Shawcross today announced a $3,000 reward for information about the whereabouts of their daughter, who disappeared Tuesday while driving from Winnipeg to Thunder Bay. Miss Shawcross, who was due to pick up a friend in Kenora, never arrived and has not been heard from since. Police in Manitoba and Ontario have discovered nothing to indicate foul play. In a brief statement, James and Bettie Shawcross said they love Stephanie dearly and will meet with anybody who has any information about her disappearance. According to police, Miss Shawcross drove a blue 1960 Buick LeSabre. At the time of her disappearance the weather was clear and road conditions were good. Although police originally thought that the young woman may have changed her mind and simply failed to inform her parents, it has been three weeks since she left her apartment in Winnipeg.

Miss Shawcross, who graduated from High School in 1964, was to have started work in Thunder Bay with Bristol Bay Pharmaceuticals, where she had been hired as a marketing trainee. Officials at the company confirmed that Miss Shawcross has not shown up for work or communicated with them since her disappearance.

A had appended a note saying he knew I'd want to know anything else I could about the story and he'd checked for additional references to the Shawcross woman. All he could find was a brief mention a year later to a letter from her parents complaining about police inaction on Stephanie's disappearance. A Google search for Stephanie turned up nothing significant.

A didn't know the significance of the article, nor would Alex, not unless she'd dug into my background after she moved here, but the person who had inscribed the accession number on the concrete walls of the underpass had chosen well, and had known something about me that neither of them did. And now I, too, knew why I had been selected. It hit me like a knife stuck into an old wound, and twisted. And for a moment the shock of it almost made me stop breathing. All the agony, the terror, the endless anxiety, and the sheer horror of a missing child came flooding back.

I have three children. Two of them have settled down, in good jobs and apparently successful marriages but I don't know where my little girl Cindy is and I haven't known for fifteen years, ever since she disappeared at the age of 16. She was beautiful, she was wonderful and she was a joy to be around even at 16. But one moment she was part of our life and then suddenly in a split second she was gone. Like the Shawcrosses, Linda and I offered a reward, and appealed to people for information, through newspapers, radio and TV. And I did some poking around myself.

Like the Shawcrosses I found that the police, initially helpful, soon lost interest. To them, she was just another runaway. They had seen it all before and it was nothing new. They sympathized but there was basically nothing to do. She would turn up or she wouldn't. I never believed that she had deliberately left home for one moment. Linda and I tormented ourselves helplessly, unable to turn off the images of the last time she ate with us, the last time she went to school, the last time she went to a dance. One moment she was a living, breathing member of our family and the next she joined the hundreds of other young people whose pictures are on posters in washrooms and bus shelters. Have you seen Alice, have you seen Jennifer, have you seen Alison, Rachel, Annabelle, Robert? And like all those parents of uncounted missing children, we lived every day not knowing if she were alive or dead. If alive, what she was doing and where? If dead, how did she die, when and where? There's no worse misfortune for a parent than having a child disappear and never knowing the child's fate. Perhaps you can imagine how great the agony is, but you can never truly experience it unless it happens to you.

I sat staring at the computer screen for a long time, wondering about how I was going to deal with this. Part of me wanted to curl into a ball and howl, then, when the tears dried and the fury abated, as it would, to forget about it, call Alex and tell her I'd decided to stop chasing idiotic clues in the woods and get back to real life. The wound never heals and yet you do, eventually, learn to get on with life, to live with it. And I didn't want to have that wound opened again. And yet, this was no longer a game. This was real now and I had a chance here, surely, to put an end to a puzzle: whatever happened to

Stephanie Shawcross? I hadn't been able to solve my own daughter's disappearance but perhaps I could solve Stephanie's. But it was well over 40 years ago. It would be formidably difficult, yet I had an unseen someone working with me, obviously keen on my solving the mystery of why she had vanished. I thought of the number with the email again. It was crystal clear now. The numbers were a code, each number representing a letter of the alphabet. If it was a simple substitution, then there were only four possibilities: it could be a seven-letter code, two different six-letter codes or a five-letter code, and since C is the third letter of the alphabet I didn't have to guess the rest: 3, 9, 14, 4, 25 spelled C,I,N,D,Y. Why hadn't I realized that earlier? But I knew the answer – I'd been too dazzled by the prospect of riding the locomotive to bother with that deadly little clue at the bottom of the email. Right at the start he'd told me he knew about her. Did this mean he had information about Cindy, or was he just using her name to get me to do his bidding?

As I thought about it, I had a sense of something darker roiling the surface, glimmering foully at me in the recesses of my thoughts. Why dig up the past of 40 years ago? What was the point of trying to get me to do that? Her parents might well be dead by now. Who would benefit from knowing what had happened to Stephanie? There was still something deeper here, something I didn't understand, some purpose larger than finding a body, if that was even possible after all this time. What clues could possibly remain after so long a period? And yet!

I knew in my mind that my daughter was dead, had probably died long ago, probably unpleasantly and yet my heart always yearned for her and hoped, day after day, that she would call or one day just be standing there. "Hello, Dad," she would say, "It's been a long time." I would rush to her and hug her and lift her off her feet.

Such events change the world unalterably. No matter how well you learn to cope, the scars remain forever. For a long time Linda and I had wanted to move away, because every location, every room in the house carried vivid memories that haunted us every day. Still, despite the pain of remaining, we were afraid to move in case she called or came back suddenly and then, finally, because it was all we had of her, those haunted rooms and places. In the end, though, we had to move, for job reasons, no choice in the matter and strangely we found the new place empty, as if only when we moved had she at last been permanently cut out of our lives.

I paced up and down the room in the basement where I had set up my office long ago. It was crunch time, I told myself, time to get serious or time to bale out. Obviously, whoever had sent me the email knew about my daughter. It wasn't any nonsense about the red hiking boots that had caused him to single me out, but something far deeper than that. And what the hell was his game? I didn't like being reminded of Cindy, didn't like it all, and didn't really see any reason why I should do anything he wanted me to. But why go to all that trouble with the locomotive, the leased car and the clues planted everywhere to drive me to this point? I was angry with him for manipulating me this way, no longer amused and entertained but furious. Yet although I didn't trust the motive of the manipulating son of a bitch who was behind this, would like nothing more than to take a baseball bat to him, I had a strong desire to see it through if I could. If at all possible I would find out what had happened to Stephanie on her way to Kenora in 1965. And if he did know something about Cindy, which is what he seemed to be implying, well I'd find that out too, although I understood that whatever he had to tell me would remain untold until I had done everything he wanted me to. I vowed then and there that when all this was over I would find out who was behind this whole sick game he was making me play and when I did, I'd find a way of dealing with him.

7

WEST HAWK

Alex and I came to West Hawk** on a dreary wet day in July, with low clouds and a cool wind out of the north.

I couldn't help smiling despite the bad weather, the anti-tourist in me coming out I suppose. Now that school was out, the city hordes had descended on the place but instead of buzzing about in their boats and splashing around in the water, they'd be shivering in their tents! Still the dull weather wasn't the greatest stimulus to start what I suspected would be a long-slog investigation. A bright sunny day would at least have given me the confidence to expect success. On this day, I had no such force to counter my increasing doubt about the whole business. Sure when I first realized that I was after a missing woman I'd gritted my teeth and decided to do it, despite how it opened my own personal wounds. But now I wondered why on Earth I assumed I could possibly get anywhere. The trail was over 40 years cold for a start. And who was I to find what presumably police and parents hadn't been able to when the case was new? I was simply an amateur detective, bumbling around. So far I had been led around by the nose. I'd discovered nothing on my own. At some stage, whoever was leaving the clues was going to step back and expect me to do some of the work myself. But the fact was I had neither investigative authority nor any particular skill to bring to bear.

In this depressed and doubting mood I parked the Audi in the parking area above Crescent Beach which curves along the shore just past the town centre. The beach was deserted and on the lake the water was flat and grey. Nothing was moving there except a few ducks paddling about and uptailing occasionally.

Up past the deserted marina the shore curved outwards forming one edge of the bay at the base of which the beach lay. Behind that shoreline was the campground with the wet, shivering tourists and at the tip of it, where the land curved away and out of sight again was an area of water with buoys marking a diving region. Nobody was diving either today it seemed although whether it was sunny or dull would make no difference 120 feet down, where the water was dark as night forever.

I looked at the sign at the top of the steps that led down to the sand. It proclaimed West Hawk's fiery birth 175 million years ago when a meteorite had smacked down here and blasted out the deep 2.4 km basin that became the lake. It was hard to imagine that on a day like today.

After a little while, Alex drove up in her beaten up Sentra, parked, got out and joined me in the Audi. She was wearing a drab grey jacket with a hood, jeans and red hikers.

"Ah, lovely West Hawk," she said.

"It is rather melancholy, isn't it!"

"So what's the plan, oh master sleuth?"

"You mean, you need a plan? We could sit here and look at the water, be glad we weren't thinking of going for a swim or sunbathing," I suggested with a grin.

"Cloudbathing isn't as much fun, I agree," she said. "A good way to start might be to get some coffee, start asking around."

"What? Anyone know this girl, pass across the picture, that sort of asking?" I responded. "That your idea of a plan?"

"Well, what's yours Sherlock?"

"We master sleuths don't need plans," I explained. "We rely on our finely honed instinct: that and a sharp nose."

"Oh, you mean we're just going to blunder around and see what turns up?"

"Something like that!"

I hissed back up the wet road in the Audi and stopped at an ice cream place that was surviving on selling coffee today. It looked soggy and bedraggled in the wet and we were the only customers. We drank the coffee in the car, with water dripping onto the roof and windshield from the trees and the windows misting up. It was snug and comfortable inside but it was time to get moving.

I drove her back to her car. "I'll go to the Museum," I suggested, "Why don't you check out the gas station, restaurants, motels. I'll catch up with you later."

The Museum was a log cabin, basically a space surrounded by wooden walls, floor and ceiling. There was a screen door and inside a wooden desk and chair behind which sat a young woman, whose name badge said she was Carla.

Carla was young, probably a college student in a summer job here; the place closed when the tourists left I figured. She was also on the chubby side, a side I suspected she'd never been on the other side of and probably never would. She was wearing a uniform, a drab green outfit consisting of slacks and shirt and she wore a Park cap on her head, brown hair spilling out around it. Her eyes were set high in her face and fairly wide, her nose was generous and her mouth pudgy. Although she wasn't going to win any beauty contests, her eyes looked alive and interested.

"This meteorite HQ?" I asked her.

She laughed. "Kind of, although it's mostly ecological stuff to be honest, native fauna and flora, watch out for bears, global warming."

"Ah yes, the inevitable, inescapable, forced down your throat until you scream global warming mania," I said, revealing a bit more of my own cynical attitude than I should have.

She put her head on one side and looked at me without saying anything.

I put the picture of Stephanie down in front of her and told her I was looking for information about this young woman. "Stephanie Shawcross. From around here or somewhere nearby I think. Disappeared 40 years ago. Ever heard the name?"

She shook her head, still giving me that you've-spoken-against-the-holy-grail look that global warming devotees adopt. I wondered if she'd ever heard of Richard Dyson or any of the other myriad of real scientist doubters that I could name. Probably not, or had dismissed him as an old crank.

"Probably went to High School here – is there one?"

She laughed again. She was quite pretty when she did that I thought. "Not in West Hawk," she said. "There's an elementary school in Falcon Lake but no High School. I know because I'm from around here myself. My parents live here, run the motel opposite the beach. My friends and I went to Whitemouth High. That's where we go around here, always have done as far as I know."

"The name Shawcross mean anything?"

She thought about it then said no.

I asked her if there was a library here and she said there was one in Falcon Lake. "It's not very good though," she admitted.

I looked briefly at the pictures of wildlife and a large map of the lake. There were a couple of posters about the meteorite. They told me that it happened about 100 million years ago – seems the sign at the top of the stairs to the beach was bragging a bit. Scientists estimate it was about 450 feet wide and came in at 36,000 mph.

I thought about that. Today was wet and cool. Maybe it had been wet and cool that day too when that big rock came rumbling in from out there somewhere, nudged and jostled by the gravitational force of other planets until it hit the atmosphere. It would have been hot and glowing, slowed by friction with the air but still moving fast. Animals may have raised their heads at the noise and light and then all hell must have broken loose as it hit like a kinetic super bomb.

"Must have been pretty warm around here then," I said nodding my head towards the posters.

She laughed and said that they were still doing research, drilling down to the fractured rock beneath the lake bed. "That's why this lake is so deep," she said. "Most lakes in the province are shallow but not this one. It was blasted out by the big rock."

I thanked Carla for her help and went outside. I was working on a hunch that Stephanie had gone to school around here but I needed some confirmation of that. I had Arthur looking for her parents. There was no Shawcross in the local telephone directory, so if they had ever lived here they certainly didn't any more.

As I walked back towards the Audi I had a crawling feeling, as if someone was watching me. I looked around but it was the kind of day which, had it been sunny, would have been alive with people, but instead had only a few sorry looking campers walking aimlessly about looking rather forlorn. There were a couple of vehicles moving past slowly and a cop car and that was about it. Anyone paying special interest to me would have stood out but there was no one who was doing anything other than visibly regretting having left the city for this.

I decided to leave the car where it was and walked across to the motel Carla had mentioned. There was a wooden building in front, painted green and white, with a sign marked office and others offering ice cream and gifts. Ice cream wasn't doing too well today and the gifts weren't exactly moving either. Behind it was a motel strip set higher than the office behind a long wedge of upward sloping lawn. There were a couple of vehicles parked in front, but all in all it didn't look like a busy weekend.

I opened the door to the office and went in. A bell rang as I stepped inside. There was fishing gear, a few food items, a half-hearted collection of videos off to one side, and a freezer displaying mostly full containers of ice cream behind glass on the other along with a couple of stand-up fridges full of pop. After a while, a middle-aged woman came towards me out of the gloom at the back. I could see where Carla got her avoir dupois from easily enough, but the woman was pretty in a way that had missed her daughter.

I told Mrs. Campbell – Mildred she informed me – that I'd met her daughter at the Museum. If she was disappointed I wasn't a customer she hid it well.

"It's nice having Carla here for the summer," she said. "Saves her money for college fees and it's just nice having her around," she admitted.

"Slow weekend," I observed.

She nodded her head resignedly. "Late June, early July's often bad," she observed. "Last year was miserable, but then it turned out all right, was a good season after all."

"Mrs. Campbell, I'm looking for information about a missing person, Stephanie Shawcross, and I wondered if you'd ever heard the name, the family name."

"Shawcross? It's an unusual name, isn't it. But no it's not a name I remember, and I remember names, that's one thing I do well, remember names. We've been here 20 years, bought the place from the people who built it."

"Well this was 40 years ago Mrs Cambell, 1965 to be precise."

"Oh, my goodness," She said. "I do know one thing," she informed me, "this was the main highway then, you know, this road here, believe it or not, used to go right across into Ontario. This winding little highway, can you imagine that!" She laughed at the idea of it. "They'd go puttering along right beside the lake. You can't go there now you know, I'm sure you do. Up the road it just comes to an end and there's a barrier. You can see the tracks of it winding away through the weeds though."

I thought to myself that 60s vehicles didn't putter but that was beside the point. The information shifted the picture I'd been building up about Stephanie's last road trip. Instead of the four-lane Trans Canada highway she'd have been on this road then, an altogether more meandering, slow and narrow thing. It might have been easy to fall asleep and wander off the road.

I thanked Mildred for her help and suggested I might be back to buy an ice cream sometime.

She looked towards the currently underappreciated stock and smiled. "It'll pick up," she said. "It always does."

Alex and I ate lunch at the burger joint and reviewed what we had learned.

They served milkshakes in metal containers, the old-fashioned kind and I hadn't been able to resist. The French fries were cut from the whole potato and crisply fried. I hadn't been able to resist those either.

Alex had been to the Esso station, the motel beside it, the ice cream shop on the other side and a fancy, licensed restaurant, once also an ice cream store, which was closed.

"I've learned something important," she said. "The past extends back to about yesterday. Apparently that's about as deep into the past as anyone can go around here. Today is all, yesterday doesn't count. Nobody knows anything. So your master plan has in fact achieved precisely nada," she added. "It's the weather. On a nice day this would all be looking a lot brighter!"

"Gosh, what a brilliant observation. Worth the trip out here just to hear that!"

"Park the sarcasm!" I told her.

"I did pick up something that might be useful, though," Alex said. "At the Esso station the guy who owns the place told me of an old woman who lives here and used to teach at the High School. If Stephanie was ever a student there she'd know it, he figured. Thought her name was King something or other."

"King Something - unusual name!" I said.

"Smart ass!"

"Still, it's a lead at last! I learned something interesting too," I told her. "A 400-foot boulder makes a hell of a bang! It certainly altered the landscape around here!"

After we thought about that idea for a while I said, "I learned something else. Not from the young woman who works at the Museum but her mother, who owns the motel across from the beach. She told me that in 1965 the road here still was the main highway. That may change things."

Alex gave me a puzzled look. "How does it change things?"

"Well one question we have is why West Hawk. We were sent here for a reason, but what is the reason? Somehow West Hawk must figure in Stephanie's life, and is tied into her disappearance in some way. But exactly how is it tied in? I figured it was because Stephanie lived here but if this was the road she took that day and not the current highway further south then she may have been killed here, assuming she was killed that is, that it's murder."

The campers were leaving their soggy tents now and the place was getting crowded. I paid the bill and we reconvened our conference in the Audi.

"There are only three things that can have happened to Stephanie," Alex said when we were settled in the seats of the car. "One, she went away of her own accord. She wanted to disappear and she did so. Two, she was taken and murdered, most likely for sexual reasons. And three she was taken but is still alive somewhere where we'll never find her in a million years."

"She might have had an accident and been injured," I suggested.

"Sure, but then she'd have been admitted to a local hospital somewhere and there are only a couple of possibilities around here. The police are bound to have checked that out, that's pretty basic stuff, check the hospitals first for admissions. So it's not likely. Besides they'd have found her car in that case."

"OK, but there's still another possibility. Remember that this is the road she must have taken, this windy, narrow thing, often with thin or even non-existent shoulders. It was early when she drove from Winnipeg according to the newspaper clipping, so it would have been dark. She could easily have fallen asleep and just gone off the road."

"And what, just disappeared, her car swallowed up and never found? Unlikely, isn't it?" Alex said. "Someone would have found the vehicle sooner or later, surely."

I conceded that it was a long shot. "I like your point about their being three possibilities, if we exclude the long shot then."

"But," Alex said, with a grin.

I nodded. "But indeed. Let's face it, one and three we're never going to get anywhere with."

"So it's murder most foul we are tracking, probably an opportunistic snatch and snuff."

I thought of Cindy then and wondered if she'd been a grab and snuff, also, deeply sad at the idea. "Christ, that sounds terrible!"

"It probably was!" Alex said.

"But early in the morning on this stretch of highway? And don't forget it was 40 years ago. It would have been mostly god forsaken stretches of road with no one on them. Not likely anyone would even have been around."

"But it only takes a single person, Colin. Out here, hitching. Back then it wasn't as frowned on as it is now. She might have felt sorry for someone, knowing his chances of getting a ride would be pretty slim. Or maybe it was someone she knew. She picks him up, and later he overpowers her, does things with her and kills her."

I sat thinking how it might have been, trying hard not to think of Cindy, to concentrate just on Stephanie, someone I didn't know, wasn't emotionally entangled with. Alex was suggesting that it wasn't murder, thought out in advance and planned, but a killing, sudden and unpremeditated. Perhaps that was how it was, but I couldn't see the email guy wanting us to figure that out. Why send for us if that was what it was? Just to find the body? Did he figure we could do what he hadn't been able to, and if so, why would he think that? And what was so important about finding her body after all these years?

"We have to factor our puppet master in this somehow," I said. "What's his motive? Why did he go to all this trouble and expense? Somehow it's got to be more than just finding her body, figuring out what happened to her. There's something else going on here, something that we don't know about, something that perhaps he doesn't want us to know about. Still, you're right," I added. "It's murder we're after and it's got something to do with West Hawk."

The mood that thoughts of murder inspired matched the gloomy day. We drove back to the beach, got out and walked

along it, thinking it through, turning over the ideas in our minds. A few brave souls had spread towels on the sand and were pretending to enjoy a day on the beach. If anything the day had deteriorated. It wasn't raining any more but a cool wind had sprung up and was blowing off the water. Despite that, a couple of people were swimming. Several boats were out on the lake now, fishing probably, and far out a wind surfer was cutting a wake through the rippled surface. You could smell wood smoke from cabin stoves.

"Feel like taking on the cops?" I asked Alex

"You figure on my master lawyering ability or my sex appeal to get on their good side?"

"Whatever it takes, Alex, whatever it takes."

She raised an eyebrow at me, smiled, looked at her watch and suddenly frowned. "Sorry," she said, "I'd like to help but I can't. I have to get back, some stuff in the office must get out by the end of the day, Saturday or no Saturday."

"No sweat," I said. "I appreciate your help. I'll call on them myself maybe."

"You realize that they probably won't want to cooperate in any case? It's a cold case, long cold and we're just amateurs. Why should they tell us anything?"

I shrugged. "You're probably right. But it's worth a try."

"The downside is that it lets them know we're poking around," she pointed out. "That may not be the best move. And I thought you were against involving them. Look how you took on about Corporal Simard when you got the ride on the loco!"

Two gulls came low over the water screaming at something or each other. I looked up at that them and thought that if I were a gull on a day like today I'd probably want to scream too.

I thought about what Alex had said. The police probably would be hostile about our looking into Stephanie's disappearance, on the basis that amateurs shouldn't poke their noses into police business. On the other hand, it had been 40 years and the cops weren't going to solve it any time soon. They might not like us investigating but I didn't think they could stop us. The worst they could do would be to refuse to cooperate. Of course they might be curious about why we were doing it and I wasn't sure I wanted to try to explain that any time soon. Still, the police might have information that would be useful to us, information such as where her parents lived, things like that.

"I think it's worth a try," I said.

Alex nodded. "I agree, but maybe you should just have a simple, disarming cover story, like you're checking into it as a favour for a friend who knew her and was in the area."

"That's the only troubling thing, though," I pointed out. "We don't know the connection between Stephanie and West Hawk. There must be one because otherwise why were we directed here, but we sure don't know what it is."

"Maybe explain what we mean if they ask by saying that we heard she disappeared around here and this is the nearest RCMP detachment," Alex suggested. "And if that doesn't work, I'm sure you can just wing it, because, well, that's your usual approach anyhow!"

I laughed then told her that I was going to start writing this stuff up, the stuff we'd talked about on some whiteboards. "Next time you're free come over to the house and help me with that, will you? It's time for us to start getting methodical about this."

Alex said she would and then left to drive back to her office.

8

FALCON LAKE

I got into the Audi and set off for Falcon Lake, in quest of
the supposedly not very good library.

There was a string of transports wheeling along the
highway, but I passed them one by one in the Audi, passed Alex
as well, who had opted to tuck in behind one of the trucks and
match speeds. This section of the highway was only two lanes, a
carry over of the Ontario section, not turning into a four-lane
highway until after Falcon Lake, but the Audi passed traffic
effortlessly and securely.

It was still too early in the season for Falcon to be busy on a
crappy day even on a weekend. The golf course had a few cars,
not many considering how strong the pent-up demand must be
for getting back onto the course after the long winter. The
restaurants and the shopping centre were almost deserted.
Slow time in the sticks I thought to myself. I almost wished I
was on vacation, strolling the beach perhaps, lying on the sand
with a good book, although probably not on a day like today,
instead of chasing the illusive trail of a long-dead woman.

After moving up and down the main street a few times
without spotting any sign of the place I was after, I parked the
Audi and went into the drug store to ask directions. Nobody in
there had heard of the library and I began to wonder if perhaps
the woman in the West Hawk Museum had been mistaken.
Maybe nobody around here reads, I thought to myself, perhaps
explaining why the library might not be very good, as Carla had
suggested. Finally the store manager gave me some vague
directions and I set off again. In the end Falcon doesn't

have many streets and there are only so many possibilities.

The Library was tucked away down a side road that looked as if it would peter out any moment and just end in trees. It was almost as if it was an ugly secret, guiltily pandering to readers, fostering the ugly art of literature. Even when I arrived in front of it, I was unsure I'd come to the right place. I parked the car at the side of the road and got out to check. There was only a notice printed letter size stuck in a corner of the window advising on Library hours to mark this as The Library. There was a single door, with a single chute in it for after-hours returns. Must be drafty in winter I thought. There was no sign in town pointing to it, nothing to mark its place for those not in the know. And maybe that was the point of it – if you were a resident you'd know about it, and if not, well you didn't have any business there. Wouldn't do to have some tourist grabbing that new best seller you'd hoped to take home to read in bed!

Through the door was a large room, L shaped, with a hefty desk to the left, tables to the right with a couple of computers and the rest of the space more or less filled with racks for magazines and books – oh and videos. Behind the desk sat a woman who looked up at me eagerly when I entered. Otherwise there was nobody there.

Linda Evans was fortyish, had large glasses, an enthusiastic demeanour and laughed a lot. I introduced myself, said I wasn't a resident but hoped she could help.

"Oh," she said.

I gave her my best smile, which I've been told isn't up to much at the best of times but I had to try. "I'm not planning on borrowing anything, just want to do some research in your archives," I told her.

"Oh, my, Mr. Therman. Archives! You have a sense of humour I see."

"It's High School yearbooks I'm interested in," I said.

She nodded. "Yes, yes. I have made a point of keeping High School annuals and I know - when I came, there was already a collection."

"It's 1964 I'm particularly interested in – the graduating class."

"Oh yes," she said breathlessly, as if this was the most exciting thing that had happened to her in a long time. Perhaps it was. "I'll just get the key." Then a serious look came over her. "I don't know for certain that we have that year, you appreciate. I'll have to look. I suspect that was before this library existed, but often some keen local collects these things and donates them, although sometimes I think they think we're a museum not a library, but yes, yes, I'll see what I have."

"I'd appreciate it."

"If you'd like to sit at one of the tables." She pointed to an area where three wood tables with small upholstered chairs were grouped around a pair of long curved tusks reaching up to the ceiling. Was this Falcon's counter to West Hawk's big rock I wondered.

I eyed the flamboyant dental work doubtfully, pulled out one of the chairs and sank down into it. The polished wooden floor creaked.

I could hear Linda clanking about with her key out of sight somewhere in the main part of the room. Apart from that, it was silent, not even fan noise to soften the quiet. Behind me the computers were mutely displaying Internet sites That was great for modern stuff I thought to myself, but being here, looking for rural school information forty years old, I realized suddenly how vulnerable are the traces of history. So much stuff accumulating – who is going to keep it all, who will pay for its retention and preservation? And but for the efforts of little people like this, volunteers, low-paid staff with enthusiasms for life's left-behind and cast off stuff, the clippings, postcards, scrapbooks, the past can just slip away, like last year's leaves crumble into dirt. If this didn't work, my only hope would be the memory, clippings and hoarded mementos of old-time residents, people who had raised children here and who had salted away records of that time, out of habit, or for the sake of reawakening the memories in the long winters.

It was taking Linda a long time I thought. When she did appear she seemed upset, flustered. "Mr. Therman, it's very upsetting and I'm embarrassed." She looked at me earnestly through her glasses. Her hands were together, twisted together in distress. "They are all there, all in good order, just as I knew them to be ...."

"But not the 64?"

She shook her head. "No, no, the 1964 volume is missing. And you understand we don't sign them out. They don't leave the building. This is where they belong, we're very firm about that. I'm upset Mr. Therman, I really am."

I could see that she was, but there was nothing to be done about it. She would keep on looking for it, I knew that, just from the look of her.

"Was anyone else asking for that year?" I asked, hopefully, but she shook her head.

"I wondered though, if possibly the 1963 issue might be useful." She looked at me hopefully, as if she longed for me to accept her consolation prize. I nodded acceptance and she went to fetch it.

I noticed children's art works on the painted cinder block walls, curling at the edges and full of their naïve enthusiasms, reflecting a world in which young people didn't disappear or get murdered on a lonely highway.

They didn't do High School yearbooks then the way they do now. In a way graduation was a bigger thing then than now but they didn't make as much fuss about it. Today it means less but is made more of. Of course, there was less money around to make fusses about many things back then.

The 1963 yearbook wasn't much more than some faint mimeographed pages, the paper brittle. The paper itself looked funny, as did the type, and the way it was written uncool. There was a photograph of the graduating class, barely resolvable, and a list of students for each grade. Except for the page containing the grade 11 students! That had been carefully cut out, neatly excised from the volume. The missing 1964 evidently was no accident. Someone was purging history, and had anticipated this line of enquiry and shut it down, wanting the past to stay just as it was, nicely obscure, hidden in the fog of past tense.

I showed Linda the neat line where the page had been. She gasped and said, "Oh dear. Oh dear! I don't know how that could have happened. No one has ever looked at these to my knowledge. This is terrible, just terrible, I simply don't know what to say!"

"Someone doesn't want me to know the past it seems, Ms. Evans. I suspect you'll find that the Grade 10 page is missing from the 1962 issue as well."

She put her hand to her mouth then fetched the volume before coming back looking crestfallen."

"It's not your fault," I told her." Thanks for your help."

She was in great anguish at not being able to help me, at having been found wanting in the face of a determination to obliterate the past but there wasn't much I could do about that. I'd made her a day a bad one but someone else had made mine bad too.

Were the missing annual and the missing pages clues, or was this just a coincidence, nothing to do with me or my poking around? Somehow it didn't have the feel of a clue. The clues usually had been in a series, one leading to the other, but there had been nothing pointing me here. But that didn't mean it wasn't connected I realized. I was investigating one bizarre set of circumstances and the odds were against my intersecting another but separate bizarre set of circumstances. So it was connected although I suspect it had been done long ago, perhaps because of some other investigator or just a precaution, the result of a long, careful weeding of the signs and fingers pointing. But the question was, why? What was he trying to hide? Was it Stephanie the High School annual thief didn't want me to know about or was it someone else, perhaps her killer, if, in fact, she had been killed.

I had concluded it wasn't a clue, yet in a way it was. It told me that whatever was going on had something to do with the High School and with Stephanie's graduating class in particular. I'd come up empty handed, no further ahead in terms of my knowledge, yet strangely it was like another giant clue. I felt I had progressed because for the first time I had seen the hand of the killer, almost as strongly as if he had sent me a note saying look for the list of names. So the absence was also a presence. Still, I was stymied, my road ahead blocked. Until I had the list of graduates I would be unable to start to piece together who was who. Where are you, you bastard, and who are you?

The local police detachment for the area was also located in Falcon Lake, so after saying so long to the librarian I decided to pay them a visit. I didn't expect that they would be particularly helpful but I certainly had to try.

There were two police cruisers outside the white wooden building, but when I went through the door and approached the desk, there didn't seem to be anyone around. There was a bell on the desk, so, feeling guilty as I always do when there's a bell, I hesitated but when no one came, rang it. After a while a young constable stepped out of an office at the back and asked me if he could help me.

He was tall, lean, young, seemed tired. His blond hair was short. His eyes were blue, but looked somewhat bloodshot.

"On May 4, 1965," I told him, "Stephanie Shawcross travelled down the highway from Winnipeg to Thunder Bay. She was supposed to stop for a friend in Kenora. Only thing is, she never made it. Somewhere along the route something happened to her and she disappeared. There must have been an investigation of sorts and I'm wondering if there's anything you can tell me about it."

It seemed to rock him back on his heels a bit and he looked at me blankly for a moment and then smiled. It wasn't a terribly open or friendly smile but the lips did move. "You press?"

I shook my head. "My name's Colin Therman," I told him. "A friend told me about Stephanie and I promised to see what I could find out. As I was in the area.."

"As you were in the area," he repeated and I began to wonder if he was thick.

"I know 65 is a while ago," I babbled on. "Before your time," I added, striving for a note of jocularity. Public officials rarely get my jokes and attempts at humour but that's another story.

"Long time ago," he said, underlining the obvious. "Hold on a sec," he instructed me and went back into the office.

After a while Corporal Simard came out of the office. The contrast between him and the other cop was stark. Simard was a man of a different stripe altogether, obvious in how he held himself and how he talked.

"Well well, Mr. Therman, we meet again. First a train now a dead girl. Heard you were around, driving a fancy car, wondered what had brought you to this neck of the woods. It's a cold case you're talking about here is that it?"

I nodded.

"We don't keep files that old around here. But what's your interest? Is it personal?" Simard asked.

Yes, I thought to myself. Yes, it damn well is personal, but there was no way I was going to tell him so. "I'm just interested," I repeated. "A friend asked me."

"The name of your friend?"

I shook my head. "Just a friend."

"Lots of people disappear," he said, "I'm sure you know that. And there's usually not much to be done, often no clues or hardly any at all. Many people who disappear want to do so, it's voluntary."

I had to bite my tongue hard, because of course I knew all that, had been told it so many times, by police, counsellors, do-gooders of all stripes when Cindy disappeared. I knew it well, I understood it, but I knew that Stephanie hadn't just walked out of her life, turned a page, shown her back to family and location and friends just like that. I didn't think that because I knew her of course, but because I was damn sure Mystery Man wouldn't have pointed me here if it had been that simple.

With great, even I think admirable, restraint, I told him that I knew all that and didn't think it applied in Stephanie's case. "All I want is whatever information the police found out when they investigated it," I told him. "It might help me that's all."

"You live around here," he asked.

I shook my head. "Pinawa."

"Nice place, know some people there, maybe ask about you."

I laughed. "Well just don't believe everything you hear! How about the files?"

He looked me over, as only policemen can do, and then seemed to soften towards me. "The file will be at HQ in the city. I could get them to send it out but they'd want to know why and someone like you walking in off the street doesn't work on an official form." He smiled. "But," he said, "next time I'm there, if I've a few spare moments, I'll see if I can dig it up, look it over, that do you?"

"I'd appreciate that," I told him.

"I have to tell you, though," he added, "there won't be much. There rarely is – much. I'd be surprised if it will help you any. People that long ago usually stay disappeared."

"I have a story to tell you," I said.

"Don't have much time for stories," he said.

"It's short, don't worry," I reassured him. "On Christmas Day in 1966, a 17-year old boy called Pat left his girlfriend's house with Bernie, his 15-year old friend to walk home. It was windy and freezing rain was falling. It was a two-hour walk over a mountain, something they had done many times before. The difference was that this time they never made it. They found Bernie, dead of hypothermia, within a couple of miles of home but there was no sign of Pat. The years went by. They built a highway right across the mountain, chopped down trees near where the two boys had walked that afternoon, moved gravel nearby, and started to build a new resort right there and all that time they never found Pat, although he was lying there not far away all that time. For 37 years his family never knew for sure what had happened to him, had to put up with all that horrible uncertainty, never able to grieve properly. And then one day in 2003 an employee of the resort raked some ground and dug up a couple of inches of peat and there he was, his clothes intact though crumbling to the touch. Unfortunately his mother had died a few years earlier but for other family members and townspeople who remembered how he had disappeared in the storm it was a relief to know finally for certain what had happened. Many of his 17 brothers and sisters attended the funeral."

"In Newfoundland, wasn't it," he said.

I nodded.

"So, there's always hope," he said.

"Exactly! There's always hope," I repeated.

"You sure this isn't personal, Mr. Therman?" he asked.

I thought that everything was personal in the end, just about every damn thing, but shook my head.

"See what I can do," he said.

I thanked him and left. I'm not sure what I had achieved by my visit. Now the police knew I was looking for Stephanie, they knew my name and they knew where I lived. Somehow I doubted that I'd ever hear from Simard again, but maybe he'd surprise me.

I drove the Audi back onto the highway and then pointed it west, accelerated and clicked on the cruise control, driving through Hadashville and Elma, on through Whitemouth, and then turning right and down towards Lac du Bonnet and then right again, across the bridge and so into Pinawa.

As I drove, I thought pessimistic thoughts about how easy it turns out to be to extinguish the embers of the past, or to bury them. Linda and I sometimes felt as if we were the only people who still knew that Cindy had ever existed, that the present has a great smothering tendency to obliterate its footsteps as it moves into the future. I was desperately afraid of emerging from this having achieved nothing, yet I knew that I had made real progress. The embers were gone all right but there was a black spot where they had been, a sign that the list of students was important, not a wild-goose chase, well not unless whoever did it was a lot cleverer than I thought he was. Yet I still knew nothing about Stephanie, only that she had gone missing. I knew that she must have come along the road past West Hawk but I certainly didn't know if West Hawk had any other connection to her, if she was even a student there or not.   Making me think the list of students was important, perhaps falsely, would be brilliant and ensure I would waste my time. Yet I didn't think so. What troubled me more than anything is that I still wasn't really making any progress. I was working hard, but so far no clear picture was emerging.

I spent the next week interviewing people in West Hawk and Falcon Lake. I told most of the people I talked to that I was doing research for a book. They'd look faintly interested, then puzzled, then interested again as they thought about the idea of them being in it. Most of them were willing to spend a little time with me, although not everybody was. Still I don't think any of them could really imagine a book about this place or that anyone would want to write about it, and their willingness to talk was often tinged with suspicion. I didn't tell them that I was after a killer or a body.

Interviewing people is slow work, uncertain. I worked in questions about yearbooks and student lists whenever I came across someone old enough for it to be relevant. Slowly it emerged that there was a hard core of old timers, people who had always lived here it seemed, could remember what it had been like. Most of these people remembered the old highway, and told me vividly how different the place had been then. People came and stayed, they told me. Now they come on weekends and are gone, pack the beaches and then leave. Winters were quieter then as well. There were no snowmobiles back then and folks were much less eager to travel it appeared. All said it had been quieter also, some with regret others as if they liked the current ever presence of the snarl of engines and oily reek of the two-stroke motor. Nobody had yearbooks, or knew anyone who had. Nobody remembered a young woman called Stephanie Shawcross.

If you've ever done anything like this you know how wearying it gets, asking the same questions, probing delicately, always having to hide the real reason for your interest. Encouraging people to be candid while dissembling yourself is tiring and frustrating. At the end of the week I was ready to pack it in. I felt I had got precisely nowhere, and done a lot of work to achieve that. And word was getting around fast, so much so that by Thursday most of the people I talked to had already heard I was around asking questions, told me they'd expected me. And some of them had already talked to Alex. That wasn't necessarily good. Memory is fallible and often the best and truest answers come from the unprepared. Giving people time to think about it often embellishes their recollection. People got suspicious too at my attempt to be methodical, to get it all down. I had to be careful what I wrote, relying dangerously on my memory and hasty scribbles afterwards to capture what I'd heard.

Talking about the past in general terms, reminiscing, was one thing, getting down people's names and lists of employees and ages was another thing altogether. Everyone becomes suspicious then. If I was writing a book, why did I need their names and ages? A history book? Well even so, can't say I like the idea of someone writing down my name, my age, my wife's in a little book, they'd tell me. Got to ask yourself why you're doing that. You give us a story about a history book. Easy to say isn't it? So I was raising suspicions, which told me I'd not be able to finish the task this way. People would get nervous and refuse to cooperate. I'd have to try a different tack. Ironically, it was just as I was finishing up that I heard the name Betty Kingsford. It was at the Esso station and he was probably the guy who'd told Alex about her, had remembered the name now, disproving my idea about prepared answers. He filled the Audi's tank, admired the car and told me of the retired teacher, Kingsford was her name he'd remembered, Betty Kingsford. She lived around here, he told me, and knew all the students. He didn't know her himself, was too young for that but he'd heard about her from other people. She might know something useful he told me. It was too late to do anything about it that day, but I filed the name away for future action.

9

GETTING METHODICAL

The following morning, after shower and breakfast I went into the basement and looked at the two whiteboards I had put up recently. By now Alex and I had collected enough information to try to make sense of it all. Being able to look at it would help us understand what we knew and what we didn't yet know and to identify the key things we had to do, or so I hoped.

I wrote 'Stephanie Shawcross' across the top of the first board and stuck up the newspaper picture I had of her. It was a lousy photo but for the moment it was all I had. I had never done anything like this for Cindy and briefly I wondered why, but I knew the answer – I had never had any clues at all in her case. She had simply vanished into thin air with no trail to follow, nothing at all. For a moment, a mad moment, I sensed her presence in the room with me, as if she were helping me and then it faded and disappeared. Both Cindy and Stephanie had vanished but with Stephanie there was a definite trail, although whether it would be enough to solve the puzzle of her disappearance remained to be seen.

Underneath Stephanie's picture I wrote: 'reason for disappearance' and under that '1) did it on purpose, 2) murdered, 3) accident, car & body not found, and 4) kidnapped and maybe still alive.' Those were the four possibilities Alex and I had talked about. I circled 2 & 3, not because I had any clue that they were the most likely reasons for her disappearance but because they were only ones we were likely to be able to deal with. Accident should be relatively easy to check out as well and could readily be eliminated. There could be only so many places that a vehicle could come off the road and not be noticed for 40 years!

I looked at what I had written and then went back and added two lines beneath number 2, '2a) someone she knew and 2b), a stranger.' Stranger would be harder to deal with, but the odds were that if she had been murdered it was by someone she knew. So who knew Stephanie?

Under the 4 possible causes for her disappearance I wrote a new title, 'Murder' and under that: 'who knew?' and 'motive?'. I thought about it for a moment and then added 'where?' and 'how?'.

Another key question we had was what the exact link was between Stephanie and West Hawk. To express that I wrote: 'Stephanie←→West Hawk?' and then a list of possibilities: 'work (summer student?), lived there, High School friends' and then another line: 'other?' When I'd finished, this is what it looked like:

Stephanie Shawcross

Reasons for disappearance:
1)Disappeared voluntarily - probably still alive?
2)Murder?
  2a)Someone she knew?
  2b) Stranger?
3)Accident - car and body not found?
4)Kidnapped - still alive?

Murder:
-Who knew her?
-Motive? (why kill her?)
-Where? (location)
-How? (method)

Stephanie←→West Hawk?
-Work (summer job)?
  -Lived there (parents)?
  -High School friends?
  -Other?

I couldn't think of anything else to write on that board for the moment, so I turned my attention to the other whiteboard and wrote right across the top, 'why me?'

Next I added, 'red-laced hiking boots? Personal reasons (daughter). Likes trains.'

Putting the information and ideas down like this made it a lot easier to think clearly about what was going on and to question everything. Looking at the second board I realized suddenly that I didn't know for sure that this was about me at all. Perhaps Alex was the real focus of this mystery. Maybe whoever was behind it wanted to distract her from something or to get her into trouble. The person behind this was smart enough to figure out I'd call for her help or was that just too damn far-fetched to be credible?

I walked up and down a few times mulling this over but the more I thought about it, the less sense it made. It was good to question things, but in the end this new idea didn't lead anywhere. If he had wanted to get Alex into trouble all he had to do was bust us when we were breaking into the brick building.

I went upstairs and saw that Linda was just finishing up her language studies. She's a keen linguist and works hard at it. "Why would he choose me?" I asked her.

She gave me a puzzled look and then asked, "Your mysterious agent provocateur, or maybe provactrice?"

"Yes. He's leading me into deep waters, but why, what's the point of it? Stephanie has been dead for 40 years, her parents may already be dead for all we know, so why bother after all this time, and why involve anyone else? Why not just do the investigating himself?"

Linda thought about it for a moment and then said, "I always think that if you want to figure something out a good place to start is at the beginning."

"That sounds incredibly inscrutable and wise," I said, laughing at her.

"The kind of thing only a woman could come up with, and only a smart woman at that!" she responded.

"You forgot about the gorgeous part!"

She beamed.

"You're not going to tell me what to do, are you?" I said in my movie voice.

She looked at me puzzled for a moment and then groaned, having got it. "It's a mistake ever to let you see movies!"

"Come on, what is it?" I teased her. "It's one of your favourites."

"We shall know soon enough," she said, making her voice go deep.

"Never mind the Gladiator moment, just answer the question. I'll give you a clue. It has an hilarious karaoke scene."

"Keeping The Faith," Linda said like a shot, then punched me playfully and told me to get back to work.

I grinned and went back downstairs.

Go back to the beginning, she'd said. I wasn't at the start I saw right away. *I* wasn't the beginning. I'd been struggling with why he had chosen me, but the real question was why had he chosen *anybody*? What was his motive for making somebody else do the work? On the left hand whiteboard I had written motive? If Stephanie had been murdered there had to have been a reason why. Finding out why was critical to discovering who had killed her, how and where. But motive was equally critical when it came to trying to find why anybody wanted to know what happened to Stephanie. Why did anybody care after all these years? I cared now but I had been brought to care, bribed to care you could say, by an adventure thrown at me, the chance to work with Alex, and the sheer intellectual challenge of figuring out what had happened. Not to mention the darker hint that maybe just maybe I'd learn something about my daughter Cindy. But why had somebody got me to that point? So the question wasn't why me but why anyone? After all, the mystery man knew a lot more about what had happened to Stephanie than I did.

Maybe this was the reason Alex had been so apprehensive about this whole thing, so against my involving myself and had become involved herself probably only so she could make sure I didn't go off the deep end. Considering that she had helped me break into the brick building that hadn't quite worked out but it was still her motive I suspected. She was alarmed because the purpose for the person behind this was obscure, hidden, and it was impossible to think of anything innocuous to explain it.

I thought of a few possible motives. One might be that it was dangerous or might be dangerous. Breaking into the brick building had been dangerous but that wasn't a necessary part of the Stephanie case at all, so that didn't count. I stared at the board but I still couldn't see any reason to suppose that chasing the reason for Stephanie's disappearance might be harmful to my health, unless of course she had been murdered and her murderer was still around, and still keen on continuing to get away with it.

Another possible reason was that the position of the person behind this made it impossible to look into it himself. I couldn't imagine what kind of position that could be however.

Could the murderer be behind this, I wondered. Would that make any sense? Perhaps he had finally decided to come clean after all these years. But if so then why go through this elaborate charade? Why not just confess, and have done with it? Or was he testing to see if anyone could in fact figure it out, doing it as a kind of dare?

I paced up and down some more and then turned back to the board, thinking out loud and waving the marker. I grinned to myself as another thought occurred to me. Perhaps I was looking for something complicated when it was really as simple as him not having the time or being handicapped and so unable to do it himself. But that still left the puzzle about the timing. Why wait for 40 years? Why did it still matter to anyone what had happened to Stephanie?

The key to the mystery then was finding out why the mystery man would choose someone to do his dirty work for him. It didn't matter that I was selected, but that someone else, not himself, was selected. Once there was a reason for involving someone else then it was merely a question of finding someone who could be enticed into doing it. But then why not come clean and simply ask? The manipulation, the game with clues, the train ride, the Audi lease, all suggested considerable enticement, but a dishonest kind, the true cost, the true reason being kept hidden. And that in turn suggested that if I had been approached openly I would have refused and I would have refused because I wouldn't have liked the reason why this person wanted Stephanie's case solved. It couldn't be something harmless and understandable like her father wanting to know what had happened to his daughter. I could understand why a father would always want to know no matter how long ago it had been, but then that would have been a perfectly good reason, one I could have accepted easily. That, clearly, wasn't it.

The more I thought about it, the more it looked as if the motive for involving someone was important and the more it appeared that it might be a bad one, a motive that I wouldn't like or could go along with. There was something hidden here that I didn't understand. I couldn't assume that whoever was behind this had good intentions, so I would have to step carefully to make sure I didn't advance his agenda.

I erased what I had written on the second whiteboard and instead wrote 'Why Intermediary?', then listed the reasons I'd thought about: 'too dangerous, no time, would expose him, physically unable', and 'to test if safe from being found out.'

Alex came over after supper. She was slumming today, in a ragged pair of jeans and a baggy sweatshirt. When she came downstairs and saw the charts she was impressed. She walked up to them and stood examining them for some time. "You know," she said, pointing to the Why Intermediary chart, "it should have been obvious earlier considering everything we have gone through, but this guy likes manipulating people, don't you think?"

I gave her a high five and added, 'likes manipulating people' to the list and then, under it, 'voyeur.' The whiteboard now looked like this:

Why Intermediary?
-too dangerous
-no time
-would expose him
-too old, infirm, handicapped (physically unable)
-to test if he is safe
-likes manipulating people
-voyeur

Alex looked at the second chart some more and then turned to me and said she thought we needed an additional chart. "You've asked why he wants an intermediary but we also need to know who he is. Who is behind this? It's important because, well just because but also it might help to understand why he's using an intermediary. It's important to know his motive – it might not be noble and we might not want to continue to play along. So what do we know about him, the guy behind this, Mr. Mystery Man?"

I'd run out of whiteboards but I'd bought a few sheets of poster paper. I stuck one up on the wall with masking tape and wrote 'Who Mystery Man?'

"We know," Alex said, enumerating with her fingers. "We know he can organize things. His job or his profession, or his skills allow him to set up things like the train ride, like having those clues ready for us in the brick building. You or I probably couldn't do that, so why and how can he?"

"He also knew about us, so he must be local, or someone who can find out about people," I said.

"He must also be a damn good judge of people, too," Alex remarked. "Every step of the way he has been able to calculate our reaction precisely and correctly."

I wrote down what we had talked about, and we stood looking at the sheet for a while.

"Hmm," Alex said. "One thing we missed: What's his connection to Stephanie?"

"Maybe he's the murderer," I suggested.

"Or a witness," Alex said.

I wrote 'Mystery Man ←→ Stephanie?' and under it, 'murderer? witness?' and then added 'lover? friend? family?'

When I was finished, the third sheet looked like this:

Who Mystery Man?
 -can achieve things:
        --train ride
        --clues in brick building
 -knows about people, can find out info about
 -good psychologist (reads people accurately)
 -can watch people?

Mystery Man←→Stephanie?
 -murderer?
 -witness?
 -lover?
 -friend?
 -family?

Alex and I pulled over chairs and sat and looked at the poster. "I don't like this guy," Alex said. "I think he's a creep, up to no good, malevolent even."

I shivered suddenly.

"Catching a cold?" she asked with a grin.

"A chill from him," I said.

"I still think you should give this up you know," Alex said. "Quit playing his game."

I knew that she was right, looking at it logically, but I also knew that I wasn't ready to give it up just yet. It wasn't so much that I disliked Mystery Man, although I agreed with Alex that he must be a pretty creepy guy, but that I still felt I could do some good, that finding out what had happened to Stephanie would settle something, bring something worthwhile out of this business. I should have realized, of course, that when an evil man's plans and those of a good man – well, giving myself the benefit of the doubt – align, the overall result is rarely good.

After Alex left I sat some more and looked at the charts. They were all very pretty and well organized looking but I was dissatisfied with the effort. Nothing shouted Eureka, there were no ah ha moments. The truth of the matter was that we knew diddly squat. All the whiteboards and posters showed were questions, a whole slew of them. As for facts and answers, well we knew the name of the girl, we knew she'd disappeared and we knew that somebody out there wanted me to do something about it apparently, but that was it. Everything else was conjecture, might-bes and perhaps. And over it all hung this sense of dread, of something sinister at work, something vague but unsettling.

Alex and I had spent two months on this and although we'd been as busy as bees, we had precious little to show for it. Sure we'd had some fun along the way, no doubt about that, been able to put aside the sense of something ominous about the whole affair, but now it was time to start digging deeper and harder. I had a feeling that the fun part of this was definitely over now. The clues and the games had ended and now the real work would begin, the hard slogging. How much time was I prepared to put into it I wondered? I sat and thought about this but I didn't know the answer. What I'd like to do I knew was set myself an arbitrary goal, a time limit, after which, if I didn't know significantly more I'd give it up. The problem was the guy knew something about Cindy or implied he did, and I simply couldn't risk not finding out what it was. And with that thought in mind I left the room with the whiteboards and poster, turned off the lights and went upstairs.

10

BETTY KINGSFORD

It was a different world I drove in the next morning, retracing my steps back to West Hawk. It was Monday, and most of the campers were back at work in the city, probably looking through the windows from their cubicles and cursing that the weather could be so uncooperative. Today was warm, blue and wonderful, a joy to be alive in. I was going to call on the school teacher and see what she could tell me. If the missing pages from the school annuals had anything to do with Stephanie then clearly she had at least gone to school around here. Of course it might have been a coincidence, and nothing to do with the missing girl, but somehow I doubted it.

The Audi moved smoothly down the road, Mozart playing quietly on the CD player. There were a couple of farm trucks trundling down the highway. Off to my left the narrow Whitemouth river muddied its way west. Old barns, some sagging towards collapse, dotted the farmland. One had a sign on it saying Red Diamond Farm, need a bull?

Not this morning, thanks, I thought.

Hay was being cut and rolled, encased in plastic. I still remembered when the fields would be dotted with myriads of little square bales. Now monster wheels were the norm, giant cakes of hay. In some fields canola was beginning its run to that perfect, impossibly bright yellow that paints the land when it is fully in bloom. Near the river, the land was folded gently, as if in time past the flow had been much greater than it was now, the faint boot prints of the ice age. In the depressions formed there, cattle grazed amidst scrub ash trees and oak.

At Whitemouth a work train stood on a siding, a long line of beaten-up white passenger and freight cars. An SD-40 idled nearby.

I remembered what Mrs. Campbell had said to me in West Hawk. The Trans Canada highway that now lay south of here didn't exist 40 years ago. Instead the road I travelled now was the main route across the country and even it had changed substantially from what it was like when Stephanie Shawcross came down it on her ill-fated trip.

I knew that there were sections of the old highway that still remained, abandoned fragments of the old route, cut off and left to die alone off in the bushes. With a sharp eye, and travelling slowly you could make out the old stretches of road here and there. I'd used one of them to get to the CN/CP rail crossing. One of the ideas we'd written on the whiteboard was the possibility that Stephanie had come off the road, been killed and never been found. I thought that was pretty unlikely but if it had happened that way, it would probably have occurred along one of these abandoned stretches of old asphalt as it was farfetched to suppose her car could have remained undetected anywhere else.

Just past Whitemouth, where the highway turns east and runs away from farmland, there's a bridge across the brown Whitemouth River. Near it were signs of the earlier highway. I stopped to get out to look.

On each side of the river was a concrete abutment, with no span between them. It looked very much as if there had been a bridge there, eventually replaced with the current structure. Could she have come off there and gone into the river and for some reason not been spotted?

I nosed around the existing bridge, hoping to spot some marker and eventually found a round metal plate saying it had been built in 1969. If Stephanie had got this far she would have come over the old bridge then not the one on which I was standing. But the idea that her car could have remained undetected in this river for 40 years was simply ludicrous. For one thing the old bridge had stood very near the new one. Besides, the Whitemouth River is hardly deep at the best of times and in the fall, after a dry summer, it would have been impossible for something as large as a car not to be spotted. If her disappearance had been caused by an accident, it hadn't happened here.

Past Whitemouth, the landscape soon abandoned farming and took to trees, with small homesteads carved out of the forest here and there, smoke rising from chimneys. The lean-to buildings looked haphazard and mean. One of them had a boarded-up vegetable stand standing near the road. Shortly after this transition from field to forest, I spotted the first stretch of hidden highway.

It was easily visible from the road, a long section of weed-choked asphalt running parallel to the current road. I parked the Audi and walked along it. The crumbling road bed was penetrated by small trees and weeds, but the centre line was still faintly visible in some sections. Part way along it was a narrow wooden bridge crossing the Bog River, which was really nothing more than a trickle of water almost invisible in the weeds. Patches of old white paint still clung to parts of the timbers. The short wooden guard rails on both sides were intact. It was unlikely she could have come off the road here but I cut a piece of branch from a nearby tree and probed the depth of the creek. Water levels were still high from spring run off but even so the water was barely three feet deep near the bridge. I walked on past the bridge but the road soon began to peter out and up ahead I could see that it was interrupted by cultivation.

I got back in the car and drove on. I knew somehow in my heart of hearts that Stephanie hadn't succumbed to an accident. I had to check it out, of course, but deep down I was certain I was wasting my time. Stephanie had been murdered and I understood instinctively I suppose that Mystery Man knew it. Perhaps he was even the murderer himself, although why he might want that discovered was beyond me.

I found another section of hidden highway just past the highway overpass over the CN rail tracks. Here the old route ran at a higher elevation than the new highway along the ridge of rock that rose above the surroundings. Weeds thrust through the centre and crowded both edges, and fallen trees lay across one section of the old tarmac. At some time someone had driven a bulldozer here cutting ridges into a short section of the old route. The piece of old road was only a few hundred feet long, abruptly severed by the CN tracks at one end and petering out at the other although there was a cut through the trees indicating that the road once ran further although the tarmac was no longer visible there. I walked up and down the stretch of old road but there was nothing here to suggest that she might have come off the road and could have remained undetected. I shrugged and walked back to the car.

There were other sections of hidden highway further along but somehow I had lost my enthusiasm for checking them out. I was pretty certain that Stephanie had been murdered. Mystery Man wouldn't have laid on a train, paid for a car lease, left clues in a building and under overpasses just so I could find out where Stephanie had come off the road in a deadly accident. Mystery Man knew something, that was for certain, and he also wanted me to know it too, but without telling me straight up, face to face. I couldn't figure out why and that was another critical part of this whole business. Figuring him out and especially why both Alex and I thought of him in terms of evil was as important as figuring out what had happened to Stephanie all those years ago.

Maybe I'd go back to the highway sections sometime. They had always interested me, and I'd often stood on them and imagined the traffic travelling down them in those days, along the narrow and twisting lanes. For the moment, however, they would be for another day, another time. Right now I was keen to call on the teacher to see if I could persuade her to talk to me.

Betty Kingsford still had traces of an English accent. She greeted me at her doorway at first with anxiety and then relief when she understood who I was. I'd called ahead of time of course, having found her name readily enough in the local phone book. When I'd spoken to her on the phone she soon admitted she had taught back in the 60s and 70s.

She was stooped now, with a deep hunch to her back, her hair tied in a silver bun, and strong glasses perched precariously on a long, sharp nose. She may have once been beautiful but it was a stretch. She was thin and bony and didn't look as if she'd ever had much flesh to her. What I liked about her right away were her eyes, which were alive and inquisitive. She'd become a teacher because she was interested in things she'd told me over the phone and I sensed that she still was.

The house was small, warm and dark. She seemed to like it that way. Two cats were about, thoroughly comfortable with the look and feel of the place.

"I don't often have visitors," she apologized. For what I wondered.

The dingy living room into which she led me was stuffed with furniture, small pieces all covered with doilies and coverings and cluttered with things, ornaments, plant pots with mostly thin, uninspired looking plants eking out a bare existence. Book cases stood in two corners, but the hard-backed volumes all appeared old and old fashioned. There was no TV here, no music, in fact no noise at all in the house, and I realized suddenly that there were no photographs anywhere, no smiling husbands, grinning babies, beaming kids and relatives. I had a sudden sense of something drying out, the house, the cats, the woman desiccating gradually, fading, fading. I shook it off and smiled when she announced that we'd have tea of course.

While she got that ready in the kitchen, I nosed around the room, looking to see if the photos had been removed for my visit. If so, she'd covered the traces expertly. Not only was there no room for them, there were no tell-tail dust marks or cleaner looking sections of doily to suggest the arrangements had ever been other than they were now.

I'd never been in a house without pictures before and it made me feel odd, as if there was something about Mrs. Kingsford that wasn't quite right. I fantasized that there'd be something in the tea and I'd be kept here, comatose, forever, unable to escape the silent, grey, smothering world she lived in.

I smiled and shook it off as she came back into the room with a small tray containing tea pot, cups, milk, sugar and a small plate with precisely four biscuits. She set the tray down, poured tea and sat down, easing herself carefully into her chair with a soft sigh.

"Now then," she said sharply, "you didn't come for the tea."

"Ms. Kingsford, as I explained on the phone I'm trying to track down some students from the 1964 graduating class. I'm investigating something that happened a long time ago and I need to find out who was there and then I need to see if I can find them to ask them questions."

"Something happened?" She looked at me expectantly. Clearly she wasn't going to be fobbed off with glossed-over explanations.

I sighed and put down the tea cup. "The following year," I explained, "one of the students disappeared and hasn't been seen since. I'm trying to find out what happened."

"Who?"

I told her what I knew.

"Why do you suppose it has anything to do with her classmates?" It was a good question, delivered as she looked at me over the top of those thick reading glasses.

"I'll be honest, it's just a hunch. And I have to start somewhere. I thought if I could find out who she went to school with, maybe track some of them down and talk to them, I might learn something useful." I spread my hands as if to say, what else could I do? I told her the rest, how I'd gone to the library, discovered the 1964 yearbook missing and the grade 11 page cut out from the 63 yearbook."

"Someone trying to obliterate their traces? How intriguing!" she said. "And how did this turn of events lead you to me, Mr. Therman?"

"Someone remembered you," I told her. "Someone said if anybody would remember the students you would. And the police interviewed you after Stephanie disappeared."

She looked at me quietly for a moment and then offered a slight smile. "Someone remembered me, now that sounds farfetched Mr. Therman!"

"Can you help me Ms. Kingsford?"

She sat looking at me severely from behind those glasses of hers. "I suppose I might," she said at last. "I don't often like to think back to those years, but, under the circumstances I might. Of course I'll need my books, can't do it without the books."

She must have seen a worried look pass across my face because she added, "Oh, don't worry, Mr. Therman. I have the books still! I don't know why really, but I do." She settled back into her chair and gave that little half smile again.

"Every year I taught, I bought a yearbook, or got a copy of whatever they were doing that year. They weren't as fancy earlier on as they were later. Everyone got caught up in fancy stuff after a while, but at first they didn't worry so much about that. Yes, every year. Don't know why now, you know. I haven't heard from any of them in decades." She cackled suddenly and sat upright in the chair. "Decades? What am I talking about? I never heard from any of them once they left, period. Ever. Anyone. I taught and then I didn't teach and they forgot about me. I gave them everything in the classroom and out of it they gave me, well nothing Mr. Therman." She said it fiercely, but in way that didn't seem to invite sympathy.

"The world can be a cruel place," I muttered stupidly.

She looked at me angrily. "You don't know the half of it," she said, "Not the half of it!"

I looked at her, thinking that indeed I did know the half of it, but just nodded.

She got to her feet carefully, slowly, letting out an oof and a grunt as she did so, straightening her stiff old joints. "Intelligent design!" she said suddenly. "Have you ever heard of anything quite so unintelligent as the design of a person!"

She went slowly off out of the room presumably to check on the albums, leaving me with the cats. Neither had shown much interest in me but now the black one came slowly forward, reached out a paw and after a while lifted its head so I could scratch its chin.

"Here we are," she said, "1964." She looked at me quizzically for a moment then shook her head. "I'm sometimes surprised by young people today, how little they know how fast the world has changed. You tell them you used to use an icebox, not a refrigerator, that they cut big cubes of ice from the lake in the winter and stored it all year under hay, delivering it door to door in horse-drawn wagons to keep the icebox cool and they have no idea, no idea at all. The world was born with jet planes, cell phones, ipods, plasma TVs and computers in their view. But back in the preDevonian things weren't quite like that." She looked up and let out a thin laugh.

She showed me the album, really just a dozen sheets of paper stapled together. It had been mimeographed and was faded and blurred. But it wasn't the pictures I wanted, but the names.

"Do you remember any of them?"

"From 64?"

I nodded.

"If I asked you who was in your graduating class Mr. Therman, could you remember?"

"One or two, perhaps, if that," I admitted with a laugh.

"Mr. Therman," she said, "you think I've retreated here to await fossilization, for the sedimentary process to do its work. Oh, don't deny it, I can see it in your face. I haven't had much luck in life, with loves, with friends, with relatives. But I could teach. And I'd be teaching now if I could. I'm far too old now of course but I didn't even get the chance to grow old in the job." She began to cry.

I was dumbfounded. What the hell had I stumbled on? She held up her hands when I made to rise and come to her aid.

"No fool like an old fool!" she said at last when she had wiped her eyes. "I haven't cried in years. Feels good in a way, but I always say it's a mistake to let the waterworks take over!" She cackled then.

"What happened?"

"Never mind," she said. "It's none of your business! Let's concentrate on those students you want to talk to. What I was about to say before that stupid emotional outburst, was that I can remember their names and what they were like but I need the pictures to start me off. Shall we begin?"

It took two afternoons of tea and the dark, soft confines of her cocoon to extract what she knew of the students she'd taught, and known almost 40 years ago. I learned a lot about the students and her sharp, at times wicked appraisals of them, but nothing more about her. She'd been an inspired, clever, and energetic teacher, that was clear, the kind of instructor that can make a huge difference in a child's life, yet something had happened to finish her at doing what she loved and lived for. I'd raised this once, carefully I thought, considerately, and she'd told me in clear fashion that if I asked her anything about herself again she would terminate all business with me then and there. I took her seriously. On that last afternoon, when she'd finished she looked up at me with those sharp, bright eyes and said I should go. "You've sucked me dry," she said, "Oh as if I could be any dryer than I already am! You've brought back memories I'd just as soon not have, bright ones, hopeful ones. Life is a mad, wasteful business. They are all so bold and hopeful when they're young and they go on to such boring, uneventful lives, never living up to their bright potential. Some of them escape, use their wings and fly away but so many don't – can you imagine! They remain stuck like flies to flypaper, buzzing around but firmly fixed."

"Now I can't vouch for it personally," she told me, "But if you want to find any of the left-behinds, you should try the Water Rat."

"Personally, I don't much like rat, with or without water," I told her.

"Oh, you funny man, it's a tavern of course. It might task your geographic skills somewhat, as I hear it's hard to find, but they often hang out there, I'm told, from all the years. I call them the left-behinds because of course they are. Every year a few of them get stuck here, never move away. It's comfortable and familiar I suppose. They know the place, what to expect, who is who, what it all means, but I mean: to stay around here! It's a vacation place. To turn 18 and then just get stuck! Where is their ambition, their thirst for adventure? If they stayed to run a business, well a few of them do of course, take over from their parents eventually, nothing wrong with that. But if not that, and most of them don't have that, well what can they possibly do? Pump gas at the Esso station, be a waiter or waitress, clean cabins? Not much of a life if you ask me."

She looked pensive staring off into a private place. "I know, I know," she added sadly. "I made the mistake of sticking around here too long until they stuck me here forever, no escape now! But my point is, how can they stand to be forever hanging around here? Why don't they ever go away? I at least travelled the world, worked in every province in the country, made a point of it at one time, every province, even Newfoundland. Democracy needs informed citizens and if you never been anywhere how can you possibly be informed. And if you're not informed well the local politicians pander to all the local stupidities, the little local pets and peeves, parochial, inbred, incestuous petty stuff! You stay ignorant, prejudiced, knowing nothing whatsoever about the world."

She looked up at me and smiled faintly. "I do run on don't I! I used to tell them that you know, don't get lazy, be adventurous, grab life, don't just settle back, middle aged, bah, old aged before you're into your twenties. But people say oh local jobs, good to keep them at home! Rubbish! Humans didn't get to be humans by staying at home, Mr. Therman, we both know that. They were adventurous. We're built to stretch our legs, wonder what's over the next hill. Maybe the same as what you left behind but you never know until you get there, just never know. And then there's another hill after that to wonder about. That's what people are, well some of us, not all of us I suppose. The left-behinds, the sad lot of them. Stephanie wasn't one of those, and Jimmy wouldn't have been either, if..."

She stared off into that invisible place again, contemplating it. "Oh, Mr. Therman, it reminds me of something my mother used to say. My goodness, I haven't thought of her for years. She was a good woman, oh but she was hard. She had to be I suppose!" A tear filled her eyes then, fiercely fought and at last beaten back. She recited in a thin, high voice, "if ifs and ands were pots and pans, there'd be no need for tinkers' hands."
She went silent for a while and then said, "Oh I'm a silly old woman." Then she turned brisk and efficient again. "Yes," she said, "the Water Rat is where you'll find them! All the ones who couldn't quite find their way out of this place. The left-behinds. You'll find them there, some of them at any rate, wallowing in the familiar, the safe, the unadventurous, letting time tick away their options. It's a shame yet in a way I understand them.. You have to be brave to be an adventurer and many of them, well brave isn't what comes to mind I'm afraid." She smiled and shook her head. "No wonder they don't come to see me!"

"May I hug you?" I asked. "You've been immensely helpful and it has been a great pleasure to share tea with you."

She looked at me severely. "No, you may not!" she said, "but I appreciate the thought. Good day."

11

THE BOYS AND GIRLS OF WHITEMOUTH HIGH

Betty Kingsford had given me the names of twelve boys and fifteen girls, among them Stephanie Shawcross and her boyfriend Jimmy Case. Young men, young women I corrected myself, though kids in reality whatever the world may say of them, children about to go through the transition into adulthood. If they were like others before them and after, some of them entered it abruptly, too abruptly, while others took their time, underwent a more graceful transformation. But in the case of that particular class, one of them hadn't made it at all.

"I need more wall," I told Linda

"You sound like Gully Jimson," she laughed.

"I promise I'm not going to paint on it."

"That might be better than all those chicken scratches on the whiteboards," she said.

"I need to write down the names of 12 boys and 15 girls, and leave room to put down stuff about them, particular addresses and phone numbers."

"Poor Arthur," Linda said.

"Yep, he's got a lot of work ahead of him," I said with a smile. "It will be a good test for him."

I taped two more poster sheets to the wall beside the other sheets and the whiteboards. Much more of this and I really would need more wall!

Girls:
Stephanie Shawcross
Melony Timberlake
Melyssa Stoern
Kara Krupriuk
Ashley Montague
Denise Armandski
Candace Weibe
Pat Farthington
Sharon Tucker
Jennifer Doerkson
Holly Hazelrod
Cassandra Fleming
Julia Borgogne
Nichola Tess
Barbara Nicholuk

Boys:
Gerald Braintree
Jimmy Case
Arnold Nesbitt
Blake Shaniuk
Tim Surtowski
Andrew Wentworth
Stuart McFarlane
John Smithson
Robert Deslisle
Dean Croswell
Joshua Napier
Tod Penning

I'd put their names down on the list, heard Betty talk about them, but I hadn't really paid any attention to the names. I should have done of course, I realized later. It might have helped me to figure out what was going on. But instead I blundered ahead and emailed the result of my visit to Ms. Kingsford and the list of names to Arthur and Alex. Later, when I phoned Arthur, however, his voice mail came on and I remembered that he had said he was off to Europe to visit castles and museums. Alex, meanwhile had also decided to take some R&R and for some strange reason that apparently didn't involve helping me. For the moment, then, I was left to my own resources. I decided to nose around, ask questions again, see what turned up as I picked up the rocks and looked underneath.

In the park, the tourists were in full swarm. Everywhere you went their vehicles clogged the roads. The restaurants, camp grounds and motels were doing a roaring trade, and I was glad for them, if not for the visitors. The merchants were like brightly coloured flowers waiting for the bees to come. No bees, no honey, no pollination, it was that simple. There was one consolation at least: here there was at least a tourist season. They came but then they went. In some places it's pretty much all tourists all the time. Here the lake and beaches, the trees and even the water fowl could breath in near isolation part of the year, recover from the assault, the vacationers safely ensconced in their normal habitat, bringing peace back to the peaceful countryside.

At the turn of the 20th century there would have been nothing here, no roads, no cabins, nothing but the lake, unbothered by buoys for divers, boats, sunbathers or swimmers. It would have been peaceful on a summer day like today. I might have been able to walk down past the trees and look out over the water, see geese and ducks, hear the cry of the loon, see the lake in its natural state. There would have been no docks then, no cabins or campgrounds, no cell tower with its blinking red light, no power pylons, and I would certainly not have been in search of a body, looking perhaps for a murderer.

The image of the lake in its pristine state faded, difficult to maintain during the bustle of a July weekend at a tourist resort. In the midst of what was in fact a quiet, peaceful place, scenic and calm, there was however something intense and concentrated about the business of being on vacation, as if it had to be experienced intensely and stored up, as if charging a battery, filling up a reservoir that must last the rest of the year. Visitors didn't just sit and relax, lie in the sun and read a book, they shouted, they ran, they launched loud boats, they water skied, they drank beer and played games in the water, they played their radios, watched TV, unable in fact to escape at all, cramming summer into a few days or a couple of weeks, squeezing it hard, consuming their vacations aggressively, working at it furiously.

Perhaps it shouldn't have, but it all bothered me. Quiet was an obsolete, quaint notion in the country now. Noise, on the other hand was everywhere and I was sick of it. Would it have been as bad in 1964 I wondered? What was it like then? Perhaps it had been worse. The road which was now a winding, rough bit of tarmac, heaving and wrestling its way through the forest and outcroppings would have been the only road east west, the single road corridor along which people could travel and goods could move, although back then most goods moved by rail, and perhaps most people too. It would have been a much longer trek from the city, so perhaps fewer came. I tried to turn my mind back to what it might have been like but

I found it difficult. Perhaps I should give it up until the fall, when school started again and the numbers of visitors dwindled.

Of course, I was a visitor too, just as much non-native as the people in the campground, out in boats or on the beaches. I had no more right to be here than they had, and also as much.

Stephanie Shawcross had been here, I knew that now, had looked at the same lake as I now looked at, perhaps grimaced at the tourists once, just as I was doing. She had been murdered, I was sure of that, although lacking proof of it. Her body was nearby: I was certain of that also, although again with no evidence for it. Someone had killed her and the questions were who and why? What had she done, who crossed to explain why she had been murdered? And since she was murdered while travelling through here, the person who murdered her must have known she was going to be travelling here, so it wasn't an impulse killing, but something premeditated, planned. She had in short been executed, killed in cold blood.

But how could anyone have known she would be driving through here? And if she was in her car, how had he killed her? Had she got out to get gas, have breakfast perhaps, or look at the beach before continuing her drive?

The key question though was why she had been killed. What had she done to so enrage someone that he would want to kill her, and not only want to, but set about doing it, learning about her plans and working them into his own to murder her? Under normal circumstances killing isn't something that is easy. In time of war it's a different matter, although even then some men can't do it, cannot bring themselves to try to kill, even when others are trying to kill them. But in normal life, ordinary people can no more walk up to someone and stick a knife in them than they can jump off a cliff. She had to have done something to someone so enraging that that person could willingly kill her. Who could have done that and why?

I know nothing about the psyche of murderers, although before the year was out I was to learn more of that than I would have wished. I had thought this at first to be a great adventure, not realizing it would turn to evil. I hadn't yet seen the face of evil, nor witnessed its full savagery, but I was going to and a premonition of that perhaps made me shudder suddenly despite the balmy weather, the sun shining brightly and hot in a bright blue sky.

I walked slowly back to the Audi. I was going home I decided, although I had come here expecting to nose around some more. But I understood now that until the hordes had left I would be unable to concentrate, to dwell on her death, on who could have killed her, and above all on who wanted me to find her body and discover her killer. Why now, after all these years?

There was a police car idling blocking me from backing out of my parking spot. When I walked up to the car, the driver's window slid down. It was Corporal Simard.

"Mr. Therman, thinking about a day at the beach?"

I laughed. "I did think about it, but it's kind of crowded."

"I have something for you," he said. "About that young woman you were asking about. It's not much, maybe you know it all already. They checked the local hospitals but there was nothing, and they kept an eye out along the highway, asked around a bit, but there was nothing. There wasn't anything to go on at all, so they put it to bed, maybe a bit earlier than I would have done but...." He shrugged and then handed me a brown envelope through the open window. "All yours. I expect you probably don't need to read it, though, Mr. Therman," he added. "I imagine you're pretty familiar with the sort of thing that's in there unfortunately."

The way he said it I knew he'd found out about me, about my daughter. He turned his head and looked hard at me. "You see, Mr. Therman, I found another file while I was there, pretty similar to this one, one you know about already."

I nodded my head but said nothing. What could I say? Did I imagine he wouldn't check up on me?

"Now you told me this wasn't personal. To be honest, I didn't believe you. Didn't believe you then and certainly don't believe you now."

"It's not about my daughter," I said.

"Maybe not," he said, "but it's still personal I'd say. I can't stop you poking around, just don't make a nuisance of yourself, and be careful. And, if you find anything that you think might be relevant, bring it to me, all right?"

"Yes," I said, "Of course, and thanks for this, I really appreciate it. Good of you to go to the trouble."

"Take care, and have a nice day," he said. He closed the window, put the police cruiser in gear and drove off.

I got into the Audi, put the envelope on the front seat, started the engine and opened the moon roof.

He was right, of course. If it was similar to the file on my daughter, Stephanie's file would contain nothing useful, just the merest trail of police futility and impotence. I knew you stood a better chance of having the police find something in the country than in the city. In the big places, police are simply swamped, and missing people are a dime a dozen, rarely leaving clues. And with no evidence of crime, there's precious little to justify an ongoing investigation. In rural areas, however, police may be thin on the ground but they keep their eyes open, and they notice things. I felt it was pretty unlikely that Stephanie had simply come off the road and remained undiscovered for 40 years. The possibility was there, all right, but it was remote, an extreme long shot. And of course Mr.

Mystery Man just about ruled it out completely. It made no sense going to all the trouble he had, just to find that the girl had gone off the road somewhere.

I picked up the envelope and tore it open. Unfortunately, the information inside was pretty much as I suspected. The police had indeed checked all the hospitals – both on the day the disappearance had been reported and several days afterwards, with negative results. Several detachments had run the highway with an eye out for anyone having gone off the road somewhere but found nothing. Gas station attendants had been questioned in several communities, without anything turning up. Then the case had been filed away and forgotten. There was a notation marked five years after the disappearance to say that nothing further had turned up, the parents had been contacted with no results and the file was being archived. About the only useful thing in the report was her parents' address and the actual time she had set out on her trip down the highway.

It all seemed so inadequate and it brought back the outrage, the helplessness I had felt when my own daughter vanished. I remember feeling as if nobody believed that she even existed, that I was the only one who knew she was real, and that everybody else was just humouring me. At one stage Linda and I had become almost desperate to ensure everybody knew she was real, that we hadn't imagined her. We showed pictures, we got out her school reports, and then, later, we put them away again. And helplessly we watched as year after year the memory of her, the public memory of her, faded, thinned. When she would have been 21 we had a little memorial thing for her, and again just a year ago when she would have been 30 we made a cake with candles. We cried together a little that day, wept for her, for what she would have been but never had the chance to be, but we were determined that she would always be a part of our family, always with us, until the day we died.

The anger came back with full force then as I sat in the idling Audi – and the sheer helplessness. I had looked up and down, talked to people, made a nuisance of myself, spent months on her trail, and achieved absolutely nothing. There had been no mysterious trails, no strange unexplained happenings, no mysterious goings on hinted at. The slate had been clean. She had simply gone out one day and not come back, as simple as that. Nobody had seen her, nobody ever heard from her. And something similar had happened to Stephanie except that in her case, I was as certain as that I was alive that she had been murdered. Someone had killed her and my job was to find out who and why.

Perhaps I would be able to bring a killer to justice, or perhaps not, but at least I could find out the truth about why she vanished, put an end to the uncertainty. Stephanie might be a surrogate for my own daughter in some peculiar twisted psychological way, I didn't know, but then I didn't particularly care if she was. I was after her and I would find her! With that vow made, I drove home.

Once again, I stood in front of my whiteboards and posters and asked myself, why does one kill? I paced the room and thought about it. To allow a theft was one reason, but that wasn't likely in her case as she probably had little worth stealing and it hardly applied while she was travelling, unless a thief was simply after her car. But early in the morning, on a dark road through the middle of nowhere? It seemed unlikely. What else could it be? As I thought about it, alternately walking up and down, then stopping and pondering the words on the boards and poster paper, I thought about love and its evil twin hate. That was the most likely cause for anyone wanting to kill her – something to do with love or hatred. I needed to know who had loved her and who might have hated her or been jealous of her, and for that I needed Arthur's ferreting skills, Arthur now visiting the history of Europe.

12

BANNERMAN COMES CALLING

I stayed away from West Hawk but not from nearer places in the park. I spent many early mornings at Dorothy Lake, swimming or watching the day gradually develop then the peace disintegrate as visitors arrived. Frisbee man was often there, skimming his disks far out over the water against the wind and running to catch them as they boomeranged back to him. He used various weights of disk depending on wind conditions. I also encountered again the man with the three-legged dog. Dogs weren't allowed on the beaches, every beach was posted with signs attesting to that, although I'd had many run-ins with idiots thinking the signs somehow didn't apply to them. But great brutes chasing after my children on the beach was one thing, this dog entirely another. Besides, he was a local and friendly. The man and I admired the Frisbee thrower's skill, talked about the height of the water, how the summer was developing and then he would go his way.

Sometimes I stayed and sunbathed, bringing my lunch, by which time usually the beach was becoming crowded, the Frisbee man would have given up for lack of room to throw his disks and the three-legged dog would be long gone. Water skiers would appear, and sometime those cursed jet skis, their engine noise rising and falling as they hot dogged on the water. Often families would get fire pits going and smoke would drift over the beach. Boat loads of beachgoers would arrive, running their boats up on the sand outside the marked-off swimming area. By 2, I'd usually had enough, become so irritated with the noise and stupidity, the careless disregard for boating rules, people leaving their car doors open with their radio blasting, children running over you, spraying sand or water indiscriminately, beachgoers dropping refuse everywhere despite a plentiful supply of conveniently located garbage and recycle bins, that I could no longer stand it and would leave thinking nasty thoughts about my fellow man.

I walked this beach from May to October, sometimes even in the winter snow and I had a proprietary feeling for it, a sense that it was mine, that I had a responsibility for it. When I talk this way people sometimes think I'm a snob, or ridiculously possessive, but that's not it at all. I don't mind sharing the beach, the water, the park. They are beautiful and vary in fascinating ways with the seasons. But most of the visitors don't treat them as something precious, to appreciate and share; they treat them as something to devour, like a big Mac with fries. They are disdainful of rules, thoughtless of others, and insensitive to the feelings of people who live here. I think that's the big grudge against tourists everywhere – that they come and gawk and don't respect the residents and their ways. If you saw the state of the Dorothy Lake beach at the end of the day you'd see what I mean, or could hear the bedlam at this place on peak summer afternoons.

It saddened me that this place, which to me came alive when quiet, its beauty apparent most deeply when experienced silently, was so little appreciated. Sure, it's hardly a pristine wilderness. There's a road, a place to park, the trees have been thinned, the grass cut, there are places to change, a shelter to eat under when it rains, and they even dump loads of sand on the beach in the winter sometimes. It was a manmade beauty spot, I admit that. Yet instead of treasuring it, letting its peace wash over them, experiencing its power to relax the body and calm the mind, to slow time, deepen experience, visitors wanted to ratchet up the intensity. Instead of caressing it, they wanted to flail at it. I didn't mind sharing it, that wasn't the problem, but I couldn't stand sharing it with yahoos who didn't understand what it was they were sharing. And I certainly didn't want to share it with marauding hordes!

It was during this long interlude in which I made no attempt to make any progress on the case, other than looking at the whiteboards and posters from time to time that Linda and I received a visit from Constable Bannerman.

Linda had come downstairs to find me staring at the whiteboards as usual. "Sorry to interrupt the great mind at work," she said, "but there's a Constable Bannerman at the door who wants to speak to you." I hadn't heard the door bell.

I looked at her and smiled. "I'll give you a shout if I need back-up."

I'd seen Bannerman around but never spoken to him. He was a young man, and fairly new to Pinawa, his dark hair neatly cut, with a closely trimmed moustache and an impression of big shoulders for some reason. "Mr. Therman? Constable Bannerman. Falcon detachment asked me to have a word. Seems you've been upsetting some people in West Hawk and we want to know what's going on."

I was a bit taken aback by his approach, not one I'm too fond of, frankly. Not belligerent exactly but not neutral and fact finding either. I debated having the conversation standing up and then decided not to.

"Come into the kitchen and sit down," I said.

He came as requested but I can't say he did much for the ambiance of the place.

"So what is going on Mr. Therman?" he continued after he'd settled himself in the somewhat cramped confines of the kitchen eating area, not made for a guy with various pieces of hardware dangling from his belt.

"Who did you talk to at Falcon?"

"That's not the issue, Mr. Therman. We want to know what's going on."

"Ah, but it is the issue – do you have a first name Constable?"

He looked angry and told me this was a professional conversation, which in his view apparently excluded the use of first names. Personally, I've found some of the most professional and downright nasty conversations in the world have involved first names. 'Colin, we think you would be much happier (not to mention our being much happier) if you were to pursue opportunities elsewhere' was one that came to mind. Still I didn't get the impression Constable whatever-his-first-name-was was going to be too keen to debate the merits of that approach over his chosen method.

"They teach you that at the Police Academy – how to worm information out of people?" I asked. OK, I admit it: I'm just never at my best talking to someone with a gun hanging from them! When they are confrontational to boot, well to hell with them. One question deserves another so far as I'm concerned.

"Mr. Therman," he said, summoning up patience from what I suspected was a shallow reservoir, "we want to know what you are doing." He had put spaces between the words as if I had trouble following him. This guy was going to be a nuisance, it was becoming apparent. Dumb, armed with a gun, belligerent, and in my house.

"Constable won't-tell-me-your-first-name Bannerman, I'm trying to remain patient with you but you're making it very difficult. I asked you who you had spoken to at Falcon. It wasn't an idle question. I've spoken to people there. They know what I'm doing, so I don't understand your visit. Perhaps you'd care to share with me what precisely your concerns are, what exactly you'd like to know." Oh well, perhaps he wouldn't, but stupidly I was almost beginning to enjoy myself.

"One," he said, touching a finger of his right hand to the left little one, in case I was innumerate I suppose. "You've spent a lot of time in West Hawk and Falcon this summer. With that sexy lawyer. Your wife know about her?" He gave me a leer just to underline things for me, in case I was slow I suppose. "Two, - touching a second finger, you've riled the locals by asking personal questions about them. Three you've been asking questions about teenagers, school children way more than any sensible person would. You got a particular interest in school kids, Mr. Therman? Four, that's a nice car you've got out there. How'd you get that all of a sudden?"

I ignored for the moment the fact that none of that was anyone's business but mine and took a different tack.

"What do you know about the area you're talking about – about West Hawk?"

I watched him, waiting for a reaction. Nothing. He just sat staring hard at me, his face flushed. "The reason I ask," I continued, "is that I'm a writer. I nose around, try to get the feel of a place, get curious. That's what I'm doing in West Hawk and the police know it, not that it's really any of their business frankly, or of yours. To be honest, I don't know why you're sitting here asking me questions."

The Constable seemed to decide he wasn't sure about that any more either and got up from the table. He pointed a finger at me. "Don't push me!" he warned. I looked at him blankly. "I want you to report in when you go there next time," he informed me.

I'm afraid I laughed at him. "I have no intention of reporting in to you or anyone," I advised him. Then I added that I didn't want to get on the wrong side of him or anyone else from the police, but that if he really wanted to have a casual conversation about what I was up to maybe the best way would be for the two of us to go somewhere quiet and have a drink. Park the uniform and the gun and just chat about this and that. "Maybe I'd learn something about what your real concerns are, and you'd get me to chat about why I'm talking to people, what interests me in the area, that sort of stuff." I let the free advice taper off, seeing his look. Informal chats were not what he had in mind at all.

"My advice to you (since when have the police been advisors?) Mr. Therman," he said gravely, "is to watch yourself. Just watch yourself." And with that he left, closing the door loudly behind him.

"I think you made a friend," my wife said calmly, her words as usual laced with commentary and advise.

"Jesus, where do they get them from?" I said. Linda looked at me. You know, one of those looks, letting me know without saying a word that she would have handled things differently, she wouldn't have gone out of her way to ensure I made an enemy for life.

"I think he'll report back that you were uncooperative, which won't do you any good at Falcon," Linda pointed out.

I'd wanted to absorb the display, to let it talk to me, but the visit of Constable Plod had rattled me, got me belligerent instead of calm and contemplative. As I stood in front of the panels again it was hard to get it out of my mind. Why had he come? Who had complained about me and why? What was really going on here? Was an unseen hand stirring things up for me? The most puzzling thing was who had sent him. It certainly couldn't have been Corporal Simard, not after helping me the way he had. And what purpose had the visit served?

"I think we've got Mr. Mystery Man worried," I told Linda. "He sees no sign of any action on my part and he wonders: have I quit on him? Have I gone away?"

So far, he hadn't put a foot wrong. Effortlessly he had guided me like a puppet on a string. But now he'd shown impatience, uncertainty. And in doing so he'd shown me more about himself than he meant to perhaps, for who could send a policeman on that idiotic visit but another policeman or someone connected in some way with the law? It had been weeks since I had spoken to anyone in West Hawk so it was no fresh provocation on my part that had brought Bannerman to my house. It was *lack* of provocation that had triggered his visit, that was clear. And it suggested that Mr. Mystery Man wasn't very far away. Maybe that explained the feeling I had much of the time of being under observation. And whatever this guy wanted me to do it didn't seem to allow for taking time out.

A couple of days later, freshly returned from vacation, Alex came to visit. She seemed to have caught a cautious virus while she was sunning herself on the beach. "I'm having second thoughts about all this," she said. She was looking especially good, had a nice tan on her and seemed more relaxed than usual.

"I have second thoughts every day," I pointed out, "but in the end that doesn't stop me. I want to see this through."

Alex and I were drinking coffee in the kitchen while she expressed her misgivings. She was leaning on the table, coffee cup in both hands, looking at me intently. I thought she was a very desirable woman but then I was married to the best woman in the world.

"You want to see it through to what, Colin? Have you thought about the possible outcomes? You assume success, that you'll find out what happened to her and maybe why, but what if you don't, what if you can't find out, that the trail just peters out and gets you nowhere?"

"With Mr. Mystery Man helping me, that's not likely is it?" I asked her.

I finished my coffee and rinsed out the mug, dried it and put it away. Linda and I have never used a dishwasher, much to the derision of our children.

"Maybe our friend doesn't know any more than you do. When do you decide that you've done as much as you can and there's nothing more to be discovered, that you're not going to be able to solve the mystery?"

It was a fair question of course. I'd wondered that myself on occasion: When do I decide I've failed? But somehow I knew I'd be able to tell if and when that time came.

"But not yet," I said, articulating carefully and precisely, "Not yet!"

Linda snorted. Alex hadn't got the movie reference but then she tends to miss things like that.

I took Alex' mug and washed it up by hand. "I'll know I've reached the end when I stop making progress," I said, "When things stop happening. Sure nothing has happened recently but that's because we stopped poking around. And then Constable Bannerman came calling just to remind us that there really is a Mr. Mystery Man out there, prodding us into action." I hadn't told her yet about the mysterious and unsettling visit of Bannerman and she wanted to hear all the details.

"Jesus, Colin, you do know how to make friends, I'll say that for you!" she said when I'd finished.

"That's what happens when you are irresponsible and abandon those who depend on you, for the sake of vacation," I said.

Alex ignored my sally. "I agree that he wouldn't have come on his own, wouldn't have come at all even if Falcon detachment had asked him." She stopped and considered what she'd just said and then shook her head. "Well, no, he'd have come but he'd not have acted as stupidly as he did. Someone put him up to strutting around like a little tyrant. He must have known it wouldn't get him anywhere, that you might even have grounds for a complaint, not that I'd advise it. No point riling the local constabulary."

"Linda figures I've already done that in how I responded. I admit I was a bit aggressive."

She laughed. "Why am I not surprised!"

She got up from the kitchen table and told me to come with her. "We need to look at the whiteboards."

I followed her down the stairs. She pointed to the Mystery Man board, picked up the marker and wrote – 'works with police' and then a series of points after that: 'police, judge, politician?'

We stood back and looked at the new version.

"I wonder why he did that?" Alex said. "Why expose himself like that? What did he achieve?" She shook her head. "It doesn't make sense! He gave far more than he got."

"I figure he's in a hurry," I said. "I stopped working for a month and he panicked."

"After 40 years, he's suddenly in a hurry? Something doesn't add up."

"So what do we do? Start compiling lists of policemen, judges and politicians?"

She looked at me carefully. "You're still set on this aren't you!"

"Yes, ma'am."

"You know that this might yet turn dangerous! Someone who can pull strings like that must be powerful and could be dangerous. Is it worth taking a risk, any risk for an unknown girl long dead?"

"Powerful yet impotent, or he would have done it himself, so I don't think he's all that powerful." I argued.

"But he might be dangerous, Colin, that's the thing you seem to keep ignoring. We don't know what his game is. It's certainly not aboveboard, there has to be something sinister in it, or else why do all this stuff he does? So why play his game, Colin?"

"What did you do with my co-adventurer, the young woman who broke into a certain building in the dead of night?" I teased her.

She put her fingers to her lips and said, "Jesus, Colin, shut up!"

"Well, if you can find her anywhere," I said, "tell her I need her to help me find the Water Rat – that's where the left-behinds as Betty Kingsford called them hang out."

"The illusive, mythical watering hole in West Hawk?" she asked. "Yes, I've heard of it. Hmm, well maybe I can have a look around see if I can induce her to come along. Still, I hear she's pretty busy keeping people who just want to go rushing off ignoring their lawyer's advice out of trouble. Full-time job around here, it seems."

And then Arthur rang. "I need you over here," I said.

"You want to see my vacation pictures?"

"Not exactly! I'd like to show you some whiteboards Alex and I have been working on."

"OK, I'll be over as soon as I can."

He rang off and then Alex said she had to go. "Clients you know. Phone me about the Water Rat!"

Arthur showed up a few minutes later. He's a little guy, with a brush cut haircut – don't see many of those these days – and freckles. He was wearing tan slacks and a white short-sleeved shirt that was too big for him, bagging out around the waist. I suspect he's in his mid thirties, although I've never asked, and he still lives with his parents, which makes some people look at him askance. He once told me that the way the economy is going, everybody is going to be doing it pretty soon. It was the wave of the future and he was the vanguard, showing the way.

He has an infectious smile, too, but he's not really into small talk or conventional social niceties. The thing you must understand about Arthur is that he's an information freak. To him, information is alive, something with a pulse, and its organization and retrieval fascinates him. He can talk about databases, how to organize them, and the challenges of retrieving information from large databases at the drop of a hat, so if you're smart, around him you keep your hat firmly on your head!

The reason I'd asked him over was something he'd said to me once that really impressed me. It was that knowing where an information request is situated contextually – I think that's how he put it – is key to retrieving relevant material and excluding noise. He'd summed it up like this: "Show my why you need it and I have a better chance of finding it."

"All museum and castled out?" I asked him.

He looked at me as if I had gone mad and then ignored the question.

"Let's see these whiteboards of yours."

I took him downstairs and reviewed the information that Alex and I had written. I didn't go into details. "In brief, we think Stephanie Shawcross was murdered and that her body is around West Hawk somewhere or somewhere along the road to

West Hawk. I want to find her body and who killed her and why. Moreover I think the key is what we can learn about and from her High School classmates."

He didn't comment on the chain of logic involved. One of his strengths – besides his uncanny way with information – is that he knows what he isn't. So he spent no time worrying about why I had concluded that her classmates held the key. His job was to check that out.

"I learned one surprising thing that might be useful," he said after a while, with a little grin on his face, as he often gets when he's about to deliver useful information.

"Go on," I encouraged him.

"Well," he said, "Stephanie wasn't the only person to go missing that day, along that highway!"

"What! What do you mean?"

"On that same day, also early in the morning, two salesmen set out from Winnipeg. They were supposed to stay in Kenora, visit some friends and call home. Only they never did call, that day or any other day."

"You mean they too just disappeared?"

"Exactly. They never found the men, they never found their car. I'll send you the details."

"This changes quite a few things, doesn't it," I said.

"I think it does," Arthur agreed.

I looked at the first whiteboard again. It no longer made any sense to consider the possibility that Stephanie had just walked away from it all. Three people doing it on the same day seemed highly unlikely. I put a line through it and wrote 'improbable' after it. As for it being an accident, with car and body undiscovered for 40 years, well now there would have to be three bodies and two cars that had gone undiscovered after having coming off the road. That was stretching probability too far also, so I put a line through that notation also.

At first this seemed helpful, because it was narrowing the range of possibilities. Sure, I had been working mainly on the idea that Stephanie had been murdered but the other possibilities had still been there to haunt me and make me wonder. Now they no longer would. At the same time, however, the new information complicated things enormously. If it was murder, it meant that three people had been murdered. But why? What was the connection between Stephanie and the two men? Or had she just ended up in the wrong place at the wrong time, stumbled across two men being murdered and so had to be murdered herself? If so, all my checking around to try to figure out who had murdered her and why was pointless. Instead I should be looking into the disappearance of the two men.

But the clues that had brought me here hadn't been about the two men: they had involved Stephanie. It was *her* disappearance that brought me to West Hawk, not that of these two guys. I needed to think about this, maybe bring Alex over again and get her thoughts too.

"Kind of helps and doesn't help," I admitted to Arthur. "For now at least, let's stay the course, Arthur. Concentrate on finding Stephanie's classmates and seeing if they know anything that may help us."

"It's a tough assignment finding those names," he told me with a dismissive shrug as if to say tough maybe but for him not at all impossible. "I've already done some checking, thought you might want some info about them, but these aren't the kind of people who use Classmates or Facebook typically, so they are hard to track down. A couple of them are dead, at least I think they are. Some of the names are fairly common and you need to figure out how old they are to be sure. The women are the hardest, because sooner or later they usually change their names. If you don't know what their married name is you're screwed. Still, I've tracked down a couple of women you could try." He looked up at me with that little grin of his as if to say, look what a clever guy I am to keep pulling rabbits out of the hat. "One's in Calgary, the other in Moose Jaw – convenient I suppose, can make a trip of it. As for the men, look in the phone book, one of them is there, at least the name is the same."

I thanked him and told him to keep on looking. I was particularly keen on him finding some of the men if he could. He promised to concentrate on that for the moment and then left.

13

THE GIRLS FROM WHITEMOUTH

I needed to think, and I've always found driving a good way to do that, at least in the country, away from traffic. I told Linda I was going to Falcon. She was struggling with Hebrew again and just waved.

The Audi was always a pleasure to drive, something to look forward to. Getting into it, even walking up to it to get into it was satisfying, and put a little shine on the day that it wouldn't have had otherwise. Turning the key, starting it up was a thrill. Putting it in gear and effortlessly pulling away was exciting. So I drove once more to Falcon Lake winding through Whitemouth and then down the straight blacktop past Elma and Hadashville, and then setting the cruise to 110 on the four-lane divided and listening to Schubert this time. I had a bone to pick with the Falcon Lake detachment.

As I pulled off the highway at the exit for Falcon Lake, I saw Corporal Simard in his cruiser turning onto the road out of town. There was another man with him, an older guy I thought, with his cap pulled well down, so I couldn't really see him properly. He was by in a moment, looking away from me.

At the station there was only the rather slow Constable Timmins who turned his indifferent eyes on me with a look of utter boredom.

"Good morning, I'm looking for Corporal Simard."

"Out," he said.

"Who was the other guy with him?" I asked.

"The Chief," he said.

"Didn't know you had a chief. What's his name?"

"We just call him Chief."

"It's top secret, is it? Must be exciting to have a chief with a top secret name!"

"You a smart-ass or something?"

"Probably (especially around policemen, I thought to myself)."

"Looked like an older guy," I suggested.

The Constable snorted. "Old is putting it mildly. He's been around here for decades I think. Don't know how he gets away with it – not being transferred around, I mean. Going to retire soon, I hear." He stopped and looked at me again and a change came over his face, as if he'd realized suddenly that he was fraternizing with the public, wouldn't do at all! "What's it to you?"

I didn't intend to tell him that right now everything was something to me. Every little piece added something to the puzzle. It was like a jigsaw with a big difference: first you have to find all the pieces. Only then can you put it together. And some of the pieces I was finding probably don't even fit. The Chief probably was one of those, a piece that was totally irrelevant, belonged to some other puzzle, perhaps, not mine. But he may have been old enough to know Stephanie or know something about her, have heard of her.

"He shy?" I asked eloquently.

Constable Timmins had obviously stopped fraternizing. His face had lost its brief amiability and was frozen in indifference. "Was that all?" he asked.

"One more thing," I said, "He any good with a computer?"

"Jesus," the cop said. "If we were any good with a computer we'd be doing video games, wouldn't we, earning big bucks, instead of....."

"Ah, but think of the bad guys who would go unpunished then, Constable."

"I was right," he said. "You are a wiseass."

"Thanks for your help," I said, then added, "Oh, and when Corporal Simard gets back, tell him I was in to see him would you? Therman, Colin Therman."

I came out of the office and thought that that was a wasted trip, although no trip in the Audi was exactly wasted. On a whim, I drove over to West Hawk, taking the slow, winding road again. Crescent beach was a going concern. I parked near the change rooms and walked over to the parking area above the beach and stood at the rail looking down. The sand was covered with families and singles, the swimming area well occupied. What was it like in 65 I wondered. I felt like a swim but it was too crowded for my taste. Back in September I thought.

Past Whitemouth they were combining already, the big behemoths prowling the fields with long dusty wakes. Farm trucks you never see the rest of the year waited by the side of the fields to carry the grain to storage bins. Overhead, geese were flying practice sessions, as if getting the kinks out of the formation routines. The month was drawing to a close with that gathering sense of desperation and melancholy that marks the near end of vacation time and summer holidays.

Back home I discovered that Linda was out. Her note said she had gone shopping and would then go to the library.

I checked my email and found Arthur's details about the two women he'd mentioned. Chances are if I was to get anything useful out of them I would have to visit them. First I'd check them out by phone. I would have to call them before visiting them in any case.

Jennifer Doerkson answered the phone right away. I introduced myself and told her I was looking for anyone who might remember Stephanie Shawcross, class of 64, Whitemouth School.

"Are you someone from her family?"

Jennifer sounded much younger than someone who must be in her 60s if she was the Jennifer I sought.

"No, Mrs. Doerkson. I'm trying to find out what happened to her, that's all. I understand you went to High School with her."

"Stephanie? Yes, yes I did. My that's a long time ago. My goodness I haven't thought about her or any of them for a, well a very long time. What was it you wanted to know?"

"Anything you can tell me about her."

"She was beautiful you know. Truly beautiful." She said it as if she was discovering it all over again, marvelling at it. "All of us envied her and wanted to be her friend, all the girls. The boys, well the boys wanted more than friendship!" She laughed. She sounded as if she hadn't laughed in a long time, as if it caught her by surprise, something she simply wasn't used to any more.

"Any special boy?"

"Oh, well, Jimmy was the one of course."

I looked at the list of names on the Whiteboard. "Jimmy Case?"

"Yes, Jimmy. They were a special number, planned to get married. None of the other boys stood a chance, although they all worshipped her, every single one of them. The only chance any of us had to get noticed was to stick around Stephanie." She laughed again as she thought back to it, briefly young again in her mind.

"Did you ever see her, afterwards I mean?"

"No, no I never did. She was in West Hawk and I was a Whitemouth girl and well, our paths never crossed again. There was talk of a reunion I seem to recall. It was a few years ago now, but, well, I don't really remember. And then, um, I believe she disappeared. But that was ages ago wasn't it? I read something about it, made me wonder. Did you know about that?"

I told her that's really what I was trying to find out: what happened to her, where and why."

"Oh, my!" she said.

I explained that I was trying to contact anyone who was in her class at High School and asked her if she knew the whereabouts of any of her classmates.

"No, Mr. Therman," she said. "I never kept in touch with any of them. I went to the Prom with Andy Wentworth. My goodness, I'm astonished I remember his name all these years. He wasn't my boyfriend or anything, but you had to go with someone. No, Mr. Therman, they all just disappeared from my life afterwards, all of them. I couldn't even tell you who most of them were after all this time" She wasn't laughing any more. She was back to whatever her reality was and it didn't seem to include much laughter.

I gave her my phone number and asked her to call me if she thought of anything about Stephanie or any of the others, anything at all. I said I would send her a list of the people in her class. Perhaps it would jog her memory. She told me she didn't want to do that. "I don't mean to be unhelpful but I don't want to think about those times. It was all so long ago." She paused and when she resumed her voice was sadder but firmer, more determined and decisive. "It was a different place, a different time, a different world. How stupidly optimistic we can be when we are young, Mr. Therman!" And with that she hung up the phone.

Clearly, I would not be going to Moose Jaw. Pity! It's not a bad town as prairie towns go.

Pat Farthington was the Calgary name that Arthur had found. She didn't answer her phone, nor give me a chance to leave a message. I would try her again later. And indeed I did, many times, but in the end I never did manage to track her down or talk to her.

So far my skills as an interrogator were looking shabby!

Next I picked up the phone book. West Hawk numbers are listed under Falcon Lake, together making up 8 pages in the regional phone book. Jennifer had said that Jimmy Case was Stephanie's boyfriend. I let my fingers do the walking and there he was, Case, Jimmy with a West Hawk address that meant absolutely nothing: block something, lot something. Most of the addresses were like that, cottage-country nomenclature.

Then, one by one, I ran through the names looking for any that matched any of the other surnames on the list. I had to make several passes through the pages, crossing off names as I checked them. It was tedious and unrewarded work as there were no further matches, unfortunately. But if Jimmy was Stephanie's boyfriend and Jimmy still lived in West Hawk, who better to talk to about Stephanie? Or from whom to find out about any others from their High School class that might still be in the local area! And if the left-behinds do indeed congregate at the Water Rat, well to the Water Rat I would go.

I checked my email to find that Arthur had sent me some additional info about the list of names. He'd added deceased to two of the girls and one of the boys. Denise Armandski had become Denise Stevens and had died two years ago in a car crash along with her husband while holidaying in California. I didn't ask him how he could find out the married names of women. There must be a way; it was just that I didn't know it.

As for Kara Krupriuk, an excess of rs if ever there was one, not to mention ks, she had died in Montreal from breast cancer a dozen years ago. And Tod Penning had dropped dead, no cause of death given, five years ago, while working on a construction project. Arthur's email said he'd just toppled from a platform ten stories up but it wasn't the fall that killed him, as he was dead before he hit the ground they found out afterwards. His information wasn't all doom and gloom, however. He said he had promising leads on a couple of the boys and hoped to have more information later today or tomorrow.

I went to the whiteboard and wrote **deceased** after the three names and put a line through them. The girl at the top of the list was dead too, I knew, although I couldn't prove it yet.

And that got me thinking. Where could her body be, and her car? It was similar to the problem I had trying to figure out where the car could have gone if she had lost control and gone off the road. If someone had murdered Stephanie, where had he put her? And where was her car? West Hawk lake itself would be a perfect place to put them except for one thing – how to do it without being noticed? In theory the killer could have driven her car through the camp ground and over the edge near where the divers go. It was very deep there. But the divers would certainly have found the vehicle at the bottom of the lake in that spot by now. And any other location where it would have been possible to take a vehicle would similarly be a poor place to hide anything. It had to be somewhere off the beaten track and that reminded me again of the hidden highway, the old road that still lay in sections here and there in the woods. My initial survey of possible spots hadn't been too promising, but perhaps there was somewhere along there where even now Stephanie's car and her body, or what was left of it after all these years, rested. And maybe, just maybe, there was someone around here who knew the road better than I did. It was time to put my extensive list of contacts to good use, well all three of them: the librarian, the school teacher and the museum lady.

I hesitated about the librarian, really I did. Did I really want to ask her something she might not be able to deliver yet again? If I did, I would have to wrap it in something she could provide, so it wouldn't seem like another failure. And would the school teacher really want to see me again, with my painful stirring up of the past? As for the museum lady, well she was too young I figured, far too young to be interested in the past. Funny that, it's as we age that we appreciate more what went before: when young we just want to blaze a path ahead. It handicaps both groups: the old because it stops them thinking of doing new things, the young because they don't learn. This rumination was interrupted by the phone. It was Simard, wanting to know why I'd gone to see him.

"You were out with the chief, Mister top secret," I said.

He chuckled. "Timmins said you were curious about him. You're a curious guy, Mr. Therman. Curiosity can get you in trouble sometimes. What did you want with me?"

"You didn't tell me about the two men who disappeared the same time as Stephanie Shawcross," I accused him.

"Nope," he said. "Saw no reason to. It can't be connected. Far as anyone knows, they didn't know each other."

"I'm surprised you didn't tell me though. Somehow I think their fates are intertwined."

"That's your seasoned investigative skill coming into play is it?"

"And Timmins said I was the smart-ass."

Simard chuckled again. "Frankly, Mr. Therman, I didn't think the other thing was any of your business. But if you find out anything about it, too, don't hesitate to give your friendly local constabulary a call, you hear."

"You bet! Oh, and if you ever find out the Chief's name, let me know, would you."

"You're the smart-ass, Mr. Therman!"

"There is one more thing, Corporal."

"There are bad guys waiting to be caught, Mr. Therman."

"The hidden highway, the old road bits of it lying here and there, know anything about it?"

"I know it's there. Kids build fires down there sometimes, toke up and drink, have to chase them out."

"Do you know anyone who is a real expert on it, knows every section inside out."

"Nope, keep you in mind if I run across anybody though."

When he rang off I wondered why he had called me back. I hadn't expected him to. I'd left my name with Timmins as a joke. And Simard wasn't investigating me so far as I knew, and I was sure I had nothing to do with anything he was working on. It wasn't normal for the police to just chat like that, call you up, leave messages, return calls, not normal at all. So the question was why. I doubted it was just because he liked the look of me, wanted to help. Maybe he was sweet on Alex, figured keeping in my good books wouldn't do him any harm.

14

THE HIDDEN HIGHWAY

The next day I decided to call on my trio of contacts to see about the hidden highway. Bombing back and forth to West Hawk was getting to be a daily routine. Perhaps the Audi looked forward to the outings as much as I did, a chance to stretch its legs, strut its stuff. I settled into the leather driver's seat and made the car come alive. The car now fitted me like a glove and I realized I'd be in deep trouble when the three-year lease was up, would hate to surrender it.

Falcon Lake is a community, not just a collection of cottages that comes alive only on weekends and the summer months. It has houses, quite a few of them, an elementary school, a couple of churches. But situated as it is, miles from anywhere, Winnipeg a distant couple of hours in one direction and Kenora as far in the other, with nothing much in between, it always seemed a puzzle to me what the people did for a living. Perhaps they were simply all retired people, although the town never seemed particularly geriatric. One possibility clearly was simply the local businesses, the restaurants, school, drugstore, grocery store, gas station, golf course, highway maintenance depot, police station, doctor, park employees and so forth. The employees and owners of these places had to live somewhere and they could hardly commute. Still I didn't believe that could explain all of the houses. There was something I was missing somewhere. But then Linda says that's often the case with me.

Whatever the reason, the socio-economic reality, the houses were there, neatly laid out on a rectangular grid of streets. There were no monster homes, no architectural fancies there, just basic dwellings. Amidst this collection of homes was a simple bungalow, painted white, with green trim. There was a car port containing a couple of bicycles, a lawn mower, snow blower, garbage bins and a blue Suburu that had seen better days. The front lawn was weed free but brown from the dry summer.

In the end I had plucked up my courage, had gone to Linda Evans the librarian yet again, hoping against hope that she might have some clue to give me, and she had come through in flying colours, much to our mutual surprise. "Oh, Mr. Therman, goodness, you don't know how relieved I am to be able to help you," she had said, with a wide smile.

Mr. Osborne, a dapper elderly gentleman who now answered the door of the white house with green trim was the result of her help.

I introduced myself and told him I was looking for someone who could help me with the pieces of the old highway that used to be the main road. I explained that Linda Evans had told me about him.

"The old TC, yes, yes, well come in, come in."

He was a short man with a thin whisp of white hair, a little goatee, barely over 5-feet tall, with brown eyes behind thick glasses. He was a dapper gentleman, dressed somewhat formally, in grey slacks, and a white dress shirt over which he wore a dark-blue sweater with a monogram on it.

Mr. Osborne and I never did get beyond the Mister stage. On several occasions I invited him to call me Colin, but he never did and he certainly didn't encourage me to use his first name, which I had discovered from Linda Evans was Reginald.

It was a name that fit him to a T, but one I never got to use. Formality suffused the man. It was very much part of who he was.

He led me into the living room and invited me to sit down. "Tea?" he asked.

"Please." I'm a coffee man myself but I never argue in someone else's home.

The room was simply furnished, but there was a piano along one wall and sheet music out on the stand, as if it were played regularly. Perhaps I'd interrupted him. The furniture was old, overstuffed, somewhat shabby but clean. The hardwood floor needed redoing, but the area carpet was attractive. There were pictures on the walls, mostly landscapes, nothing that stood out as art, and photos on all the tables, along with a pile of magazines. A large, fat tabby cat prowled nearby treating me with complete indifference.

After tea, I told him I'd long been fascinated with the old highway – the hidden highway I call it, although it's not very hidden.

"Actually, some parts of it are. Hidden I mean," he explained. "Or, quite well hidden. If you don't look carefully you can easily miss them. It was left behind in 1969 you know. Well of course most of the road around here, as far as Rennie at least, is still the original road. You can imagine what it must have been like having that heaving narrow strip of road as the main transportation artery. It's only from Rennie on that you find sections of the old road."

"I've walked on some of the sections," I admitted. "And thought about what you just said – the cars rushing along, twisting and turning around the rocks, trees and lakes."

"You had to drive more slowly then, it was essential," he pointed out. "So of course you actually saw something of the countryside, had a sense of being somewhere, not like today settling back with the cruise on and trying to avoid falling asleep." He laughed, a deep, rather loose laugh deep in his chest. "Still," he added, "it must have been a real bother getting places. On the other hand, well you know I think people had more time in those days. Less money but more time, Mr. Therman." He cleared his throat again.

We sat thinking about that for a moment.

"Mr. Osborne, in 1965 a young woman called Stephanie Shawcross disappeared somewhere around here while driving from Winnipeg to Thunder Bay. We do know that she never reached Kenora."

"Over 40 years ago! No trace of her?"

I shook my head. "None at all. Her parents never heard from her again and the police know absolutely nothing."

"Oh dear, that's dreadful. Do you think she disappeared or.."

"I think it's the or, I'm afraid," I said. "Very much the or!"

"Ah, I see. And she would have come along the old road, yes of course, that was all there was then. Of course they were working on the new one at that time, did you know? Typical highway project of course, lots of signs extolling the beneficence of government, taxpayers' money at work and precious little progress." He cackled again, giving me an almost irresistible urge to clear my throat.

"I think someone killed her," I said. "And whoever did it had to put her car and her body somewhere and he can't have taken her far surely, so I thought perhaps he put them somewhere nearby but where they wouldn't likely be found."

"Good god," he exclaimed. "Hidden nearby for all those years, is that what you are saying?"

I nodded. "I thought that if you know the road that well you might be able to think of places where he might have put them: the car, the body."

"Ah, yes, coming to the point now are we, yes indeed." He stood up and looked at me. "Are you dressed for it," he demanded.

I looked at him questioningly.

"For beating about the bush, tramping over crumbling tarmac man?"

I looked at him in astonishment. I thought the question a peculiar one. He was the man with the fancy clothes, not me!

"I'm game," I said.

"Not what I asked you," he said. "Come," he added, "I have a map. We'll plot our strategy."

I wondered what this man might have been like when he was young, a whirlwind certainly!

He rushed upstairs leaving me in his wake. When I followed him up to the second floor I found him in a small bedroom that had been converted into a study, with a desk, filing cabinet, a couple of chairs and bookcases and a map table, its surface angled for display and study of large-scale maps. There was a big map spread out on this table and he was examining this closely.

"Ah, there you are," he said as if I'd taken a month to get here. "You can see the current road here and I've drawn in the sections that still exist of the old highway in the region between Rennie and Whitemouth. There are exactly twelve of them, none of them longer than about a mile." He pointed to the map and tapped it where the sections were drawn in.

"Ready for an outing then? Shoes up to it?" He looked at my footwear dubiously.

"You drive, I'll show the way," he commanded.

I felt out of breath already. He hadn't once asked me why I was on the trail of a probably long dead woman: apparently all that mattered was that I was interested in the hidden highway.

We got into the Audi. He'd brought a pair of highly polished but sturdy hiking boots, very professional looking, with thick, grippy soles, as well as a thin jacket with hood. "Bugs," he said, as if I had asked him about the jacket. He put the boots and the jacket on the back seat, did up his seat belt. I started the engine and drove off.

The transition between the old road and the new road happens abruptly at the park gate just east of Rennie. One moment the road is twisting and dodging, dancing around like a meandering river, the next moment it widens, straightens and becomes flat.

In Rennie there was a tanker truck filling up the no-name gas bar, a farm truck parked at the tavern, a police car idling by the side of the road and a couple of pick-up trucks at the grocery store. A CP train was rumbling through on the main line, an endless line of grain cars going east. At Alf Hole, the sign said there were 492 geese in the sanctuary.

"It's just that I think I might have missed a spot or two, on the old road, that's why I need your help," I reminded him as we drove.

"I know for certain you've missed some places," he asserted. "There are a couple of places nobody knows about, nobody except me."

"I want you to think carefully about where you might put a body near the old road. Well, a body and a car, so that nobody likely would find them."

"Stop while we talk this over Therman," he ordered, so I pulled over onto the sandy shoulder and brought the Audi to a halt.

"Don't want to overshoot," he explained.

He sat and thought about what I had said, or I assumed he was thinking over what I'd said. No way of knowing what anyone's thinking, that's the truth of it, and he might just as easily have been going over this week's grocery list for all I knew.

After a while he turned to me. "Ever seen how a road is built, Therman?" he demanded. "Or a building for that matter, same thing in a way."

I shook my head.

He looked at me as if he really wanted to demand that I answer yes, sir, or no, sir, instead of just moving my head.

"It's a mess," he said. "A complete mess. Old things get ripped up, there are masses of rubble, old concrete, excess tie bars, barrier timbers, packaging, worn-out tires, empty barrels and pails, broken tools, just endless stuff. And it has to go somewhere. Some of it gets ploughed under, some of it gets dragged away. They try to be a bit neater about it nowadays, tidy up afterwards, recycle stuff more, although it's still an amazingly wasteful and messy process. It proves the physics of entropy you know, to create order you need energy and work and first you make chaos."

"Interesting," I said.

"But you didn't come to me for a physics lesson, right Therman?"

I laughed. "Something like that."

"There's a point to my rambling, though. The point to it is that there's always somewhere nearby that is convenient for dumping stuff. Usually it's a pond or stream or some wet low-lying area where the contractors can get away with dumping stuff. They aren't supposed to do it, of course, but for them it's a lot easier than sorting it and carrying it back to some depot or other to deal with. And nobody is going to go looking in such a place. If there is a body or an abandoned car somewhere along that old road, it's most likely in a spot like that."

Traffic was light, mostly campers with retired people, a couple of trucks pulling boats, the time between vehicles measured in minutes. The police car passed us moving fast.

"Carry on Therman."

I pulled the Audi back onto the highway and accelerated to 110.

"You're going to proceed over the CN overpass and then slow, look for a small clearing on the left maybe 500 yards on."

As we neared the overpass there was a CN train throbbing towards it, glimpsed in snatches through the trees, a mixed consist of double-stack containers, tank cars and car carriers.

There was an old ruin off to the right, a chimney sticking up from a pile of rubble, stubs of walls. As we passed it he told me to slow, then put his hand out to signal stop and pointed to the left. I could see nothing but did a U-turn and parked on the shoulder.

Reginald Osborne reached to the back seat for his boots and put them on. "Hope your shoes are up to it," he said again, as if to emphasize the vast superiority of his footwear.

We tramped through the tall grass at the side of the road, and then through a thin frieze of trees and found ourselves standing on the edge of a section of old, crumbly tarmac that dodged left then right and disappeared over a rise. Grass grew at both edges and in patches in the middle of the road. White lines were visible here and there. It looked as if with a bit of cleaning up it could easily be carrying traffic once more. The old road fascinated me for reasons I couldn't figure out. Perhaps it was that it was hidden, cut off from the rest of the highway system, abandoned, yet still apparently serviceable. Standing there, I could almost hear the sound of old-fashioned engines driving motor cars along the road. What I could really hear were the croak of frogs, the whir of dragonfly wings from a late hatch, the honk of geese flying overhead.

Reginald marched vigourously along the road, striding ahead in his superior boots with confidence and no concern for my gawking. I hurried to catch up with him. After five minutes or so of walking, he stopped and moved over to the left side of the road and pointed. Just visible through the trees was a glimmer of oily water. Here the sound of frogs was louder and mosquitos began to bother us.

"If I were a betting man, Therman, that is where I would look for your body and car, right there."

We walked up the edge of the pond. The water was dark, impenetrable, with an oily sheen on it. Old tires and plastic bags littered the edge of the pond. The surface of the water traced out a shape that was long and narrow, twisted into a flattened S-shape. Surrounded as it was by trees, it looked lonely and abandoned. I had a sudden image of my daughter Cindy, getting ready to go to a High School dance. She had been a popular girl who got on well with just about everybody. Her face was gleaming, her eyes shining and she was excited as only a young teen could be about life. I stopped and stared, scarcely able to breath.

"You got a funny look there for a moment, Therman," the old man said.

I shook my head, barely able to keep back tears. I looked at the pond again and hoped against hope that this wasn't the last resting place of Stephanie, this scummy pond full of construction junk hidden in the trees.

"This was one of the main dumps during the highway construction. Anything of no value was discarded here," Reginald told me. "Of course if you start dredging it all up you might find more than you bargained for. Don't necessarily want to do that – not unless you're absolutely sure." I thought to myself that being absolutely sure was a condition in short supply. "There's another spot that was used," the old man said, "But this is your best bet."

"I'd never noticed this section of the hidden highway," I admitted.

"No one is interested in it," he said. "I've suggested it be preserved, made into a protected place. Not just this piece but all of them, but they scoff at the idea, Therman. If you want to thank me, write to your MP, tell them about this."

I said I would indeed, although to my shame I never have.

We walked back to the car. There was a police car idling behind the Audi but as we emerged from the woods, it pulled back onto the road, did a U-turn and disappeared. I thought I saw a glimpse of the chief riding shotgun but couldn't be certain.

"Looked like the chief," Osborn said.

"You know him."

"He takes an unhealthy interest into my old-road mania that man. I told him once that it was none of his business. He seemed to think that that was funny. He comes from around here, knows this place like the back of his hand. Another time I asked him to help me ensure I'd got all the pieces of the road identified but he just told me he was a policeman not a cartographer or explorer."

I drove Osborn back to his home and thanked him. He took his boots and jacket, got out of the car and walked up to his front door. As he got there, he turned and raised a hand, then went inside.

I was now in possession of secret knowledge and probably an unofficial member of the fraternity of the hidden highway. I also knew the probable location of Stephanie Shawcross, assuming she really was dead and really had been murdered around here. Knowing where she was, was one thing, but being able to do anything about it another entirely because what I didn't have were any arguments that would persuade forensic specialists to go digging into the oily pond Osborne had shown me.

With one thing and another it was dark before I finished up in Falcon Lake. The one thing had been the trip to Stephanie's probable grave. The other was running into Bettie Steffer in the restaurant in Falcon Lake where I'd decided to have a bite before heading home. The restaurant was a big, echoey cafeteria-style place with hard tables and chairs. Betty was behind the counter and took my order for an old-fashioned milk shake and a hamburger with fries. Linda would have had a heart attack about me having a heart attack but then if there was anything particularly healthy on the blackboarded menu I hadn't spotted it.

By now it had become routine to ask anybody I met questions about Stephanie. Bettie was plump and looked in her late fifties, early 60s, old enough to be someone who might actually know something of the past. Her hair was under a sanitary cap and most of the rest of her was covered by an apron. She had a pretty face, with a dimple and cheeks you wanted to grab and squeeze. Her eyes were a slightly bloodshot green.

"Steffie Shawcross?" she said. "Holy cow, I remember Steffie! She was a few grades ahead of me in school. We went to Whitemouth you know."

"That must have been quite a ride, especially in the winter."

Bettie laughed. "Hell, we didn't think anything of it at all then. We were young after all. Now.." She shook her head. "Now I shudder. Long, cold roads, snow sweeping across the highway. Amazing we survived!"

My burger, fries and shake were ready. She told me she'd come to the table as soon as she could, so I took my food over to a table by a window and sat down. A few minutes later, Bettie came over and took a seat opposite me.

"Not too busy this time of the year, this time of the week, this time of the day."

I smiled at her.

"So," she said. "You know Steffie?"

I shook my head. "She disappeared in May, 1965. I'm trying to find out what happened to her."

"Disappeared! No shit – pardon my French. Boss tells me to watch my mouth sometimes. She was beautiful you know, I remember that, absolutely gorgeous, the envy of everybody. We all wanted to be like Steffie!"

"I heard that," I told her.

"And now you think she's dead?"

"I figure she is, but I don't have any proof."

"Trying to put things to rest are you?"

"Something like that. What I really want is to find anyone who was in her class."

"Oh wow," she said. "That could be tough. There's Jimmy of course, Jimmy on his big bike. You'll find him at the Water Rat most likely, if you can find the Water Rat."

"I'm still looking," I told her.

She laughed and clapped her hands together. "Well," she said, "Don't tell anyone I told you but I'll tell you how to get there. It's just down Starfish Drive, that's it! It's actually not that hard, just that most people don't keep on the road long enough, think it peters out, but it fools them, seems to narrow to a couple of tire tracks in grass, goes round a bend a bit and then opens up again for a stretch. And there it is, your stinking Water Rat, an overrated watering hole if ever there was one, with a lot of deadbeats in it, including good old Jimmy. Jimmy was her boyfriend of course, everybody knew that. They'd been a couple as long as I could remember, all through High School, maybe climbed trees together as little kids, who knows." She sighed as if thinking back to old days, days when the future probably had more to offer than a job waitressing at the Falcon Lake Restaurant.

All this time I'd been chewing away appreciatively on my deadly supper. For stuff that could kill you it sure tasted good!

"Honestly, I don't know of anybody else though. Well, let's face it, I've forgotten most of them. Do you remember who was ahead of you in your High School?"

I laughed and shook my head. I admitted I could hardly remember more than a couple in my own class, people I'd graduated with.

"And most of us have managed to escape this place, except for a few. It's not really a bad place, you know, but it's not exactly the big wide world! It's funny though. The summer comes and the tourists flood the place and soon you can't wait until they leave, they irritate you so much. Then they go and you start thinking about next year, gearing up for when they come again, anticipating it, even looking forward to it. It's why we are here, after all, that's the truth of it. Without them, we wouldn't be!"

She smiled as if to tell me that it was fine for her, she was content. "So," she continued. "I'm OK with it, never wanted much more than what the place has to offer, and it is beautiful sometimes, even in the winter, but it's no good for most of us. Most of us have to get out. Well, let's be honest here, letting our back hair down as we are, sometimes I wish I had, yes I do, just sometimes. Wonder what I'd be doing now, where I'd be. Probably chatting to a nice customer like you, just somewhere else probably." She laughed.

I thought she was finished, I honestly did and then she said something that stopped me from continuing putting the dishes back on the tray.

"Something I do remember," she said. "They always had this big party you know, on the beach, after graduation. They put a stop to it the year I graduated of course! Isn't that the way of it: you look forward to something and as soon as you qualify, bam they shut it down!" She laughed again, then continued. "But I used to hear about those parties, how wild they were, how loud. Back then, the police looked the other way about it. I think they must have thought it was about as safe as you could get given how wild everyone was at graduation. But something happened that year, I remember. I heard these rumours about something bad having happened on the beach that night. I'm sure it was her class, because I know Jimmy and Stephanie were never the same afterwards, in fact they split up completely. I heard about it from my friends and it was all over the school in September when we all met up again. You have to understand we're pretty scattered, rarely see each other in the summer. Something bad happened and it broke them apart. It amazed everybody but it seemed to be hushed up so I never found out exactly what it was that went on then."

I thanked her for her help and gave her my card, asked her to call me if anything else occurred to her. I've rarely had anyone call me afterwards but you never know, and besides, as Alex would say with a teasing toss of her head, it's what investigators do, even if they are amateur ones like me.

Bettie said it had been a pleasure talking to me.

I fired up the Audi and set off home. The road was dark and lonely, its curves hiding what lay around the corner. The worst danger here was running into a deer, so I kept the speed down although the car wanted to run.

As I was passing Dorothy Lake, on an impulse I pulled into the parking area, brought the Audi to a stop and switched off the engine. With no moon out it was pitch black. I closed my eyes, opened the door and got out, then opened them again. I felt my way carefully over the grass towards the beach and sat down at the table, the one I considered my table, although for most of the summer it was confiscated by tourists.

I thought about that for a while, how the world lives on and we just pass through. Overhead the dust of the Milky Way spread its awesome veil over the black of space. Faintly I made out the slow progress of a jet, high overhead, its lights moving steadily across the sky. I wondered if there were similar scenes on other planets, spaceships on long, slow trade routes between the stars or whether it was all empty, lifeless, a vast void unobserved. I felt the world turning, and tracing its year-long orbit, the sun moving in its spiral arm, the galaxy rotating, and falling its long, slow fall towards Andromeda.

After a while, I took off my shoes and socks and walked on the beach. The sand was cool and faintly damp. There were a couple of lighted cottages further along the shore, too far away to have any illuminating effect. Now and then a car passed, telegraphing its presence by its headlights. I thought about going for a skinny dip, but I had no towel with me, and it was a bit too cool to wait around to dry off. If the moon had been out or I had been younger perhaps I might have done.

I thought for a second of doing it with Alex and smiled because I'd done it years ago with Linda, on the spur of the moment, on a dare. It had been fun I remember but cold and sandy. But we'd never done it again. Once was enough for her apparently.

A loon cried, invisible on the water and then a chorus of rustles and protests from geese.

I went back to the table and sat again, thinking now about Stephanie and whether she was in that oily pond. Something about this whole situation didn't add up, that was clear. My only hope now was that probing the beach party would shed some light on what had happened and why. This made Arthur's work critical – that and visiting the Water Rat. I put on my shoes and socks and drove home.

I spent the next week chasing down classmates of Stephanie. This was the kind of work that gives investigating a bad name: slow, slogging even, and repetitive, yet it can be exciting in a way, digging up the past, drawing dots between where people were when they were young and where they are now, how they've turned out even. Of course it was often frustrating, yielding nothing useful after hours of work.

I kept calling Pat Farthington, but she never answered her phone the whole week, and in the end I decided to write her a letter. I also sent a letter to Jennifer Doerkson. She had told me that she didn't want to talk to me any more about Stephanie but I urged her to reconsider and sent her a list of the boys and girls in Stephanie's class. Arthur had sent me contact information about a couple of additional people: Robert Deslile, who now lived in New Zealand apparently, and Dean Croswell.

Dean lived in New Brunswick and told me that he had just retired. "I worked at a pulp mill and got out just in time," he said. "Business is going to the dogs right now and I'd have been laid off for sure. Not much else to do around here and I don't see myself going to the oil patch at my age." He chuckled at the idea of it.

"I'm trying to find out what happened to Stephanie Shawcross," I explained. "I understand she was in your grade in High School."

"Steffie? Yes! God, that's a long time ago. She was a sweet kid, I mean gorgeous but sweet is what I really remember about her." He chuckled again. "Everyone was sweet on her too, every single boy in the class and all the other classes too! But she belonged to what was his name, er Jimmy, that's it, Jimmy. I remember that, no other boy had a chance and we all knew it."

He went silent for a while and I began to think that he'd put the phone down but then his voice started up again. "Funny, weird really. I can remember Steffie's name, and Jimmy's and Nichola Tess, too, well I should remember her's because I married her, did you know that? Funny thing is we weren't sweethearts then but I met up with her later on, a few years afterwards, after school, at a training course for something or other and we hit it off. Yea, funny thing."

He went quiet again but this time I just waited, realizing he was thinking back to it, remembering it. "I was saying I remember their names but you know I can't for the life of me remember anybody else's, not a one. Isn't that a wonder!"

I told him I couldn't remember most of the names of the people in my graduating class either, then asked him about the beach party, if he'd gone.

He paused again then laughed loud, rumbly in his throat. "The famous beach blast, yea, but you know I didn't go to it, I don't know why. Isn't that crazy! There must have been some big reason for me not to go. That was a tradition then. The High School was miles away but everybody would come to West Hawk for the beach party, bring beer, music, and have a blast. But I didn't go to it that year, my final year, wonder why? Can't think what it was. I did hear that Steffie and Jimmy stopped talking to each other after the party, so something must have gone down at the thing. Must have been powerful to make that happen, to split those two up!"

"That's one of the things I want to find out," I told him, "what happened at the beach party. I wonder if your wife might know."

"Nichola, yea, that's a thought. I wonder if she went. She's out right now but maybe she could call you?"

"I'd appreciate that," I told him, and gave him my number.

"What is it with Steffie anyway?" he asked me.

"She disappeared a few months later."

"No shit! Just vanished?"

"Exactly. I'm trying to find out what happened to her."

"Well jeeze, good luck." he said.

I thanked him for his help and rang off. I decided to send him a list of the students in the class with a note asking him to jot down anything he could remember about any of them.

New Zealand is an awkward country to call; well anywhere in the southern hemisphere is. Everywhere is a day wrong and seems to require a challenging mental calculation of what time it is there. I managed to do the arithmetic successfully and got hold of Robert Deslisle. He was a long time answering and when he did his voice was weak. New Zealand also seems to have less than robust telecommunications links with the rest of the world too, if the low quality of the line was anything to go by. I turned up the phone volume and told him what I was after, a spiel that was becoming somewhat routine by now.

"I've just had a stroke, you know," he told me.

"Oh, I'm sorry to bother you."

"It's OK, don't worry. I'm OK too, it's just that it takes me a little time to think things through now. I can remember fine, just fine, don't you worry about that. Stephanie, eh? I remember Stephanie. I had dreams about her, I can remember that, the dreams. You know what kind of dreams young boys have I'm sure and she was in them all right! But I suppose we all had dreams about her."

"Can you recall anything about the beach party?"

"Beach party? Oh, yes. Yes, I remember the beach party too, I really do. It's good to remember things, well some things anyway, don't you agree, Mr. Therman?"

"Yes, yes I do. What can you remember about the beach party?"

"You know, I get tired remembering," he said. "My mind seems to be slow these days, I'm afraid. It takes me time to get the remembrances out, to talk about them. I don't think I can talk much more."

"Could you write them down, just write down anything and everything that comes to mind about the beach party?" I asked him. "It's important, very important."

He agreed that would be best. I gave him my address and said goodbye. I wondered if he really would write to me, if he'd remember to do so, if he really could remember back that far. I decided to send him a follow up letter as well.

"Ah, the glamorous world of the master sleuth," Linda said, coming into the basement room, or master sleuth HQ as she had taken to calling it sarcastically.

"Want a job?" I asked her. "I'm afraid it can only be entry level until you've developed some skill at it, but it will put you on the ground floor of a promising career."

"Anyone who can master Hebrew should be cinch for your work," she laughed at me.

"You call that mastering, do you? As a Master Sleuth I would have called it something else!"

She swatted me playfully and then said she had to vacuum, code word for disturb me, force me to move my chair and suspend what I was doing. One of the things I learned early on in marriage is that vacuuming takes precedence over anything and everything else. Nothing, it seems, is more important than dust control!

That evening Nichola Tess, now Croswell called me. "Hello Mr. Therman. Dean said you were asking about Steffie and the beach party. Something happened to her, is that right?"

I told her she had disappeared early the year after graduating and I was trying to find out what had happened to her.

"Just vanished, puff, gone that sort of disappeared?"

"She was driving from Winnipeg to Thunder Bay and somewhere along the route she vanished. Something must have happened to her, but nobody knows what or why."

"And you think it might have something to do with the party?"

"To be honest, I don't know if it does or not. All I do know is that something happened at that party, or so I hear. I don't know what it was, but whatever it was it was big enough that Stephanie and Jimmy, who had been an item all through High School, I'm told, stopped being an item. I don't know if that had anything to do with her subsequent disappearance or not, frankly, but I've got to start somewhere."

"Yes, I see," she said. "Well, of course I'll help you if I can. It might take a while, talking about the party. I remember it pretty well. Funny, the music brings it back you know, the memory of the music we played. Perhaps I can call you in the morning, when I have more time, am less tired?"

"Yes, of course. I'd really appreciate it."

"I'll talk to you tomorrow, then," she said and cut the connection.

True to her word, Nichola called back just after ten o'clock the next day. I'd been staring at the Mystery Man poster sheet wracking my brain for ideas about who he could be. There had to be a connection between him and Stephanie, although not necessarily a murderer-victim one. If I could figure out what the connection was I might be able to zero in on the guy. Yet what brought me up against a wall every time was the time period – the fact that it was over 40 years since she disappeared. Why would anyone wait that long to start investigating her disappearance? There was something here, something critical that I wasn't seeing. Although I knew a lot more about the case now than I did when I started, I seemed as far as ever from having any clear answers about who had killed Stephanie and why. The fact that I was amassing information but that none of it seemed to be doing anything useful was beginning to irritate me. I knew that the most likely suspect in Stephanie's murder – assuming again that it was murder – was her boyfriend, just because murders are usually done by people the victim knows. She and he had stopped talking after the beach party and apparently had called off their relationship as a result of whatever happened that night. But then if Jimmy had killed her why had he done so and above all why had he waited until the spring of the next year before doing so?

Nichola said she was ready to talk about the beach party. "It's the music that I remember more than anything else." She laughed. It was a pleasant sound, clear and uninhibited. "Music! Can you believe it! The Beatles were big then, all the top songs were Beatles songs. I can hear them in my head, see what we were doing when they were playing."

"And what were you doing?"

"We'd been to the High School for the graduation ceremony itself and the awards, and then there'd been a dance afterwards. That must have gone until midnight I suppose, and then we all came to West Hawk for the beach party: well, most of us did. I'd gone to the prom with a boy called Stuart."

"Stuart McFarlane?"

"Yes, that was his name. He was a nice kid, a bit shy, with blue eyes, beautiful eyes, quite handsome. I wasn't going out with Dean then. We were friends but nothing special. That didn't come until later. In fact Dean didn't even go to the beach party. Most of the boys brought beer and a couple brought music systems and plugged them into an electrical outlet at the marina with long cords and we just danced on the sand. It was a calm, warm night, and the bugs weren't bad, so it was perfect. All the boys wanted to dance with Stephanie of course and she let some of them. Jimmy tolerated it all right. He wasn't the possessive type, besides he had nothing to be insecure about. Everybody knew Steffie was his girl. I danced with Jimmy a couple of times, I remember that. I think we danced to Sweet Dreams. I used to like Patsy Cline. I was sad when she died in a plane crash a year or so later I think it was. And From a Jack to a King, I liked that one. Of course I danced with Stuart. I didn't mind. I didn't owe him anything but he was a nice boy and he danced well, especially the slow ones. Some of the kids got pretty drunk but they were just silly and making noise. It was Beatles as I said. Can't Buy me Love, Love, Love Me Do. We played some Elvis as well. He was still pretty popular. Stuff like I Want to Hold Your Hand, and Return to Sender. I remember though something weird. I was just talking to my friends, Julia and Candace. The House of the Rising Sun was playing. I always liked that one too. I may have been singing along as well and there was a scuffle of some kind. Well it was hard to see really. We'd got a couple of fires going but it was dark beyond their immediate circle and I remember there was a fight or something. I'd probably had too many beers by then myself. I certainly don't have a clear recollection of what happened." She laughed again. "And it was a long time ago. Stuart was getting amorous and I was getting a little annoyed. I think he wanted to make out and I didn't want anything to do with that. A couple of kids had gone skinny dipping, although the water must have been pretty cold at that time of year still. Joshua

Napier was stark naked, came into the fire zone, sloshed and without a stitch on him."

"The fight?" I prompted.

She didn't say anything for a while and then sighed. "You know, I don't know what happened. I have the impression that something happened, there was a disturbance, some shouting, some screaming. It was down at the other end of the beach, near the marina. We had gone to the other end for some reason. Sharon came running up, Sharon Tucker and said Jimmy had been fooling around with another girl and Steffie had caught him at it and whacked him one. I wasn't aware of it being any big deal but I didn't really see it myself. I think after that the party kind of broke up. It was 3 or 4 in the morning, even a hint of dawn. Parents were coming by to pick us up. Some of us just went to sleep on the sand, lay down and snored. The police came by and offered to escort people home who weren't in any shape to drive or didn't have a ride. Oh, and Ring of Fire, that was another one. Johnny Cash." She paused again. I didn't say anything and the silence stretched out and then she added. "When I think back to it, it's hard to believe. I was 18 then, so young, so young."

"Thank you," I said. "Are you still in touch with anyone from that class, or know where they are now?" I asked.

"No, not really. I – well, I did keep in touch with a couple of the girls, for a while. I used to know where Candice was, her and Julia. We were great friends then. They went to college. I never did, but they did and I stayed in touch but then we sort of lost interest. They came to West Hawk once. I'd stayed there and worked at the campground in the summer and for the gas bar the rest of the time. When they came, it was disappointing. I remember I'd looked forward to their coming, planned what we would do together, was really excited about it but they had changed, they were different people, we talked a lot for the first little while and then it sort of dried up and then we didn't know what to talk about any more and they seemed bored. I can remember it to this day, how that felt, the sadness that came over me, that we didn't mean anything to each other anymore." She let out a long sigh and then a little self-conscious laugh, as if to pretend that it didn't really hurt. "You know they never, oh I don't know, I never ever saw them again, that's what I meant. After that we just sent cards at Christmas and then that stopped too."

She paused again, thinking about it, remembering, the hurt and disappointment of friendship that had evaporated. "Funny how people just don't bother to keep in touch." She laughed again, a little self-consciously, aware of having perhaps shown more feelings than perhaps she had wanted to.

I thanked her again. She hadn't really been much help, when I thought about it, but she had at least confirmed that something had happened at the party. The trouble is, it didn't sound like something that would explain a murder. Nor was she a useful lead to others who were at the party.

Still, I had enough new information now to start another poster board. I labelled this one '**Beach Party.**' And then wrote: '**Who was there?**' and under that, '**Music: Beatles, Elvis, House of Rising Sun, Patsy Cline, Johnny Cash.**' Finally I added one more line, '**Beer, music, dancing, some skinning dipping, drunks.**'

When I looked at the result it hardly seemed worth bothering with. But something had happened there, at the beach. Maybe that something wasn't what had got Stephanie killed, or at least led to her disappearance but I didn't know that, and in any case I didn't have any other leads. Rule number one in sleuthing, I thought to myself: work on the leads you have, not those you don't!

I went over to the list of names and put a tick beside those Nichola had named and others I had learned about first-hand who had attended the beach party. I ticked Jimmy, Stuart, Robert and Stephanie, Nichola, Julia, Candace, and Sharon. So far it didn't look like much of a party! There must have been others there. I decided to send Nichola a list of the names of her classmates and ask her to indicate any she could remember being at the party. Perhaps that way she would remember more about what happened that night.

The rest of the week I spent around the house. There was a lot to do, including cutting grass, getting the garden ready for winter, getting up on the roof to clear leaves that were clogging up the eavestroughs and downspouts, putting garden tools away, getting down snow shovels, and washing the garage floor. I went to Dorothy Lake a couple of times on sunny warm September afternoons, enjoying the practically deserted sand. Sometime recently they had taken away the lines marking the swimming area. Geese were still around, waddling with evident annoyance back into the water when I arrived, squawking in protest. One day the man with the Frisbee was there. We talked about how nice it was when the tourists left.

Saturday evening was Water Rat time. I asked Linda if she wanted to come along.

"As what? Your chaperone, your protector, your witness?"

"Keep me out of trouble."

"If you mean supply some brains to the operation, I could do that," she told me.

"We have plenty of brains," I responded indignantly.

"Oh? Is Alex coming along then?"

"Of course Alex is coming along!"

"Well, no, dear. Three's a crowd you know."

"Besides there's that Hebrew to master," I teased her.
She rolled her eyes.

15

THE WATER RAT

When I picked her up in the Audi, Alex looked more like sex than brains. She was dressed in tight black slacks and a short, cream-coloured blouse abbreviated at both top and bottom, showing her midriff and plenty of her breasts. She also had on a black leather jacket so I didn't realize quite how daring her cleavage was until she got into the car and flashed me.

"Jesus, Alex!"

"What, you don't like it?"

"That's not the point!"

"You mean you do like it?"

"Yes, it's just that I don't think the clientele of the Water Rat are probably used to that kind of stimulation."

"Oh, good, then I'll certainly have their attention."

I got onto the highway to West Hawk and put the car on cruise control.

"How's the plodding going?" she asked, deliberately changing the subject.

"So far I've found out that there were 8 people at the party, five girls and three boys, and that they played the Beatles, some Elvis, Patsy Cline.

"God, Colin, that sounds so 60s doesn't it! I can't imagine it, just can't: Elvis and the Beatles! And 8 people! Can't have been much of a party."

"I agree, and I'm working on trying to flesh out the numbers. So far nobody has told me anything particularly helpful frankly. I suppose that's not surprising. It was a hell of a long time ago. I don't remember what music was played at my grad party I can tell you that! It's all lost."

"Let's hope the party does really hold the key. It would be a shame to put all that effort into it only to find it's irrelevant."

"They teach you that sort of trenchant observation in law school do they?"

She laughed, threw her head back and laughed. It made me feel good to see her laugh like that and I realized I'd missed her by my side as I worked through the painfully slow business of trying to piece together what had happened so long ago.

"Actually," she said, "They teach you that irrelevant is good. Adds up the billing hours!"

"Not to mention the rebillable expenses!" I said.

Once we got to Rennie, I clicked off the cruise and took the car through the long twisty stuff to West Hawk with my foot on the gas pedal, pushing around corners and easing up over particularly heaving sections. The road wore patches on patches, with here and there new sections of paving that had already developed the slumping and heaving unevenness of the rest of the road. It was hard to imagine that it had ever been the main east-west corridor in this country, the only way for cars and trucks to get across the nation. This was the road down which Stephanie had come that day in May in 1965, driving her car attentively along this tortuous route, watching the curves, careful not to get too close to the unforgiving edges, usually bereft of shoulders. Somewhere along the way she must have stopped. Perhaps to fix a flat tire, or she'd run out of gas, or the engine boiled over, or she'd seen someone she knew. And someone had killed her.

I mused all this out loud as I drove. Alex reminded me that I had absolutely no proof whatsoever that Stephanie had been murdered. "All you know is that she disappeared, period, oh and that they must have had an argument or something at that beach party; big deal, who doesn't have bitter arguments at some time or other. So far, you have nothing but supposition, Colin. Frankly, we've taken a long time to get precisely nowhere."

It was true in a way I suppose, but it didn't feel like that to me. "You're forgetting about Mystery Man," I responded.

"Maybe somewhere someone is having a big laugh, watching us dance around getting absolutely nowhere just because he sent us a series of little puzzles and challenges."

That set something off in my mind, the idea of someone manipulating us, sending notes. Who else had he manipulated I wondered suddenly. I thought about it for a time as I guided the Audi round corners, past the Lilly Pond and its neighboring rock wall, and on down towards Caddy Lake. The thought itself though ran into a mental rock wall and then went skittering off and vanished. I vowed to make a note of it, though, to add it to the whiteboard. I also decided to mention it to Alex.

"I wonder who else he may have manipulated. He got me going by knowing about my love of trains and then the disappearance of my own daughter. He knew about me and he used that knowledge to make me do something he wanted me to do, something he either couldn't or didn't want to do himself and something I certainly wouldn't have done otherwise. Can you imagine! Us breaking into that building! Whatever else he may be, the guy is good. And I don't think he's doing that just because he wants us to run around like chickens for the sake of having us run around. He's doing it because he wants us to do something, to find something out. And why would he care unless there's an important connection between him and Stephanie."

"You're forgetting those other two people who disappeared, Colin," Alex pointed out.

"I don't think they mean anything. I thought at one time that Stephanie may have just shown up at the wrong time, wandered into something not meant for her, but I don't think that any more. I think those two guys were the ones who just blundered into something that really had nothing to do with them. I don't think they mean anything."

The conversation petered out and only afterwards, when it was far too late, did I realize how significant the idea had been. I should have run hard with it, but the reality is simply that I didn't, and like a lot of other things I should have done, it all came back to bite me.

The Water Rat is down a dirt road which attempts to deter casuals with a no-exit sign, as if the owner had deliberately set out to go broke by hiding the place where no one could find it. As Bettie Steffer had told me, the road also just petered out or seemed to and picked up again only around a 90-degree bend. Unbelievably, and as a kind of direct affront to MBA case studies everywhere, it hadn't worked, and word of mouth and regulars had seen to it that it continued to defy conventional business wisdom.

When we pulled up in the Audi, there were three small trucks, a couple of cars and a big Harley abandoned around it.

We got out of the car and walked towards the entrance. Before we went in, I grabbed Alex and slowed her down. "Park the boobs," I told her.

"Afraid of the biker?" she mocked me.

"I'm serious, Alex!" I glared at her in what I hoped was an intimidating style.

"Listen," she said angrily. "I don't tell you how to do your job – well maybe I do, but I'm a lawyer – so don't tell me how to do mine. I use the weapons I've got, OK? I'm a big girl!"

"That's what I'm worried about," I joked.

"Oh, Colin, you do love me after all."

I chose a booth near the back and sat down. How to describe the place? Well, you reach for your grab bag of superlatives and discard them all, each and every one of them, as being wildly excessive and inappropriate and when the bag is empty there it is. It was big, drab, dark and echoey, probably just the way the customers liked it, redolent of what I call Northern Ontario hick, but then I'm prejudiced.

Alex excused herself and went to the Ladies. When she came out not only had she not parked the boobs, they weren't anywhere near a parking lot. She had the kind of look about her that makes a man's hands itchy and mouth dry, not to mention her effect on other parts of a man's body.

Every head turned, all five of them, and the place fell even more silent except for the unmoved TV, still flashing some sports results, compressing the results of hours and hours of play in numerous games into a few videoclip highlights, a reader's digest of sports, all the dull stuff leading up to the excitement left out, along with the whole point of the exercise. Finally someone whistled and the noise fell back to earth.

To me, it was as if she'd put on a different persona. At the worst of times, Alex is a sexy woman, but now she was transformed and seemed to exude sex from every pore, as if she'd swallowed something marvellous. Her face glowed and her skin was smooth and shiny.

"Now we chat up the bartender," she announced.

"What's my role – boob worshipper?"

"Colin, shut the fuck up – just come with me and seize the opportunities."

"I think they are the ones wanting to seize the opportunities," I joked, indicating the men in the bar.

Alex walked up to the bar and sat on a stool. I followed her and sat a couple of stools away from her.

"Who's the guy with the Harley?" she asked the man tending the bar. He was an old geezer, in his late fifties I guessed, heavy set, somewhat shorter than he should have been, with a vague, unkempt beard and moustache that he must touch up with Grecian Formula or something. He didn't speak for a while, just silently appraised her, his eyes doing the grand circuit then concentrating on her chest.

Evidently he was the kind of sleazy guy who didn't mind when a girl knew he was looking in detail at her breasts.

He looked up finally from her cleavage and smiled. "Bikes turn you on?"

"I want to talk to the guy who rides it – if he's who I think he is." She spoke calmly and looked him in the eyes.

"Hey, Jimmy! Tits here wants to talk to you. Sorry, Ma'am," as if he'd caught a whiff of manners like a draft from somewhere.

Jimmy was sitting alone at a round table with a good view of the television screen.

He waved and said, "Come on over."

Bar tender said, "What're you having? On the house! Girls like you don't come in here very often."

Alex thanked him with a medium wattage smile, said she'd like a Sleeman, waited until he put the bottle on the counter along with a glass, then picked them up and went to Jimmy's table. I followed her trying to look submissive.

"Sit," he said.

"I'm Alex." She bent over and offered him her hand and a generous view of cleavage.

Jimmy was enough of a gentleman, or perhaps just wanted a closer look, to get briefly to his feet and shake her hand.

"And this is Colin."

He nodded to me. "Hi. Jimmy's my handle, but you already know that. Anyhow enough chit chat. What's a half-naked lady like you want with Jim boy? I mean, do I get my hopes up or what?"

His eyes were small and beady and roved constantly, not just over her body but around her and over at me. He was nervous, twitchy, not at all the kind of cool cat you'd expect to mount a Harley, or is that just another stereotype? At any rate, whatever interest he may have had before in the sports results had vanished now that Alex offered an alternative.

Jimmy was an old geezer, of course, looking even older than his actual age, at least if he was the Jimmy who had been Stephanie's boyfriend all those years ago. His skin was pitted, lined and spotted, heavy with the patina of time in sun and wind. He had a beard, too, but it was full, tidy and grey. Black roots still showed here and there but their days were numbered. He was a big guy, dressed in sturdy jeans, heavy boots, a dark-grey T-shirt, and a leather jacket free of tassels, hood ornaments, logos, or insignia of any kind and he looked mild enough, if testosterone aroused.

"Jimmy," Alex said, "here's the deal. You get to enjoy the scenery, as in look don't touch, and I get information, which I'm led to believe you possess."

"Hmm," he said. "You look soft but you don't talk it! Fact is, I like to talk, and I'm partial to looking at sexy women. Truth be told, I don't get to do much of either in here, or anywhere around here for that matter these days. This place suit you, or would you rather go someplace more comfortable?"

"Where would you suggest?"

"Well, you can come to my place if you like. It's not much, just a simple cabin, but it's more intimate than here and nosy old Frankie over there won't be straining his ears to eavesdrop. Hey, and don't worry, I won't keep you there as my sex slave!"

"Although the thought has crossed your mind," Alex suggested.

He looked deep into her cleavage, then up at her eyes and grinned. I got a funny feeling suddenly, sensing that this Jimmy thing was already spiralling out of control. Was I just the tiniest bit jealous of Jimmy? Or was it a twist of a reproving nature? Sex appeal always has defied logic, and here it was certainly riding off in a strange direction. But perhaps Alex was just turning it on, deliberately using it, just as she was using the physical appeal of her body to fool both me and Jim boy.

Just then we heard the deep bark of big motorcycle engines approaching and then being shut off.

The two men who swaggered into the Water Rat a short time later were burly guys, the sort you inevitably see near or on motorcycles – maybe it's the leather stuff they wear that makes them seem so bulky. They were indeed wearing black leather outfits. One had a kerchief on his head, the other a long beard that had lost its colour but not its vigour a while ago. As I had feared they would, they strolled up to our table as if they owned the place, dragged up a couple of chairs and sat down. No please and thank yous about it either.

"Hiya," the bearded one said. "Gimme a beer," he shouted towards the bar tender. The other guy just waved his hand. "Jim boy!" the one who could speak said. "Hiya tits," he said in Alex's direction. "You her escort?" he asked me, at least I deduced the question was aimed at me.

"We're looking for information about the disappearance of Stephanie Shawcross," I told him, like a shot between the eyes. If the statement meant anything to him he gave no sign of it, just looked me over and shrugged. "Never heard of her. Why you bothering old Jim boy about that?"

"Everyone says he and she were a number."

"Everyone says that do they?" He guffawed loudly. "Well, Mr. Escort, looks like everyone was pulling your chain, or are just plain forgetful. Looks like you chased down old Jimmy boy here for nothing."

"Well, the people I talked to were there, with Jimmy and Stephanie and they told me they were a number, that's all I know. There's no reason for all those people to lie," I pointed out.

He smiled at me. "So you say, so you say. Easy to say something, but doesn't mean it's true."

He was irritating me. "You know, I really want to talk to Jimmy about this, not two guys I don't know who waltz up to our table and barge in on our conversation." I tried to look fierce and mean, as if I might have a temper.

He just looked at me and chuckled. "You're a lippy guy, you know that. Last I heard this was the Water Rat. That's a place where I want to sit at this table I sit here, I want to sit in the bench over there I sit there. That's the kind of place it is. You probably don't understand that, so I'm going easy on you, but just because you've got a shaved head doesn't mean we can't toss you out of here just like that, we don't like the look of you. Just so you get it straight about this place."

All this time Jimmy just sat there smirking.

The bartender finally showed up, as if he'd deliberately given the two of them time to straighten things out with the strangers in their midst. He looked questioningly at Alex and she nodded.

After he brought her the second beer, she leaned forward and said, "OK, now that you tough guys have shown us how high your testosterone levels are perhaps we can get down to business. Do either of you know anything about Stephanie or are you just here to decorate the place?"

"Boobs with a mouth!" the bearded one said and got to his feet. I had a feeling this was going to turn unpleasant but just then the door opened again and Constable Timmins entered and looked around. My guy had sat back down I noted. Timmins too came over, dragged up a chair and sat at our table. "Hey, it's an old-folks reunion," he commented.

"You find out the name of your chief yet?" I asked him.

"This guy thinks he's funny," he observed. He looked at me and said, "I think you try too hard."

"These boys were just telling us how tough they are and how what they say goes in this place," I told him.

"Oh, they're tough all right, no doubt about that, but sometimes someone has to tuck them into bed, right guys?"

The two men looked at Jimmy who just shrugged.

"Yea, yea, nag, nag, like an old woman!" the talking one said. "Nice meeting you, Tits, and you, too, Mr. smart mouth."

The two men got to their feet. As he passed me, the mute one stroked my head. They went over to the bartender, paid their bill, and left. The door closed behind them and shortly afterwards I heard their bikes starting up and then growling off.

"Thanks for the cavalry act," I said to Timmins who had also got to his feet.

"Have a nice day," he said as he left.

"Grab another beer, then we'll go," Jimmy commanded.

Outside, the sun had started its long, slow slide towards the edge of the world. This time of the year the twilight would last forever. Some geese flew low overhead, honking, making for the lake.

Alex turned to me and admitted that she'd never ridden on a Harley before, even as a passenger.

The bike looked big, gleaming, and definitely male I thought, probably a potent foreplay machine. Once on the bike, Alex turned and gave me a wave and then they were off with a roar and burst of speed.

I followed them in the Audi, down the track to the highway and then along about a mile until we turned down a short stretch of narrow dirt track at the end of which was the cabin.

Others people's houses are always mysterious. In practice there are only so many ways of arranging interior space and the same old design trade-offs get made over and over, and yet with every house I've ever seen I've always wanted to know what it's like inside, and Jimmy's cabin was no exception. In truth the cabin wasn't much, a simple, grey rectangle, with an angled roof, with three steps up to a narrow porch and the front door, looking as if it had been there for fifty years or more.

The floor boards were clean but dull, unpolished. He took us through to the back and out onto a deck overlooking the lake. There was a BBQ, a metal table and several surprisingly comfortable chairs with plastic-covered cushions. We sat down and Jimmy leaned back in his long recliner with a sigh. It was quiet here, with only the faint sound of an outboard to disturb the silence, that and the gentle swish of waves.

"Funny you should be on the trail of a dead girl," he said after a while. "My girl died too. We were High School sweethearts, graduated together. We were going to go to university and I told her after that I'd buy a bike, we'd get married, settle down and live happily ever after."

He paused again and let the silence return, then gave a little chuckle and shook his head. "But that was a hell of a long time ago, hell of a long time!"

As he talked, it seemed to me that he was nervous about something, and if it wasn't about Stephanie, then what was it, I wondered. He interrupted his tale to get us coffee, fussing about inside with a coffee machine.

"What the hell is going on?" Alex whispered. "He acts as if he doesn't know who Stephanie is!"

I shrugged and suggested we just let it ride for the moment.

When we had the coffee, which was pretty good, Jimmy continued.

"She drowned at our grad beach party. Back then they didn't have safe grads and things like that, so we could do pretty much what we wanted, be as wild as we liked. I guess she'd had too many beers. It's pretty deep here and it took two days to find her."

He looked out over the lake as if reliving it and was silent for a while. We looked out too, over the water to the far shore with its few tiny dots of cabins.

Why was he lying I wondered. Alex was shifting on her chair, wondering what to do or say. Surely he must know that we knew Stephanie was his girlfriend. And I'd heard nothing from anybody else about a girl drowning at the beach party. What was going on?

Jimmy cleared his throat. "Sometimes," he growled, "sometimes I feel her on the bike. Feel her arms around me, holding on, feel the soft pressure of her body. Long time since I've had a real person back there." He nodded at Alex. "You see the hard thing is, she never did get to ride with me, not ever."

The silence came back then and lingered for a while. Jimmy looked out over the water again. There was a wind ruffling the surface of the lake, making it look as if it were moving fast. Far out a couple of sailboats shifted angles, doing their thing with the wind, their sails tiny colourful outposts in the dark blue.

"Life happens," he said. "It doesn't give a shit, so you've just got to stare back at it and get on with it."

"What happened? Afterwards," Alex probed softly.

Jimmy snorted. "Nothing much. Didn't go to school after that. Both of us were going to go. Had our applications accepted, found a place to stay, but it didn't make sense with just one of us." He grinned suddenly. "But I got the bike and just stuck around here, did some of this and some of that."

He took our coffee cups back inside and when he came out he stood standing, leaning against the rail of the deck. "I guess I'm not a very imaginative person," he said. "I just couldn't imagine being anywhere else without her."

Alex went up and touched his arm. "I'm sorry," she said.

He nodded. "Funny," he continued. "It fades, you know. You think it never will, but it does." He looked at us unemotionally. "She's been dead a long time – like your girl I suspect." He coughed again. "Anyhow, here's the deal. "I'll help you, oh yes I'll help you all right, but there's a price." He turned to me and said, "You've waved this sexy lady under my nose," He stopped, looked at me directly and narrowed his eyes. "That's partly my price. You're not his girl are you?" he asked Alex suddenly.

Alex smiled and shook her head.

Jimmy took her hand and pulled her back towards the chairs. They sat across from each other. He looked into her eyes. "Alex," he said. "I'm not a dirty old man, well not really, and I don't want to embarrass you, really I don't, but damn it woman you've got my juices going, and I sure do like looking at you." He reached out for her hands and held them. "So," he continued, "my price is this: I want you to dress for me just like you are today. And you and I can flirt while I help you out. And if something else happens, well that would be nice, but to see a pretty woman and watch her move, well that's what I want."

I could see that Alex was blushing, which I thought was pretty strange considering how she'd dressed and everything but what do I know! I was also aware of how dangerous this might be, hesitant about the tensions Alex might build in this man, with his memories of his long-dead love, and his suppressed anger at how life had thwarted his dreams. Alex looked up at him again and then smiled. "Deal," she said.

"OK," he said, getting to his feet again. "Come back in the morning. We'll go for swim, have breakfast and then we'll get to work."

"I'm going back to the Water Rat," Alex told me when we got back into the car. I started up and then looked at her questioningly, not saying anything. "There's something I need to know about why he's lying to us about Stephanie. There's something not quite right about Mr. Case," she said as we bumped back down the track towards the road.

"Yea, he's a lecher," I said. "It's really hard to see him as the lovely Jimmy pledged to beautiful Stephanie. I wonder if he's not a little nuts – besides being a bit sex crazed!"

Alex laughed. "Don't worry, I can handle him," she assured me.

"That reminds me of the skier who thinks everything is just dandy until he starts over the lip of the hill and suddenly spots the yawning crevasse ahead of him. Personally I don't trust a guy who mopes around the place where his girl died all his life. It's tough, I know, but...."

"He's wants to be a romantic, gives him a sense of purpose, but, sure he's also a dirty old man, but doesn't want to seem to be one. I can pull his strings pretty far."

"He's got you to agree to give him lots of sexual eye candy, to jiggle and wobble around him and you're pulling *his* strings?"

When we got back to the Water Rat, the place was almost empty.

When Alex walked in a couple of young guys near the VLTs looked up briefly then back to the screens.

"Slow," she said, getting up onto a bar stool.

"You like the place so much you've come back for more," the barman suggested. He hadn't learned to worry about where his eyes lingered in our brief absence.

"Mr. Case," she started.

The man snorted and said, "Take my advice and stay away from the guy."

His eyes were grey and heavily bloodshot, his facial skin and arms pasty and flaccid. He was no woman's dream.

She raised an eyebrow then indicated her glass.

While he filled it, he said, "I suppose he told you about his girl. The romantic version."

"There's another?"

He looked up from her chest for a moment as if to see who was in the bar, then turned his eyes back on her.

"You have to be careful about the stories people tell. Sometimes it's hard to know just where the truth lies. Maybe his version's true but there's certainly more than one tale about what happened that night."

"Don't tell me," Alex laughed. "You were at the beach party too, right?" She hugged her arms close to her body and leaned forward. "Tell me your story," she said softly.

He broke away from staring at her breasts and began to polish glasses. "Not me," he said. "I have a friend who was there and he sings a different song than Mr. fucking Case and his pathetic sob story he's always telling everyone." He came back to his cleavage viewing stance and stood there, silent, but I could see that his eyes weren't on her for once but were far away. I wondered if perhaps his friend was a very close friend indeed.

He began to speak, this time in a softer voice. "It was a warm night and they'd had a lot of beer. Well, why not. They'd graduated, made it through High School and had their life ahead of them as they say. There was no moon that night so away from the fire it was pretty dark. Sometime that night, his girl – he calls her Lyla in his romantic version but everyone knows it was Steffie of course – wandered off with a couple of other guys. Case was doing something with the fire and joking around with some other fellahs and their girls. So off she goes with those two other guys and the next thing you know they are helping her out of her clothes. She's excited about it and not resisting at all. Then she's naked and they are too, and they start dancing around, her breasts bobbing, their penises bouncing, and they are touching her, pawing her and she's pretty worked up, flushed, excited, having a great time when Case walks into the scene. Skinny dipping she says, but it's like an excuse, desperately thought up." He shook his head and went back to polishing glasses. "Skinny dipping! Jesus! She just wanted some wild oats, why not, before she settled down with Case, no harm in that in my mind, no reason to get all worked up about it."

"But she ends up drowned," Alex said.

He looked at her, his lecherousness for the moment seemingly forgotten.

"That what he told you? Drowned? Like I said, that's the romantic version, all terribly tragic and sad. Remember he's talking about Lyla, not Stephanie, who as I'm pretty sure you know was the real name of his girlfriend. He never admits that by the way, never. Not to anyone. Well the way I heard it, she just went away afterwards, went away without him, that whatever they said to each other that night afterwards was enough to silence them forever so that they never never spoke to each other again afterwards."

"Just because she was naked with some naked guys at a beach party?" Alex said in astonishment. "There must be more to it than that, surely!"

"There is more to it than that, the barman said. "The guy who had his hands on her boobs when Jimmy discovered them. He ended up in hospital, badly beaten and half drowned. Nobody saw anything of course, nope, not a soul."

Alex stared at him and shivered suddenly. "Oh my god!"

The man stared unseeingly across the cheap uninspiring interior of the bar, as if peering into the past. "They fought and fought hard but Case's a strong guy, was even stronger then. Anyhow, as you said, oh my God. It's 300 feet off the rocks there you know, where Case tried to drown the guy. Long way down and Case always was a swimmer. It was a near-run thing that"

"And he never moved away – or your friend either..." Alex let the sentence trail away.

He shook his head, the folds of skin on his neck shivering in the movement, making him seem old suddenly. "Funny what a thing like that does for you," he said slowly, thoughtfully. "Funny. And this place, well this place has a way of getting under your skin. Tires you out. Summer comes and for two months they lash the lake with engines and they splash and shout and buy ice creams and beer and then it all goes quiet again, silent, slow and you remember and the past...." He paused and seemed to come to suddenly, and looked at her sheepishly. "Well, it's just that the past has a way of getting its claws into you."

"What about you?" Alex asked him. "You got a sad story?"

He snorted and let his gray eyes look into hers before looking away. "What makes you think that? You imagine everyone around here has a melancholy tale to natter on about? Anyway, it's not like his, nothing as dreadful as that."

He went to work polishing the counter. He said Jimmy was lying, but I had a strong sense that he was lying too, that the version he had told us was just as far removed from the truth as Jimmy's. All we were doing here was getting entangled in lies, lies and more lies.

The TV was showing some sports results program, hundreds of athletes in dozens of games and hours and hours of gameplay squeezed into snippets of highlights, seconds of fame and glory, flashing momentarily on the screen and replaced with another and another, into a noisy, meaningless potpourri of scenes, ripped out of context and ruined, like a movie cut and cut to only the sex scene and the car chase.

"Hey, life deals disappointments, that's normal," he said. "Young folk have these big expectations about life, but you know.." He stopped and looked at her again but it was through her once more I saw, staring at something only he could see.

"Tell me," she said, touching his arm.

"My mother died when I was 16," he said, "and my Dad a year later and back then, with that, well there was no way I was going on past High School. I was smart but not enough for scholarships, so I stuck around here, married my High School sweetheart." He faltered suddenly and looked down, then away.

"But.."

He smiled bravely. "Didn't last. Oh we parted amicably enough. It was OK for a few years but then it just kind of died. It was almost as if we both woke up one day and realized that we really should have done something else. So she moved in with someone and then she moved away, and.." He stopped and got that far off look again. He laughed. "You know I don't even know where she is now." He shook his head. "Heard she had some children but don't know anything about them. Not really much of a sad story!"

"Sad enough," she said. "You were one of the boys at the beach that day, weren't you?" She looked closely at him as she sprang the question but he didn't react. "What's your name?" she asked him.

He looked at her and then down at her breasts again. "People just call me the barkeep," he said. Clearly the time for revelations, for spilling all at the confessional bar counter had come and gone. He began to serve customers now, the place beginning to fill up.

Coming out of the dark bar into the evening was surreal. Inside was a different world, man-made, sad, discordant. Outside the setting sun was embracing the whole world with its pink glow, setting the water on fire, kissing the trees and rocks of the far shore with radiance. Geese were wheeling and dipping as if practicing maneuvers and tactics for long flights south.

Alex shivered suddenly "I was just pulled back in time by a sudden memory of childhood holidays at the ocean, lobster dinners, ice cream, movies and toy stores, in the easy, carefree embrace of youth," she told me. She smiled at the sudden fond recollection.

"Disappearing women seem to be a specialty of this place," Alex said as we ate in a burger place. It was busy as if everyone was trying to compress in as much of the last bit of summer as possible before the long winter began again. Already at night you could feel its icy breath as if it was waiting just below the horizon for the signal to start its long slow reign all over again.

"Must be something about the big rock that made this place, out there still, casting its malevolent influence on the place." I suggested.

Alex snickered. "Sure, Colin. Good explanation!" She looked at me with a smile and then turned serious. "You know I just don't understand at all why my biking pal won't admit that he's connected to your disappearing girl." She looked hard at me and then away.

"Something bothering you?" I asked.

She nodded. "Where are you going with this? I need to know because, well it's getting messy isn't it, growing hair. We've discovered a stage full of weirdo, wacky characters, dirty old men most of them, malingering suspiciously around this place and telling tall tales that reek of distortions and omissions. It's not getting any clearer now Colin! Now that all the puzzles and games have stopped it's still no clearer now than it was at the start. What did you expect – that Jimmy would confess suddenly and that would be that?" She shook her head then leaned forward towards me again. "I need to know if you're serious about this Colin, or if it's just a kind of go through the motions way of saying thanks for getting a nice choo choo ride and a fun car to drive. Do you really want to solve this thing or are you just playing at it, happy to let whoever is out there lead you around by the nose, sprinkling little clues here and there before your feet? I don't know where this is going but I don't think it's going to end up at pleasantville and happy-endings-shire. Are you just having fun or are you serious?"

"Hmm," Colin said. "Mother told me to watch out for girls like you!"

"Colin, can we have a serious conversation, you know the kind where probing, serious questions are responded to thoughtfully, seriously and honestly, without flippant cracks."

"My Dear Alex, I seem to have upset you, I do apologize!"

"And enough already with the movie quotes, OK? Because, Colin, if you're just in it for the fun, I'm going back to work. If you're serious, then for God's sake let's get down to work!"

"You know we seem to have this same conversation every few weeks!" I said. "But my answer's still the same. Look, I wouldn't have come this far if I weren't serious. I'm not saying that at some point I won't say to hell with it, but I'm certainly not there yet and I won't do that so long as there's any hope at all of solving this thing. I'm in it for keeps, or until there's just nothing else I can do. That satisfy you? And another thing, while we talking seriously, Alex, I appreciate your help, I really do. Yes, I do want to get to the bottom of this. It's not just because of echoes of my own daughter, or the promise, or maybe promise of info about Cindy, although frankly I don't put too much faith in that. It's this place. There's a shadow over it, I can't explain it, but it bugs me, and I want to tear it away and let the sun shine in there."

"A hundred million years ago," Jimmy said the next morning, "a big rock fell from some god-forsaken inky cold place out there, moving through space for eons and then down, down, hot, white, through the air and walloped into this rock like a million nuclear bombs. It made one hell of a bang and when the dust and fire had settled down there was a crater, huge and smoking. That's how this place began – in smoke, flame and uproar. It dug itself a huge, deep lakebed and of course in time water came and covered the scars."

"Tell me about Stephanie," I demanded after we'd thought about the meteorite for a while.

"After our swim," Jimmy said. "You did bring swim suits I hope. Now me usually I swim naked. Nobody can see or cares even if they do around here, but in deference to you my dear, it's swimsuits today." He nodded to Alex.

Alex wore a string bikini, the cups unlined, unstructured, small and dangerously insecurely tied with tiny connections. The bottom was Rio style, high cut and revealing. Jimmy whistled when he saw her and I stared.

"Are you out of your mind!" I whispered to her.

Alex just looked at me with knowing eyes.

As for Mr. Case, he wore the briefest men's bikini I'd ever seen. His body was unmistakably old – no matter how hard you work at it, you can't fool the old tick-tock clock – his skin alligatory in places, but this was a man who stayed in shape, and his body was hard, well-muscled, and amazingly smooth for a man his age. I wore a Speedo – can't stand the long droopy draggy things that are fashionable currently, but it was modest indeed compared with Jimmy's.

Jimmy looked Alex over appreciatively as she jiggled her way down the steps and onto the thin strip of sand at the base of the rocks on which the cabin was constructed. A thin, short pier jutted out from the shore. He strode out onto the end of this and dove into the water. Alex copied him but I entered the water more gingerly, walking out into it through the weeds. The water seemed cool only for an instant and then warm. Jimmy was swimming impressively, no doubt showing off to Alex who was doing a leisurely back stroke out from the shore.

I'm enthusiastic about swimming but not much good at it, and there was no question of competing with hot-shot Jim. The day was promising. There were thin clouds in the west but the east into which the sun was rising was blue and clear. Wind lightly ruffled the surface of the water making gentle ephemeral patterns, instant art works never the same.

We stayed in the water for half an hour or so. Alex and Jimmy came out of the water together. He whistled appreciatively at her as she stepped onto the sand again. He went up to her and put a hand on her waist and then moved it up to her shoulders. I was pretty damn sure he wanted to put them somewhere else. "Hey doll, next time you come maybe we can try for a skinny dip – it's a lot of fun."

Jimmy led Alex up the steps into the cabin, not paying much heed to me. I felt dangerously protective of Alex, which I knew was an inappropriate thought, sexist probably. If the two of them were going to get it on well it was really none of my business, but embarrassing even so, because to Jimmy it would be as if he had taken her away from me I knew, and he'd like that I realized. I was having increasing trouble seeing him as the perfect boyfriend of beautiful, sweet, probably dead Stephanie, but then that was a long time ago.

Inside we all swiftly got dry and dressed and Jimmy led us back outside to the deck, told us to be seated and went back inside to work on coffee and bagels. After we got that out of the way, I decided it was time for business.

"OK, enough foreplay!" I joked.

"Never get enough foreplay," Jimmy remarked.

"We're looking for a dead girl, a young woman called Stephanie Shawcross. She disappeared on her way to Thunder Bay from Winnipeg forty years ago. She was supposed to pick up a friend in Kenora but she never did. The most likely place for her to vanish, assuming she didn't just take off deliberately, was around here someplace. It's pretty lonely around here at night or in the early morning on the highway, was probably even more so then, so anything could have happened. Her car was never found either. Someone – don't know who – has led us here, made us believe there are clues or information here."

"Stephanie Shawcross?" Jimmy said. "Travelling alone?"

I nodded. "All alone, and early in the morning. She was in your class, so we thought you might be able to tell us something about her."

Jimmy settled back into his easy chair on the deck. Personally I thought it was a little chilly for sitting outdoors but said nothing.

I handed him the list of students in his graduating class.

He looked at it, looked at it and again and then laughed. "Where'd you get this?" he asked.

"A source," I told him. I was damned if I was going to tell him it was Betty Kingsford. Already Jimmy was making me angry. There was an old, vanished highway, crumbling away, hidden in the woods, down which had come Stephanie Shawcross early one May morning, many years ago, and this bastard knew all about it, I was sure, could tell me everything I wanted to know. I wanted to shake him, to force him to tell me the truth. But then, why should he? What would he get from levelling with me? He didn't care if my curiosity was satisfied or not. He had nothing to gain by telling the truth.

I thought about confronting him, telling I knew all about it, about how he had killed her, but it would soon blow up, I realized. I'd get one fact wrong, as I was bound to, and he'd know right off I was having him on. The truth was, I just didn't know how to play this. If anything, Alex's instinct to just let him run with his version, his made-up story, seemed more likely of getting us somewhere. It, too, would come unravelled, she seemed to think, and at that point he might realize that the jig was up and level with us. Or, again, he might not, might just relapse into some other fairy tale.

"Well, sure I knew Stephanie. Everybody will tell you that." He waved his hand as if everybody were just out there waiting to confirm his statement. "She was a pretty girl, too. All of us wanted her. Still for me it was always Lyla you know." He looked at me with a smile. "Beautiful Lyla!"

"There's no Lyla in this class list," Alex pointed out.

"Brains and a body," he said. "Nice combination!"

I wanted to slug him.

"But no, to answer your question, not in my grade." He just left it there, with no further explanation, almost as if he knew that the liar's great problem is saying too much, getting things too complicated.

"The way we heard it," I told him, "It was you and Stephanie, not this Lyla person."

Jimmy shook his head. "Hell you got it wrong. People say lots of things, believe lots of stuff. Over the years things drift in their memories. Doesn't mean it's true. Darned if some folks don't believe the world was made ten-thousand years ago! Doesn't leave much time for that meteorite to do its stuff and get transformed into a lake mind you, but that awkward reality never bothers them!"

Obviously the awkward reality about Stephanie and him didn't bother him either.

"At the party," Alex said, "something happened between you and Stephanie, something serious, so serious that you split up afterwards. What happened, Jimmy? You can tell us. It's OK."

Again Jimmy shook his head. He stretched out on the recliner and looked for all the world as if he just wanted to doze off. "Nothing special happened, nothing that you wouldn't expect to happen at a party where everyone was drinking. Stephanie and I danced together a couple of times, we might have groped a bit, everyone did, didn't mean anything, it was school over after all, big celebration."

He stopped and a funny look passed across his face. He swallowed once and then looked up at us with that fake smile he was using now. "Just a party," he said. "Just a party. Don't make too much of it."

"Jimmy," Alex said softly. "You and Stephanie were going to get married only something happened that night that made you change your mind. We're not here to do you any harm, to blame you for anything. We just want to know what happened, that's all."

Jimmy got up from his recliner suddenly. "Well I'm a bit sick of all your – he put on a high whining voice - 'we just want to know the truth' crap. Nothing happened! Got that straight? Nothing at all! We had a party, we had fun, end of story. Now I've got things to do. If you want to talk to me more sensibly come back tomorrow. Otherwise, our deal is off! Now scat!"

I stood up too. "We had a deal, Jimmy. Remember?"

Jimmy looked at me wildly. "If you think a ripe pair of tits and a nice ass is enough to make me listen to all this crap about me and Stephanie, well you can stuff it! Lyla was my girl and I don't care who tells you different! Lyla died that night, that's what happened. She drowned and that's all there is to it!"

"I thought you said I had a brain as well, Jimmy," Alex said but Jimmy was in no mood for smart-assed sallies. He gestured to us angrily to leave, so leave we did.

"I guess the skinny dip is off," Alex said as we got into the Audi.

I had to laugh despite my anger at Jimmy.

We drove home through the fields of fall, leaves already descending from some of the trees, and scattering in our wake as we sped past. Over to the left, there was a huge field of sunflowers standing bright in the sun and I thought of the biochemistry going on in that field.

There had been two, great, earth-transforming discoveries made by evolution through natural selection. The first had been using carbon dioxide to make sugar, driven by energy from the sun, and the second had been using oxygen to burn that sugar metabolically. On those two great discoveries, made by the blind working of evolution trawling patiently through protein spaces after stunning eons of time, all complex life depended. The processes were invisible of course, unseen marvels of biochemistry going on in that field and all the other fields around, sucking up the thin supply of carbon dioxide and locking it away in the form of food. I laughed to myself at the stupid idea that the press had started to parrot from some of the more extreme global warming advocates, that carbon dioxide was a pollutant, a poison. Try and live without it guys I thought to myself. Just try!

16

LETTER FROM NEW ZEALAND

Two days later I received a letter from New Zealand. As usual with the testimony of those who had been at the beach party, it was helpful but not as much as I would have liked.

Dear Mr. Therman,

I attended a post Graduation party at Crescent Beach in June 1964. These parties had been going on all during my High School years. Nowadays they have so-called Safe Grad parties, or even dry grad – hard to imagine - which are altogether different, but back then nothing was organized. So this party was an unstructured affair, in which we simply brought along whatever we thought we needed to enjoy ourselves. We made a lot of noise, we drank a lot of beer, although many of us, most of us probably, were underage at the time, and we ended up – most of us – pretty drunk and absolutely dead by the time dawn came. Trying to remember then an event during which we got hammered is pretty challenging. Here is what I do remember. I went with a girl called Ashley. I liked her a lot although we hadn't been going out or anything. Actually it was hard for most of us to date because we lived in separate little communities. The High School drew its students from a wide rural area. Many of my classmates just lived on scattered farms, not even in towns proper, while the rest of us lived in Whitemouth, Falcon Lake, West Hawk, Rennie, places like that and it wasn't easy getting around. The road back then was a bit of a joke, narrow and twisty and even though gas was cheap in those days, it wasn't cheap enough for most of us to be able to take the family car. So we didn't see much of each other outside of school. Anyway, I think Ashley liked me well enough, although we never saw each other afterwards. That was typical of most of us, I think, except for those who didn't get out. Some of the boys just carried on working for their Dads at their farms. Most of the girls got married almost as soon as they could. Me, I got out. I wanted to see the world so I signed up on a liner, believe it or not. They were in transition then, still doing passenger carrying as opposed to cruising. I hitched to Montreal first and got a job there since my family spoke French at home and then took it from there. Eventually, as you can see I made New Zealand my home. I think it was easier to get in then than I hear it is now.

For the party, I brought a record player with some big speakers. I'd borrowed the key to the marina office and opened it up so I could use the electrical outlet. My Dad had driven me in his truck. I played all kinds of stuff. I liked Duane Eddy back then, even though he didn't have any hits in 64. He'd had a couple a year or two before and anyway I liked his music so I stuck in some of his stuff. But it was the Beatles of course. They were all the rage then, and some Elvis still, fading but still popular and lots of others, a Ray Charles thing or two. And we danced.

It started out with us just talking about what we were going to do now – first for the summer and then afterwards. I think afterwards had a capital letter starting it in our minds: Afterwards. Now that we had finally managed to get through school and emerged victors what were we going to do? That seemed to occupy us a lot. I remember Stephanie was dead keen on going to college. So was Jimmy. They were both pretty bright people, at least in our little universe. I never went to college and managed to get on all right but I met up a few years later with Tod Penning. I think I heard somewhere that he's dead now. I don't even remember how Tod and I came to meet again, but I do recall vividly his saying how amazed he was when he got to college - I think he went to Queen's - he was a smart boy too - amazed to find how smart all the other kids were. In High School he had stood out, but at Queens he was very ordinary stuff he said. He'd had to work like mad to get good marks.

Who was there? Among the boys there was Blake, Tim, Jimmy of course and Tod. Also John, Andy and I think Gerald although I don't remember anything he may have said or done, just that I think he was there. Gerald was a quiet one, nobody knew very much about him, didn't open up much, shy, OK in class, not much in sports. In that school if you wanted to be on a team you pretty much got on the team. It only took being there, attending practices. But he didn't do anything, I remember more because of what he didn't do than what he did. As for the girls, well of course Stephanie was there. I still remember her, how stunning she was and at the same time how sweet and gentle she was, considerate. I was sad to hear she disappeared and I hope you find out what happened to her, although I don't suspect it will be anything nice will it, after all this time? Ashley was there of course, Nichola. She was a nice girl, quiet, down to earth, reasonably good looking, went in for most sports, don't remember her as excelling in them. I was probably the best basketball and volleyball player in the school, nothing like seriously good, but the best in that little world and I remember who was into sports and who wasn't. Nichola was one of those enthusiastic people who aren't much good, but every team needed them to fill out the roster. Jennifer now was pretty good. She was a ringette girl. They didn't play hockey back then, not the girls, it was ringette,

and volleyball she was good at it too, quick, aggressive, smart
on the court. She had big breasts, I shouldn't say this I
suppose, as they weren't the main reason I liked her, but of
course I noticed them, was interested in them, I was 18 after
all! I can't imagine she necessarily looked on her spectacular
breasts as an asset though. Who else? Melissa, or did she spell
it with a y – can't remember now, and Sharon, Julia, Candace,
Ashley, and Holly. I may have missed one or two. Even in a
small class you don't necessarily make friends with everybody,
especially when you only see them during school hours. I
suppose I remember mostly the kids who played sports,
because you saw more of them, went on bus trips with them,
sometimes stayed for a night or so with them in another town.

Anyhow we talked. I can't for the life of me remember
what they said about what they were going to do After. Some
of us were going to farm, stick around where we'd lived all our
lives. That always struck me as insane, to want to go nowhere,
just to stay where you had already been forever. What was
the adventure in that? Some of us, a few of us were going to
go to college, mostly U of M. One or two wanted to learn a
trade, be apprenticed, go to trade school. One of us wanted to
drive a train, Arnold I think. I used to laugh at that. It
seemed dirty work back then. I think steam had pretty much
gone by then, but it still had that black, oily reputation driving
a train. I don't remember for sure who it was though, I'm sorry
to say. There wasn't anybody else quite like me, who couldn't
wait to get out of the place. It seemed so stifling, so ordinary.
Nothing would ever happen there, it would just go on in the
same old way, or at least that's how it seemed to me. Maybe
I'm making more of how we talked than was really the case. It
certainly seems significant to me, what we talked about, our
various ideas and how nobody had much interest in seeing the

world, as if West Hawk and Whitemouth were the centre of the universe. Well, no, maybe that's not how they thought about it, but they were mostly pretty satisfied, that's what it was, satisfied. I suppose most of them had no ambition, that was the problem. It wasn't that I wanted to make money or anything, but I did want to have some adventures and I knew that adventures weren't going to happen sticking around.

After that we started dancing, cuddling up to our girlfriends or dates. Jimmy and Stephanie went off by themselves somewhere, down the beach a way. Tod got drunk fast and went into the water, splashing around, making a fuss, dragged a girl in with him, I think it was Holly.

It seems to me looking back that we formed a couple of groups. I had to hang around the record player, keep putting records on, and Jennifer and a few others hung around near me, and then the rest of them grouped around where Jimmy and Stephanie were. It was pretty dark. We had a couple of Coleman burners running to provide some light and we made a fire on the sand but even so it was fumble around dark there, so after a while I really didn't know what was going on. I saw Harry briefly, hadn't seen him all evening, in fact I hadn't realized he was even at the party, but Harry was like that, always in the background. He emerged from the trees near us and then went down the beach and shortly after that I heard screaming and shouting coming from down the beach. I didn't think anything of it, just supposed it was all part of the party. When we got sloshed like that we could get pretty rowdy and there had already been a couple of fights, nothing serious, few punches thrown, some wrestling on the sand. Stephanie came running over to where we were and then past us into the trees and I didn't see anything of her after that. I thought she had been crying and she was carrying something but I couldn't make out what it was. There were some shouts and taunts but it's all formless after all these years, like a blurry picture. What surprised me to tell the truth is remembering the names, didn't think I would but they came right away when I thought back to that year. I'm sorry to disappoint you but I never did hear what it was that had happened. I don't think it was anything much, but that may not be right because I seem to recall an ambulance showing up some time later, can't be sure now though, it's all rather fuzzy. I did hear that Stephanie and Jimmy broke up afterwards but people do that all the time, after school. People change and they don't always change together if you know what I mean, they change differently and then find they just aren't interested in each other anymore. Well, I'm speculating now. The plain fact is I don't know what happened and I don't know why they split up or even if it had anything to do with what happened at the party. I left before it was over. My Dad had come with the truck again and I had to pack up the music and records and go home with him.

I remember how nothing else moved on the highway except that an ambulance came past us in the other direction, siren going, lights flashing. I don't know if it had anything to do with the party or not. Apart from that, we were the only vehicle driving along the road, so peaceful, dark, lonely, driving with my Dad. We had given Jennifer a ride as well. She lived on a farm not too far from us, but as I said I never saw her again after that, no idea what happened to her, or to any of the others. I left my Dad and went out into the wide world but I always wrote to him over the years, until he died, dropped dead on the farm one day, just keeled over and that was that. I suppose he was disappointed I didn't want to stay and farm with him but frankly I never regretted leaving. I've seen most of the world and been glad for the chance to do so and finally settled down in this place. It has its faults, like most places have, one thing being it's so far away from anywhere else, except Australia, but it sure is beautiful.

Mr. Therman, I'm afraid I have rambled on excessively without being of much use to you, but I've put down anything useful I can remember and I hope it helps you. Good luck.

Sincerely,
Robert Deslisle

I thought to myself that the letter was typical of everything I was turning up in this investigation. Each step was a tiny one, each person I talked to presented a small step forward. There were no giant revelations, no huge advances. I had hoped for more but he had given me something useful, mainly the names of the people at the party. If anything really nasty or significant had happened to explain why Stephanie was murdered (if she was murdered I reminded myself dutifully) it certainly hadn't been apparent to anyone I had spoken to who had been there. Maybe the beach party was a red herring, and I was making far too much of it. Still there had been screaming and there had been an ambulance, although whether they were connected or not wasn't clear.

I looked at the list of names and ticked off some more of them on the whiteboard, going through Robert's letter carefully. But when I finished I had one name left over: Harry. Who the hell was Harry? Harry wasn't on my list. Had Betty Kingsford made a mistake about the students? I remembered how careful she had been, examining each picture and then looking through the names printed there to find one that went with it. She had counted the pictures carefully, so I doubted that she had goofed. The more likely explanation was that Robert just got the name wrong or that it was a Harry from another occasion, not the beach party.

I decided to call him to see if he could tell me any more about Harry. I looked at the clock on the wall above the whiteboards. It was a good time to call a place hanging upside down, as I always thought of it, illogically. Not only upside down but a day ahead of itself. I got through, not always a sure thing for New Zealand, but when I said who I was and asked to speak to Robert, I was told that he wasn't able to talk to anyone. Apparently he'd had another stroke, this one much worse than the first. I said I was sorry and rang off. 'Harry Who?' I wrote on the whiteboard.

I thought about Jimmy, who was lying his head off about Stephanie, which just made him seem all the more likely as the suspect, the probable murderer. Surely he must realize that his lying just made us more suspicious. I hoped he wasn't under the mistaken idea that we would swallow his nonsense. Even the bartender had got into the act with his nonsensical version of the beach party. Did they take us for idiots, I wondered. It might be worthwhile to see if there had been anything in the local paper – if there was one – about the goings on at the party. I decided to pay the friendly librarian another visit. And as for Harry, well the best source for dealing with that was Betty Kingsford. No wonder Mystery Man gave me the Audi – all this driving to West Hawk and Falcon was certainly putting on the miles! The environmentalists wouldn't be happy, that was for sure!

"I swear Colin, that car and you have an unhealthy relationship!" Linda said when I told her that I was heading back to West Hawk and Falcon Lake. "You should rent a cabin there; it would probably be cheaper than all the gas you're using going back and forth."

I kissed her goodbye and got back into the Audi.

17

BETTY KINGSFORD AGAIN

When **Betty Kingsford** came to the door she was as boney as ever and wearing an eye patch. I stifled a chuckle for she looked all the world like a miniature pirate, albeit an old one. "Ah, Mr. Therman, come back for some more of my cookies have you?" She looked at me sharply as she led me back into the living room, which was as gloomy and cluttered as I remembered it. "Yes," she said, "I've had an operation on my eye, so now I'm Long John Betty. It is supposed to help me see better. I think all it does is make the surgeon see his way to retirement a little better."

It was hard to keep a straight face with this geriatric pirate vision in front of me. The cats had come to sniff me out and then pad softly back to wherever they snuggled up.

"Well, then," she said when at last she had come back with the tea tray containing precisely the same contents as on the previous occasion, including four biscuits, two for her and two for me.

"We've talked to Jimmy," I told her. "He claims that a girl called Lyla was his sweetheart, not Stephanie and he says nothing happened at the beach party."

She looked off into the distance and shook her head. "Poor Jimmy. He's lying of course. I wonder why. Perhaps he just can't face the truth. I don't know what it was that kept him here all this time, though, why he became one of the left-behinds."

I told her my theory. "I think Jimmy killed Stephanie and that her body isn't all that far away. I don't know why he did it, that's the big mystery right now. Something big must have happened but nobody's talking about it, that's the thing."

"I don't know," she said. "I live in this little place, shut away from the world. I go out to shop, to get a book or two – when I can read at least – and I know very little about what goes on out there, and am mostly glad not to. I shut it away. But even so it creeps in, with people like you – oh don't apologize, people need to find out, however unpleasant it may be. It's just that, well Mr. Therman, I'm an old, dried-up woman whose senses are beginning to fail. Now that's cruelty: for your brain to live while your eyes and ears and everything else dies on you." She waved her hands as if to dismiss any protest I might make, or any expression of sympathy. "Mr. Therman," she said fiercely, "It's not me that counts. My life is almost over. It's my children, the children I taught, all the children that I care about. I remember them all so vividly you see, all of them. It was a long time ago but I still remember them, although I imagine they've long forgotten about me. But I know what young people are like, how the possibilities stretch before them, if only they would grasp them. Many of them simply don't. They just give up while they still have a chance at something. I never understood why then and I certainly don't now. The future is there to grasp and they just won't reach for it."

She stopped suddenly as if replaying what she had just said, and then continued. "Oh, listen to me, babbling on like, well, like an old woman, isn't that what they say, Mr. Therman! Now I'm not such a dried-up old bag that I don't know you came not only with information but with a question. You have that look in your eye. You sit there patiently, drinking my tea and eating my biscuits, but you're like a coiled spring. Shall I remove the catch?"

I liked Betty immensely, although I wasn't sure why exactly. I didn't envy her. I thought it was a mistake to live as she did, shut away, in this dark, depressing little house, encaged with her two cats in a little world marked only by the ticking of the clock and the occasional forays for groceries. It was far too confining for my taste, yet she was a brave woman it appeared to me, brave and hard. She had shown her love only to children, school children, who mostly don't have much time for teachers, toss them away, discard them like last year's clothes. Clearly she'd had precious little thanks for all her love. Maybe one or two of them might remember her, even think of her as significant in their early life, but they'd never tell her, never let her know. But that's often the way of it: the fairy tales and movies of the recognition finally given to great teachers are just that, imaginary reworking of reality. They represent what we would like to have happen, but what in practice rarely does. Something had happened to Betty long ago, something that had been like taking a two-by-four to her love of teaching, something that had sent her reeling back to this cocoon. I wanted to know what it was.

"Mrs. Kingsford, fifteen years ago my daughter disappeared. She had gone to school as usual, she was in grade 10 at the time, and came home afterwards to tell my wife that she was going to the hockey arena with two of her friends. She assured her she'd be home in time for supper and off she went, period, end of story. We never saw her again. It was as if she had never been, had been sucked up from the earth. I don't think anyone who hasn't been through something like that can have any idea what it is like: the terror, the fury, the despair. The police investigated, everyone was interviewed but no one had seen anything. She had been at the arena with her friends and then one time when they turned to her, she was gone. No one had seen her. There had been no strangers in town – it was just a place to meet up. There was no ice there any more, no team from out of town, nothing like that. Simply put, there were no clues as to what could have happened to her. We have other children but that makes no difference at all, except that possibly it kept my wife and I together. We thought she would have wanted that and for the first few horrible years it worked like a glue and after that, well we learned to live with the scars. But you know, well it was worse at first of course, but even today, sometimes, if I'm not paying attention, my mind is wandering, I will suddenly feel as if I expect her to be walking towards me, or that she will open the front door and yell that she's home. I'll feel a swelling of joy in my heart and then of course I come to my senses and tell myself not to be a fool. But maybe today she'll be at home, it's always there, like a faint, but never extinguished possibility."

Betty was looking at me intently, respecting me with silence.

I sighed, dragging myself back from the painful past. "I tell you that not to get your sympathy, Mrs. Kingsford, but so you know, you understand, that I have pain too. I know what it is to suffer. What happened?"

She sat there still, silent for the longest time and then she moved slightly, then got to her feet, collected the cups and saucers and the plate that had held cookies and took the tea tray back to the kitchen. When she came back, she sat down again and shook her head. "You know Mr. Therman, you're a brave man. I told you the last time you were here that I would throw you out if you ever brought up the subject yet here you are bringing it up and before you've even asked your question. Rather silly of you, actually, to risk not having your question answered! I'm sorry about your daughter, Mr. Therman, really I am. Life can be unbearably cruel and there's no appeal court to give you a second chance when horrid things occur. You want to know my story, well it hardly compares in bitterness to yours yet in some ways you seem to have weathered your storm better than I have mine, I must say."

Her uncovered eye had misted. She wiped at it and said, "Oh, drat." She composed herself and began. "Years ago, I was a teacher. Well of course you know that already. And I loved it, and I was a good one, I really was." She looked at me as if to dare me to suggest otherwise.

"I already know that too," I said gently.

"Well then I was almost fifty at the time, had been teaching for many years, still enjoyed it. I wasn't itching to get ahead, to become a Principal, had no ambitions that way. I just wanted to teach. And then the rumours started. I don't know how. There was never anything to them, just rubbish, lies. But they persisted, hinting at unsavoury things between me and my students, ugly things. I could never get at them. They were like smoke, vapours that wouldn't go away. I could never find out who spread them, or even why that was the worst part, simply not knowing who started them or kept them circulating. Surely, I thought, nobody could possibly believe those things about me." She paused and let out a despairing laugh. "Oh, Mr. Therman, I was naïve, because of course they could believe them and did! I ignored them and kept hoping that they would go away. I was summoned finally one day by the Principal. He started off pleasantly enough but he soon got to the point that I was bringing disrepute down on his precious school. But they are lies, I told him. You know they are lies! That's not the point, he told me, not the point at all. Parents are concerned. They hear these things and they call me. What am I going to do about it they want to know. I begged him not to listen to the lies, to talk to the pupils in my class they would soon set him straight. And that's when he poleaxed me because he said he had done, he'd talked to several of the boys and they all hinted that there was something to the rumours after all. I hardly knew what to say. I was bereft, heartbroken. How could those boys lie about me like that, because of course that's what they were doing — lying. After that, it was all over, my teaching career destroyed. I made the mistake of appealing directly to the school board, which held an in camera hearing. If anything it was more unpleasant than when the Principal had spoken to me, because none of them cared a jot about me that was clear. It was the school that mattered, nothing else: the school and its precious reputation. Their responsibility wasn't to truth, to support a wrongly accused teacher or to punish someone who started the beastly, lying rumours. Not a bit of it. Their responsibility they informed me was simply for the school and for the safety of the pupils as they kept sanctimoniously insisting. But what kind of school is it, I asked them, if it allows teachers to be wrongly accused and does nothing. But they were deaf to such entreaties. Oh, I'm boring you, dear me, I surely did not intend to run on about this. So, Mr. Therman, that was that. They wanted me to go and go I went, it's as simple as that. My teaching was over, and all because of lies, cleverly spread and somehow — I'll never understand it — substantiated by my very own students."

I shivered suddenly. "I truly am sorry, Mrs. Kingsford," I said. "That was terrible, tragic. I understand how it must hurt."

Curled up in her chair she looked so vulnerable I felt heart sick for her.

She sniffed and said, with a little self deprecating laugh. "I was so silly. You know for several years I kept thinking, hoping, that one day I'd hear a knock on the door and the Principal would be there saying, oh do forgive us, it was all a terrible mistake, please come back. But of course he never did come knocking, not even to apologize. Someone destroyed me. I don't know if they meant to, but they certainly did a good job of it, intentionally or not. Now then, Mr. Therman, let's turn away from this and consider the question you wished to ask. What was it now?"

"I want to know about Harry," I said. "Harry was mentioned by one of the students you identified in Stephanie's graduating class who said he was at the beach party here in West Hawk. Unfortunately that student can't tell me any more because he's had a bad stroke."

Without saying a word, Betty climbed stiffly to her feet and presently brought in the albums and sat back down. "I taught 28 classes in my career. Some people think that each class must blur indistinguishably into the next, but that is like telling a parent with many children that they must all seem the same. Nothing could be further from the truth. In each class I find there is always someone around to whom the whole class seems to gravitate. This is how I could recall the faces and put names to them when you came to see me before. Stephanie was one such person. She was beautiful. That is what I remember: how good looking she was. Yet she was a sweet girl, successful academically and in sports, popular of course, not outwardly affected by her physical good fortune. Of course the boys swarmed around her, but so did the girls. Everyone wanted to be her friend. Jimmy was special of course. Now I put the names to the faces did I not, each face named and there was no Harry."

She paused for the longest while, remembering I supposed, sifting through her brain for all the links to Stephanie. "There was one boy who was mad about cars," she continued, with a little smile now. "Of course most of them were back then. The models were still changing every year, superficially at least I seem to recall. That was Tim. Arnold now wanted to be an engineer. Drive a locomotive I mean. Gerald was a farm boy through and through, and so was Stuart. He was big and slow and good with his hands. I can remember something about them all, at least all except Harry, and there was a Harry and what seems strange to me now is that I know now that there was a Harry and I can't recall anything about him!" She opened the 1964 annual and turned to the pictures. She touched each face once and matched it with a name, once more going through the process she had used before. And then she reversed it, going from the names to the picture. At last she looked up triumphantly. "I have your Harry!" she said.

I leant forward eagerly to see his picture but she shook her head. "Not his picture. Harry Cunningham – his name's right here, but he's not in the picture. And I remember now Harry was the most secretive little boy, well young man, I have ever encountered. Never wanted his picture taken, went to great lengths to avoid being noticed, volunteered for nothing. Harry was always in the background. Harry was the kind of person who is always there and never noticed. I thought it just a strange quirk at the time I suppose, but now it strikes me as extraordinary, creepy, unhealthy."

"You have come through once again for me, in flying colours," I told her. She seemed flustered by the praise.

"All I have Mr. Therman, are my memories. Once those go..." she shrugged.

I thought of all the things I could say to her, how I could commiserate for her mistreatment by the school board, the unfairness of life, but I knew that whatever I said to her would hardly make up for what had happened, her personal catastrophe. She was a brave soul, but injured, bearing up as best she could. Words from me would do nothing to change anything, would be trite, insulting even, platitudes. Everyone in the end wants to be respected, to do well in their chosen career and then, at last, when it is time to retire, to have everyone gather round and remind them of their success and importance, to let them go out with the warm regards of those with whom they have worked. Some people think that's sentimental twaddle but for most of us it is deeply meaningful. Instead of that nice ending, which she greatly deserved, Betty got turfed, had to creep away in disgrace, everything that she had done for class after class ignored and forgotten. It wasn't fair but there was nothing to be done about it, and nothing that I could say would undo the hurt. So I stood up and she got up also and followed me to the door. "Come again, Mr. Therman. Come for tea and perhaps some biscuits."

I said I would and then, without thinking I put my arms around her small frail body and I hugged her, gently hugged. We stood for a moment like that and then she moved back and said, "Good bye Mr. Therman."

After I left Betty's house, I drove the slow way back to Falcon, over and around the narrow, twisty road, under the overpass carrying the thundering main highway overhead and around the lakeshore.

When I walked into the library, Linda Evans was again behind the desk. She looked scrubbed and polished today, her hair down her back and wearing a brightly coloured blouse with beads. She looked up and smiled.

"Mr. Therman, come to check our archives again?"

"Actually I have," I admitted. "The local newspaper, if there is one, old copies."

Her face fell and then she gave a laugh. "Oh, Mr. Therman, I'm so sorry. You do have a way of finding our weak spots don't you! For a moment when I saw you I had hoped we might redeem ourselves with our collection, but I see that's not to be. Ah well. There *was* a paper, the SouthEast Clarion it was called, but it went out of business about five years ago. And we certainly did keep back issues, had a large collection but.."

She paused and took off her glasses. "Well it was most upsetting at the time, I almost resigned over it. But the chair of the Library Board developed a mania for circulation data. It can be useful of course, I admit that, but in his hands it became everything. Had to make way for the new, he kept saying. If it doesn't move, just remove was one of his slogans, I remember it well." She looked at me and laughed.

"Every holding had to justify its existence. Well how can an archive justify its existence? There's no circulation data because the holdings aren't circulated of course. But it took up a lot of space. Ironically, the High School annuals survived, except for the issue you wanted of course, but the newspapers didn't. News is ephemeral, he said and the board went along with him, would have been hard not to, he had up a good head of steam over the issue. I almost resigned, as I said, but I didn't. It didn't seem quite the issue to get all principled about. And of course a Library does have to weed, that's a reality, no matter how large. And the more readers want the latest books the more the old stuff must go. Someone is always upset no matter what you do."

"Of course I knew full well that to get at the minutiae of a small community like this, the local newspaper is indispensable. The city papers don't cover places like this in any kind of detail, if at all. If you want to find out what happened you need these little papers published weekly or monthly. I knew that, knew they were important because of that, so was stubborn, at least for a while."

She sat and thought back to how it had been. I waited patiently. I could see it was important to her to explain it to me, to have me understand why she had failed me this second time.

"He didn't bully me over it," she continued. "If he had done, I think I would have resigned. He listened carefully, he was patient, but he was relentless. Something had to go. If we didn't discard the old newspapers, it would have to be something else, perhaps the encyclopaedias."

She took off her glasses, rubbed her eyes and then replaced the spectacles. She looked up at me and laughed. "Talk about going on about minutiae," she said. "The grubby reality of library operations! Not what you came for I'm sure, Mr. Therman."

"It's all right," I said. "I'm interested."

"Well I should have chosen the encyclopedias, I can see that now. Even then they were all on the Internet or CD-ROM."

She suddenly looked flustered and laughed again self consciously. "I'm sorry, Mr. Therman," she said. "You were looking for old newspapers and I've given you old news."

I laughed, despite my disappointment. Linda was an amusing woman and I decided it was fun even to be disappointed by her.

"Well, it was a long shot," I admitted.

"There's worse news, I'm afraid," she added. "Ordinarily, well we wouldn't be the last resort, but the building they used to publish the newspaper itself, the one that went broke, burned down not too long ago. I'm told that they still had old copy but it all went up in the flames, made a big bonfire.

"The past does have a way of obliterating itself when I'm around, doesn't it!" I observed.

She looked at me sharply and then smiled. "I'm sorry to have disappointed you again," she said. "It's quite upsetting not to be able to help." She paused and took a deep breath. "But, Mr. Therman, nobody used the old papers, nobody at all. You must be the first in years."

"And I don't even live here," I said. There wasn't much I could say really. She was upset and I couldn't undo that, no matter what I said or did. She thought she had made a mistake and she was probably right, when you thought about it. The newspapers were irreplaceable, now forever gone, never to be restored. The alternative of encyclopaedias or anything else weren't, it was as simple as that. But then we all make mistakes. She would dislike herself for making that one because in a way it was against all her library training. It was unprofessional. She felt she had weakened in the face of pressure, not stood up for what was right, taken the easy way out, oh I could see it clearly.

She must have sensed what I was thinking because she smiled.

"I understand," I said, and I think she believed me. I told her not to worry about it, that I'd find what I was looking for one way or another. "Maybe one day, I'll come back and just want to borrow a book."

She beamed and said that would be nice.

18

FINDING STEPHANIE

Ever since I'd toured the hidden highway with Reginald Osborne I'd known I would have to dig around in the spot he'd fingered as the most likely. I'd been putting it off, hoping for some other lead but one thing that was driving me now was the season. It was getting on for winter, and soon there would be no chance at all to go digging into ponds hoping to find buried cars, or buried bodies for that matter. I just didn't want to wait until May or June again; it was simply too long. To some extent I had worked up a head of steam now and didn't want to lose the momentum I had going.

I told Alex what I wanted to do and she said she couldn't think of anything she'd rather do than get muddy and wet, not to mention freezing cold, sticking poles down into muck. So on a chilly depressingly dead day in October we set off down the highway once again in the Audi.

I had borrowed a small rubber boat from a friend, strapped it to the top of the car and brought some ski poles as probes. We parked the car at the side of the road and struggled with the boat and poles through the trees to the oily pond that Reginald Osborne had identified as the most likely spot for someone to hide a car and a body.

There was a bitter wind blowing across the surface of the water. There seemed little chance of it warming up appreciably later on. October is a month I could gladly skip, a transition month that is neither winter nor summer, one that often starts out well but ends in misery, with no leaves, no birds and everywhere grey and cold. The warmth of summer already seemed a distant memory. The only good thing in the miserable litany was that there were no insects.

We put the boat into the water, got in and pushed off from the shore. Neither of us were experienced with boats and we soon found that the wind kept driving us back to where we had started unless one of us struggled constantly to hold us on station with one of the poles. After a bit of this we agreed we'd better adopt a different plan.

Luckily I'd brought a long coil of rope and we finally hit on the idea of paddling over to the far side of the pond. There I attached one end of the rope to a tree, got back into the boat and let the wind push us slowly to the other side while controlling our progress with the rope. Next we discovered that the ski poles were far too short to be useful as probes, so we paddled back to shore once more and I clambered out again. I cut down a couple of aspen branches and stripped them down to long narrow spears. Out on the water again, Alex suddenly looked around and laughed. "What, Colin dear, just what the hell do we think we are doing!"

"Do I know how to show a girl a good time or what!" I responded as we pushed the poles into the water. The bottom of the pond felt as if it was covered by loose blocks of something. Every time I pushed down I felt the tip of the probe slide off something and then sink into sediment. Whatever was down there was small, however, certainly not like a vehicle. We did one crossing and then tied the rope to another tree several feet away from the first and were on our second probe run when a voice hailed us from the spot where we had started.

"Need a hand?" It was Corporal Simard, out of uniform.

I waved and let the wind push us back to him.

"I thought it was you guys," he said. He was wearing a blue sheepskin-lined bomber jacket, a blue watch cap and hip waders. He shook our hands and said he'd gladly help us. "Looking for the missing vehicle, is that it?"

"I found a guy knows the hidden highway like the back of his hand," I told him. "When I challenged him to think of a place where someone might try to stash a car, this is the spot he fingered."

"So you figured it was your best bet, is that it?"

I nodded. When we weren't talking there wasn't a sound, no cars passing by on the highway nearby, no birds, no noises of civilization at all, just the wind stirring dry leaves. As we talked, our breath steamed out of us as if were mini steam engines idling in the station.

"Well," he teased us, "it's interesting to see how you investigators do things. Always things to learn, yep something new every day!" He turned serious. "If you want to do your boat thing, I'll wade out and try my luck. First one to find something gets breakfast bought."

"Thanks, Corporal Simard, I appreciate it!"

"Hey, it's John, come on!"

We resumed our boat, wind, rope trick while Simard did the hip wader thing. As we worked, a thin sun had appeared. It was doing nothing to warm us but it made the task a little less gloomy and forlorn. We were on our sixth trip when Simard – John - suddenly let out a whoop. "Come over here and give me a hand," he shouted. We paddled over to the spot he was probing and went to work. By making repeated stabs with my probe, I could tell that there was definitely something large and flat down there and a lot nearer the surface than most objects. "Could be the roof of a car," he suggested. We continued stabbing at whatever it was under the surface and at last concluded that it must be a vehicle.

I reached down with my right arm, pushing it as far down as I could and finally felt it with the tips of my fingers, a smooth, flat surface, something metal certainly under a thick layer of ooze. We paddled back over to the tree, untied the rope and let the wind carry us once more to the other side. I got out of the rubber boat and coiled up the rope.

"Thanks," I said to John.

"Tell you what," he said. "I'll get the boys in here on Monday and we'll drag out whatever it is, how's that?"

"Great," I said. John gave me a hand to drag the boat out of the water and then stripped off his hip waders. "Easier than a boat, unless it's too deep," he said.

"You know, I really appreciate your help," I told him.

"But you're wondering why I'm helping you, right?"

"Something like that. Actually it's a broader question than just you," I explained. "Alex and I were in the Water Rat the other day when some of Jimmy's cronies, biker guys, came in and started to muscle in on the conversation, make a nuisance of themselves, swagger a bit and suddenly there's the cavalry, in the form of Timmins."

"They're not bad guys, those pals of Jimmy's you know, not bad types at all, might look a little rough, I suppose," he responded. "I think they like that, to look rough but they're pretty harmless, might swagger a bit as you say, but I don't think they'd do anyone any harm. Unless you were rude about their bikes, that might be a different story!"

I laughed and thought to myself how neatly he'd avoided answering my question. Well, I wasn't going to complain. If the cops wanted to help me, so much the better.

We drove to Rennie for breakfast at the hotel. Wood walls, cheap furniture, a pool table, some VLTs and the smell of beer and musty carpet: you've seen it all before. Still, the service was friendly and the food hearty and reasonably priced. We'd all worked up a bit of an appetite and dug into the ham, sausages, eggs and toast with enthusiasm.

"This what you do on your days off?" I asked. "Help folks like me with their amateur investigations?"

John laughed. "Never had a situation like this before," he admitted.

"Neither have I," Alex said. "This is not exactly lawyering as it's taught in school!"

"How did you two get on to this, anyway?" John asked. I'd never told him about the email and the trail of clues that had led us here and I wasn't about to start now.

"Disappearances always get my attention," I explained. "Not hard to figure out why. And I came across this one and thought it might be interesting to poke around see what I could find out."

"You ever find anything about your daughter?" he asked.

I shook my head. "Not a whiff."

"Must be rough. I'm sorry."

I nodded, not really wanting to talk about it. "Timmins tells me the Chief has always been around here, never posted anywhere else," I said to change the subject.

John laughed. "Naw, what does Timmins know! I think the Chief's pulling his leg. He's got to follow the rules just like everybody else, it's just that he keeps coming back." He looked at me as if to tell me he knew I'd switched the topic on him but was willing to let me get away with that this time. He smiled then and sat back in his chair and drank some more coffee. "He's rotated away for a while and then he's back again," he added. "Seems he just can't stay away. Must like the place I guess!"

"And his name is top secret!"

"Oh Timmins has a way with him, doesn't he, likes to pull your leg I think. But no he doesn't like his name used, or his picture taken for that matter, says it's a question of security, as if he's made some enemies and wants to keep out of the limelight. But you know, he's a good cop, keeps his eyes open, knows what's going on."

After breakfast we parted company. John told us to come by the pond Monday morning, say coffee time. "We'll be out at first light and with any luck we'll have something for you then."

I thanked him again and then got into the Audi and drove Alex to my place.

"Rubber boats, ski poles, warm clothes! I don't know, affairs aren't what they used to be!" Linda said.

"Ha, ha!"

"We found something, though," Alex told her. "Maybe Stephanie's car."

"Or maybe it's just a wreckers paradise," I countered. "Maybe every damn pond along that hidden highway is littered with abandoned wrecks!"

"My aren't we the pessimist!" Linda laughed.

Alex and I went downstairs to the whiteboards again and stood staring at them. They stared back. There was nothing on the boards yet to show it, but we were getting somewhere at last, or maybe we were.

"I think it's significant that Jimmy didn't want to talk about the hidden highway, the possible spots where you could hide a vehicle or a body," I said.

"I'm not sure that means anything." Alex responded. "Jimmy didn't want to talk about anything pretty much except his tall tale about Lyla, fictitious Lyla."

I nodded. "I think he's afraid we're getting close and he's desperate not to give us anything at all, even to the point of distancing himself from Stephanie, making us prove his relationship, and how can we do that as it's all hearsay, people remembering stuff 40 years ago. All that dissembling to me pretty much wraps it up: he's the killer."

"Maybe," Alex conceded, "But you still don't know for sure that Stephanie is dead or that *anyone* killed her, let alone Jimmy."

Technically she was right of course, but I didn't believe for a moment that Stephanie hadn't been murdered, or that Jimmy hadn't killed her. But I still didn't know why, I still didn't know how, and I still didn't know who the mystery man was. That was the deepest, darkest mystery of all right now. Who had wound me up and pointed me in this direction? And why? Whoever he was, he clearly wasn't Jimmy, that was a step forward at least, realizing that killer and mystery man were not one and the same, or was that all a clever ruse designed to make me think that?

"If Jimmy is the killer, he must be getting pretty nervous about now, or he will be when he hears we've found Stephanie's car – if it's hers."

I hadn't thought of how Jimmy would respond to this development and it suddenly seemed like a great opportunity for prying more at his armour, clearing away all his lies.

"Is he making things up to hide his guilt, to put us off the track, or is he just mad?" I wondered out loud. "Once the car is out of the pond, I think maybe it will be time to confront Mr. Case," I said. "And I think maybe the time for pretty clothes and sex appeal is over. It's brass knuckles time."

"Oh my hero," Alex said, feeling my biceps.

"What I don't want is the police horning in on it. Once they find the car, if that's what it is and not just an old tractor or something, they might just decide to take this whole thing seriously and start doing their own interviews."

"I don't think so, Colin." She paced up and down the room, nervously poking at various points on the whiteboards, nodding at mental points she was making to herself. I just watched her and after a while she looked at me, and said, "Remember how you always kept saying you felt as if you were being watched, but could never find any actual sign of it? Well I think we were being watched – by the police. Didn't there always seem to be a police car around? You know, you look around for bad guys and you see a police car, it's almost as if it's invisible. You don't think anything of it, do you? You just accept it, oh yes a cop car, pretty normal thing to see, nothing unusual there, so you don't count it, you don't even think about it. But I think they have been watching us very carefully every step of the way."

I thought back to how it had been and it seemed to me that she was right, that there had indeed often been a police car around and of course you don't think anything of it, pretty normal thing to see, nothing unusual there. "Watching us and stepping in whenever it was needed, like the first time at the Water Rat, and this morning at the pond."

Alex laughed. "Even when they're off duty, too!"

"I wonder who's behind it. Can't be Timmins. He's just too stupid. Simard? Well, maybe. He's in on it, certainly, knows something about what's going on, but I can't see him as the brains behind it, the driving force, so who can it be?"

"Perhaps it's he who cannot be named," Alex suggested.

"The Chief?"

"None other. Mr. Top Secret himself!"

I thought she was on to something. "Maybe he's the mystery man himself," I said.

Alex said she liked the idea. "But we have to figure out why he's directing things like that. What is his motive?"

"Perhaps he knows Jimmy did it but had no proof and after all these years, getting close to retirement, he's determined to take him down, so he winds us up hoping, well hoping something." The idea had run into the sand, bogged down, spinning its wheels. I still couldn't see why he would care. Police must have to deal with lots of people they know are guilty, or think are guilty but can never nail for lack of evidence. They must be used to the frustration that involves. So what was special about Stephanie?

"Would be nice to know his name," Alex said. "Let me work on that. There has to be a way of finding out who he is. He can't work incognito."

"OK," I said, "but don't get your hopes up. Just because he's *a* mystery man doesn't mean he's *the* mystery man. After all, how could he arrange for the train, or afford the Audi lease. Cops aren't exactly rich usually!"

Alex thought about that and looked at the whiteboard again.

Linda called downstairs to ask if Alex would like to stay for supper. Alex looked at her watch, said oh my god, and told Linda that actually she had a date that evening and would have to get going soon. "Don't worry," she purred at me, "He's more a business associate than a sex stud, not serious competition."

I laughed and shook my head at her teasing approach to life.

"Before I go though there's one more thought I had. Remember that grand vision of a student database you had, way back when? Inputting every little twitch and foible of every classmate of Steffie's, and choreographing every second of the great beach party?"

"Didn't exactly work out the way I imagined it, did it!" I admitted ruefully. "People don't remember, have different versions, are irritatingly vague or simply don't want to talk."

"Or are dead!"

"There's that too."

"Sure it hasn't worked out the way you hoped it would but even so it seems to me that you're not making enough of the data you have got. Look at this."

She waved the letter I'd received from Robert Deslisle. "Listen to what he says here, 'One of us wanted to drive a train'. Did that not switch on a light bulb when you read it, Colin?"

I shook my head ruefully. In truth it hadn't. "I missed that, that's pretty bad isn't it. So maybe he did end up driving a train and that's why there was a locomotive waiting for me at the Bear Lake trail." I thought back to my ride on the locomotive and suddenly remembered. "He said his name was Arnie – the engineer! Christ, I'm stupid!"

"Exactly," Alex said. "And who knows, maybe another of them went on to become an Audi salesman."

"Christ!" I said again, remembering now the name on the lease documents: Tim Surtowski, another one of Stephanie's classmates.

"You know Colin," Alex said sternly, "there's not much point in collecting the data unless you are going to mine it."

"Yea, yea. No need to nag!"

"Gotta go, love," Alex said, "And don't worry. Every outfit needs some brains. You collect the stuff and I figure out what it means. Not a bad division of labour!"

"Get out of here!"

After she left I stayed downstairs with the whiteboards thinking about what we had figured out. Maybe it was as simple as that, that after all these years, despite the apparent lack of community currently among the long-ago classmates there was still a connection, that one of them could still call in favours and big favours at that. But then where did the chief fit in? Was he just a rogue element, operating independently of all the other stuff, with no connection between them? Or was he deeply involved somehow? It was becoming absolutely critical to find out his name.

The next day, without telling Alex, as I knew she wouldn't approve, would warn me about the possible danger involved, I drove to West Hawk to talk to Jimmy again, or to try to. Jimmy hadn't exactly been cooperative the last time we'd tried to discuss things. Perhaps without the distraction of Alex he'd be more inclined to level with me.

If anything the day was blacker than the day before, but at least it wasn't snowing yet.

Jimmy's bike was sitting near the cabin. When I knocked on the door I heard Jimmy yelling to come on back.

"Oh, shit, it's you," he said when I climbed up to his deck.

"Kind of cold to be still sitting outside," I commented.

"I like it out here," he said. "What brings you back here? I thought I made myself pretty plain the last time you and that bouncing boob bitch of yours were here that I didn't want to talk about the party, or Stephanie."

"Sure, but we've found Stephanie's car, or we think we have. The cops are going to get it out on Monday." I told him.

"Yea, big deal, good on you mate as they say and why should I give a fart about that?"

I wondered what Stephanie had seen in this big turd, way back when. The years certainly hadn't been kind to his personality but then maybe guilt had been eating away at him all that time. That might do something to a person, I suppose. Everyone said he was a nice kid and I had to believe they were right. Still he certainly wasn't a nice kid now!

"I just thought you should know. No matter what you pretend, I know that you and Stephanie were a pair, that she meant a lot to you. So I thought you might be interested in knowing that soon we should have the answer to what happened to her so long ago."

"Christ! Can't you leave a man alone! Why do you imagine I might want the past stirred up, the dead disinterred? I just want peace. I just want to forget."

His anger appeared to be draining away or so I thought but a moment later he was on his feet, finger stabbing angrily in my direction. "Get the fuck out of here!" he yelled. "And leave Stephanie alone, god damn it, just leave the girl alone." He came towards me, his face red.

I backed up and held up my hands reassuringly. "Jimmy, it's OK," I told him. "You can tell me what happened, nothing will come of it. It will be good to get the truth out at last."

He came towards me with a roar and I ran back to the car and got in. He pounded on the window.

"Scram!" he said. "Scram!"

I backed out of the dirt trail to his cabin and drove away up the highway towards home. Brilliant performance I told myself. I didn't know whether to feel angry towards Jimmy or to feel sorry for him. He was obviously confused and I hadn't helped any by talking about dragging out Stephanie's car. It would serve me right I suppose if on Monday they pull some old irrelevant wreck out of the ooze!

19

GETTING THE BODIES

On Monday morning I drove the Audi back towards Rennie. Alex had some clients who needed attention right away and had called me to say she couldn't come, much to her own disappointment I could tell. The fields were deserted, the road empty. It was another dull day and there had been a light sprinkling of snow, making the road wet and covering the rocks, field stubble and vegetation with a thin veil of white. I always found this in-between time surprisingly dead and quiet: summer had gone and with it all the cars and tourists, all the water fowl and insects and it was as if the world was waiting for something - the whine and stink of the snowmobiles maybe? It seemed as if the world was waiting to tip over into winter but wasn't quite ready.

I pulled over onto the right-hand shoulder and parked where I saw the collection of police vehicles off to the left.

Someone had cut down the screen of trees that had hidden the section of old highway and there were tire marks in the ground. Up near the old tarmac there was another area of recent tree cutting and there was flatbed truck parked nearby. Through the newly created opening in the trees I could see down to the pond where a mobile crane was growling away near the water. As I approached, a couple of divers emerged like dripping monsters. As I watched, the crane sank down on its wheels as it hoisted something slowly out of the pond. It emerged gradually, dripping black ooze, but clearly a vehicle. The front end was heavily damaged and the windshield had two huge holes. I was disappointed because the number of holes was enough to tell me that whatever this was, it wasn't Stephanie's car. And the car itself, with no fins and lacking the characteristic double headlight cluster of her model of Buick clearly wasn't the vehicle she had been driving that day.

Corporal Simard was conferring with the divers. When he saw me he waved me over.

"John, that's not Stephanie's car," I told him. "She was driving a 1960 Buick LeSabre and she was travelling alone."

"Yea I know, I know," John said. "Divers here tell me there are two cars down there. Looks like you were right when you accosted me about the files. That's probably the two missing men there and they certainly didn't just go off the road – someone had to have dragged their car here for it to end up in the pond where it was."

"And if Stephanie's car is here, well then, they must be linked." I suggested.

John frowned and looked away. "Well, don't be too eager to jump to conclusions," he cautioned me. "Let's take it one step at a time."

The crane was slowly lumbering over to the truck with its dangling cargo. I turned my attention back to the water, where the divers had resumed their work. Part of the time they were submerged and part of the time clambering over underwater obstacles. They appeared to be fixing support wires to something under the surface. As I watched I recalled the holes in the windshield and thought to myself: no airbags and no seatbelts. It was hard to imagine that it had once been the norm to drive sitting untethered and unprotected, although I could remember barrelling down the highway at high speed without either safety device myself. Nobody thought much about it then. In fact, front seat belts became standard only in 1964.

There were several other policemen around, among them Constable Bannerman. He was standing off to one side as if just observing. I walked up to him. "If it weren't for me, you wouldn't be here today," I told him, "Me and my big mouth asking questions!"

I think he actually looked embarrassed, but he worked it off by giving his gum a good chewing and looking superior. "Don't get a chance to see stuff like this out in the boonies too often," he commented.

The crane had deposited the first car on the flat bed and was growling slowly back towards the pond again. The clouds had thinned and the sun was brightening the scene. It seemed inappropriate somehow. Forty years ago death had visited this place, death delivered by a murderer and only now was his handiwork emerging for the world to see. Gloom suited this scene far more than sunshine.

Responding to the sudden light and slight increase in warmth, the snow was sliding off the rocks, melting into the dead grass and wetting the bare tree branches.

The divers had finished attaching the supports to the crane and now it was straining and roaring again as it pulled up another vehicle from its long-time bed of sediment. It came up at a slight angle, first the roof, then the windshield emerging with its single hole and finally the unmistakable fins of a 1960 model vehicle. As with the first car, the front end was heavily smashed, the hood was twisted up and back, the bumper and double headlights missing.

I felt deeply sad suddenly. Maybe it would have better to let her remain here in her burial place, forever lost, just as Jimmy seemed to have suggested. In a way we were like vultures feeding off a corpse, the police and I. I had been so keen on solving the mystery that I never stopped for a moment to wonder if it might not be better after all not to know, to have the why and how of her death forever unknown. Sometimes a mystery might be better than the truth. But as I thought about that, I realized that I wouldn't hesitate a second to know the truth about my own daughter, however ugly it might be. It might not stop the sudden moments when, taken off guard, I image her coming in the door, but it would put an end to all the questions. Or would it? I don't know that you can ever know which would be better. The truth is you never get the chance to decide. You find out or you don't find out, it's as simple as that. Nobody ever asks you which you'd prefer.

And as the mangled vehicle rose into the air, suspended from its supports, black stinky water running off it back into the pond, the reality seemed more sordid than the mystery, the knowing worse in its dreary details than the not knowing, which at least had an escape clause, the possibility that until now could never be disproved: that she might still be alive somewhere, happy even, having disappeared of her own volition. But there was no cheery possibility now, only the deadly detail of her mangled car and the hole in the windshield to mark where her head had hit as she died.

The crane was moving again, backing away from the water and turning towards the flat-bed truck. I shivered despite the sunshine which was steadily strengthening. I had got somewhere finally, made some progress and it hadn't made me happy. Stephanie had come driving down this road, this very stretch of old abandoned highway, long ago, when it was new. She hadn't expected to die that day. She had been on her way to new things, was probably excited as she drove through the early morning, watching for animals, careful around the corners. She certainly hadn't been intending to give up her life to someone who waited and watched and struck. I knew as I watched her car being deposited onto the bed of the truck that the only satisfaction I would ever get from this now was bringing someone to justice, in finding out who killed her and ensuring he was punished. Jimmy hadn't wanted to talk about the hidden highway, had shied away from it which meant that he knew about it all too well and didn't want me to find out where the deed had been done. For the moment at least, the finger of responsibility pointed solidly at him. It was time to pay Mr. Case a visit. I just hoped the police wouldn't ride fast into action.

John came up to me and told me they were wrapping things up.

"What happens now?"

"We take the vehicles into Winnipeg, let forensic go over them both. There are remains inside, so they'll check them out, try to identify them. I'll let you know. Could be a couple of days or more."

"Thanks, John, I appreciate it."

"Well," he said, "Let's face it – we wouldn't be here without you. It was you who pointed us in this direction. Doesn't matter much probably after all these years, but it's always nice to put a case to bed finally, write the end in the book."

As I turned to go, had taken a couple of steps back towards the old strip of lost highway he said something else. "Oh, Mr. Therman, there's one more thing you might like to know."

I turned and he came up to me with a smile on his face. "The Chief has announced he's going to retire soon, time to hang up his skates as he put it. He says he's not going to start drawing his pension yet though, got some other things to do first."

We started walking back towards the road. The clouds had cleared completely now and the sun was starting to make the surroundings steam. It was nice to see that in October it still had some power to it.

"We'll be having a do for him of course, thought you might like to come."

"Me!"

"Get a chance to meet him, shake hands." He stopped and looked at me closely. "He said something else, too. Funny. It was as I was leaving, was almost through the door and he said it just like a throwaway line, of no significance, only I think it was significant."

I waited patiently for John to get it out. We started walking again.

"One more thing, the Chief said. No need to keep my name secret now. If people want to know, he growled at me, well then you can just tell them. The way he said it, nonchalantly, as if it didn't matter a darn. But it had done once, that's the thing of it, it sure had done. Now, suddenly it doesn't matter." He shook his head.

I waited for him to tell me the name, had a sudden sense I knew what he would tell me, a sense of the day closing in on me.

"Harry, that's his name," John said, "Harry."

I stopped, rooted to the spot. Harry! Well that was the name I was expecting wasn't it? Was it a coincidence? I didn't think so. I thought back to the letter, of how Robert Deslisle had mentioned a Harry at the beach party although there was no Harry on the list of students. And I recalled what Betty Kingsford had told me about Harry Cunningham, how he kept in the background, didn't like his picture being taken.

"How do you like having your strings pulled like a puppet?" I asked John.

"What do you mean?"

"Come on! Harry's a manipulator, you know that. He sits there out of sight and pulls people's strings. If he's the man I think he is, he knew Stephanie Shawcross and he certainly knows Jimmy Case and he's been pulling my strings for months now, cleverly channelling me to go exactly where he wants me to."

"You've lost me," John said.

"It's too complicated to explain now," I said. "When you've got a couple of hours I'll sit down with you and explain it all. Meanwhile I've got people to see."

"Deal," he said.

I walked back to the Audi, got in and started it up. I had been planning all along to drop in on Jimmy, shake him up by telling him I'd found his girlfriend at last. Now I was determined to do it. If this didn't crack him nothing would!

20

CONFRONTING JIMMY CASE

The road to West Hawk was wet, sections of it steaming in the evaporating moisture from the melted snow. There was no other traffic and I gave the Audi its head through the twisty, heaving route of the blacktop. The sheer exhilaration of it made me forget for a moment that there was still an awful lot I didn't know. I was now pretty certain that Harry was Mystery Man, but I had no idea why he was involved, what his motive was. I was pretty certain of one thing, however: that he wasn't the murderer. It just made no sense to stir things up like he had if he was the guilty party. As for Jimmy, I still had no idea why he had killed Stephanie, or even how, although, seeing the vehicles, I now had some idea how he might have done it.

I pulled over onto a small clearing just off to the right and called Alex on my cell phone. When she answered I told her the police had found Stephanie's car and the car belonging to the other two guys who had disappeared the same day.

"Progress," she said, "Results. I don't believe it!"

"There's more! Guess what the Chief's name is."

"I. M. Guilty?" she said with a laugh.

"Close, but no, it's Harry!"

"Ah."

"You don't get it, do you?"

"No, Colin, I guess I don't. Do you have a point to make or are you just making sure I don't make my quota of billable hours this month?"

"Touchy! Do you remember that letter you beat me over the head about, used to crush my ego by any chance, crowed about how you remembered and I didn't about one of the kids wanting to drive trains?"

"How could I not, you bring it back to life so vividly!" Alex responded.

"Well there was a Harry mentioned there. We thought it might be a mistake but remember I wrote on the whiteboard, Harry Who?"

"Now that you mention it, yes, I do remember. But are you sure this is the same Harry. The guy in New Zealand – Robert wasn't it? – still might have been mistaken and the Chief might just happen to have the same name."

"I don't think so, Alex. Look, I talked to Betty Kingsford about it and she remembers a Harry too in Stephanie's class. Didn't let them take his picture at the grad, was secretive and always hanging back according to her. And all this time, the Chief has been sitting in the background like a spider hiding in the funnel part of his web, waiting for the vibrations on the web."

"Well that's good work, Colin. I'm really glad this is finally leading somewhere! What's next?"

I told her I was going to see Jimmy.

"Are you sure that's wise?"

"Talking to Jimmy?"

"Yes. If he really is the murderer, he might turn violent if you start accusing him of anything."

"It's time for Jimmy to stop hiding behind his imaginary girlfriend and admit that it was Stephanie, that's all I want. I don't have any proof of anything. It's all circumstantial. Even if I wanted to, there's no way I could prove anything against him in a court of law. The fact is, he's going to get away with it and there's nothing I can do about that. I can tell the police of my suspicions, explain why I think the finger points in his direction but it's not enough to convict him. Even I know that."

"Well, just be careful, that's all. Let me know how it goes."

I promised to do so and rang off. I got the Audi back on the road again and soon arrived at Jimmy's cottage by the lake, turned off the engine and got out. There was no sign of his motorcycle and the front door was locked. I stood looking at the cottage. There was something a little off about it I thought, something not quite right about its dimensions. It niggled at me but I couldn't determine exactly what the problem was.

I went round to the back. The boat was tied up at the short dock and the deck was empty. I went up the steps and tried the back door. It was unlocked. I opened it slowly and went in. I called out, "Jimmy!" The house was silent. I went to the front door, turned and looked towards the back of the cottage, as if I had just entered. There was something wrong with the dimensions, that's what it was that was bothering me. I opened the front door and measured the width of the house using my feet as a measure. It was hard because of the steps up and the porch but as near as I could figure it was 25 feet wide. I came back inside and looked across the width of the cottage, the inside wall. Somehow it looked noticeably shorter. It wasn't evident unless you looked carefully but now that I was suspicious it just looked wrong somehow. A fridge stuck right against the left-hand wall made it difficult but I paced out the width inside the cabin as best I could and came up short. It was at least 5 feet shorter inside than out! Jimmy, I thought to myself, you're a sneaky bastard. All this time Alex and I have been coming here and you have a secret room in your house. Either that or bloody good insulation!

Once I realized that there was a hidden room here it didn't take me long to find the way into it. The wall was panelled using wide vertical boards and on close inspection it was possible to make out the lines of a door. It was behind a chair, easily moved, and with a picture hanging in the middle of it, a poor-quality reproduction of some Van Gogh or other. There was no obvious door knob sticking out to give the game away. I moved the chair and removed the picture. Behind the frame was an indentation in the paneling with a lever action. I pulled on this and the door swung inward. There was a light switch on the wall to the right of the opening. I turned it on and then stepped into the room, closing the door behind me.

This was Jimmy's secret lair. The room was long and very narrow, with no windows and no other way out except through the door I'd used to get into it. On the wall facing me were pictures and clippings from newspapers, some letters, and on a narrow desk pushed against the end wall on the right, a collection of what looked like photo albums and a three-ring binder. I went closer and examined the items. The pictures were mostly of a young man and a young woman. The girl obviously was Stephanie, as beautiful as everyone who had known her assured me she was, a stunning and radiant young woman. The young man was Jimmy presumably. Without his beard and 40 extra years, it was hard to see the resemblance. There were pictures of them on porches, at the beach, lying on the sand, holding hands standing beside a car, on a farm with cows, always holding hands or at least smiling at each other. The letters were love letters from her, dozens of them. I skimmed one or two of them but I was in a hurry, concerned the Jimmy might come back at any moment, so I turned to the other wall and got the shock of my life. This wasn't a chamber of love as I had first thought, a hidden testimonial to their once-upon-a-time love, but a chamber of love and hate. For the other wall testified to his hatred for Stephanie. There were clippings there too and letters or notes typed on white paper, there was a copy of the newspaper article about her disappearance. There were more pictures of Stephanie here too but this time there were lines slashed through them, broad black and sometimes red diagonal lines across her face.

I turned back to the other wall for a moment, amazed at the stunning contrast between the love shown there and the poisonous hatred on the other.

"I thought you might discover this one day," Jimmy said from the doorway. I had been so engrossed in the material on the walls that I hadn't noticed the door opening again. Now he was standing there looking at me and holding a gun in his right hand. I don't like guns, have never used one and want nothing to do with them. "I think you'd better sit down," he said. I thought I had too. There were no chairs in the little room so I sat with my back against the love wall. He just stood there looking at me.

"I found Stephanie's car," I told him. "It's time for the lies to stop! And time to start telling the truth. One truth is that you must have loved her very much," I said, waving my hands at the shrine to his lost love on the wall behind me. "It would be hard to image you killed her from what is on that wall. But I saw the car. I saw the hole in the windshield."

"Loved?" Jimmy responded. "I see that wall when I come in but that's the one that really counts!" He waved the gun at the other wall, the one I was facing now, the one with the door. "When I leave this place that's the wall I see and that's the wall that matters, because you see you don't really understand Mr.Therman, you have no idea, you and that fine lawyer sexpot of yours, no idea at all!"

"So, tell me, help me to understand."

He laughed bitterly. "It was all perfect, just perfect. Everything was going as it should. We were graduating, we had plans to go to college and we were going to get married. And then in a few minutes it all went to hell, was all destroyed just like that"– he snapped his fingers. "Puff and it was all gone, like someone suddenly smashing their fist through a wonderful canvas. You are standing there admiring it, thinking it wonderful and blam, the fist comes through and it is all a ruin. Can you understand that?"

He was getting worked up and I thought I had better calm him down. "It was a long time ago." It was a stupid thing to say, me nursing my own wound from long ago but I had to say something.

He shook his head. "Maybe in time but not inside here," he said pointing to his head. "In there it's yesterday, fresh as spring, etched forever. I can feel how I felt before, how perfect it was, shiny bright perfection, and then how it all came crashing down. Have you ever had anything like that Mr. Therman, the world divided into before and after and a split second right there in the middle, dividing the one from the other? In that split second everything suddenly changes, is abruptly wrenched away from before and becomes after and there's nothing you can do about it, absolutely nothing. It is irrevocable, unalterable! Why do things happen like that?"

"Is that why you killed her?"

He shook his head. "Oh you don't know why I killed her, you have no idea. You think that just because she was fooling around on the beach that night with another boy that that was it. We were all drunk or fairly drunk, we were all wild, didn't have a clue what we were doing and she let some guy stick his thing in her and I stuck mine in another girl too. No, no, oh god, no that's not it, you don't get it, you can't. That meant nothing – I don't think it meant anything."

"So, why?" I asked again, as gently as I could.

He looked at me wildly for a second and then said, "Don't think I won't kill you if you take me in, don't think that for a second."

"Nobody's going to take you in," I told him. "I just want to know what happened. I've got no evidence against you. Anything I said would be just hearsay and the police aren't interested. So you have nothing to fear from me."

"Harry said you'd come after me," he said. "Told me you were tracking me down, would worm your way into my confidence, sap my resistance with a sexy woman."

"Harry, eh? Harry Cunningham I presume."

"Harry who the fucking else would it be," he shouted. "Harry's been a good friend over the years, a good friend, my only friend now I think."

"Jimmy," I said, "I just want to know how you killed her and why. Tell me that and I'll just go away, that's all there is to it. But help me to understand first."

"What happened was that the world fell apart. I had no idea it was so fragile. I thought we were immune, immortal, perfect, nothing could happen and then it all came tumbling down, cracked and collapsed. I think about that all the time now - how quickly things can change. Sunny day and blam there's a thunder cloud overhead. So suddenly, so suddenly!"

"How did you kill her?" I repeated.

He sat down in the doorway, still pointing the gun at me. I had no idea if the safety was on or not. He let out a sigh. "Well what does it matter now?" he said. "It's all over now isn't it. This is the end, just as Harry warned me." He looked at me and shook his head with an air of resignation. "With a tree," he said. "I cut down a tree and made a big log and dragged it to the road and let it lie there, just below the crown of a hill, so she wouldn't see it until the last moment, when it would be too late, nothing she could do. Harry told me she was coming and when but I worked out how to do it, how to kill the bitch. I used my Dad's Dodge truck. That was a great vehicle." He stopped suddenly and then screamed, "She cut me! You don't understand. She cut off my cock!"

I was stunned. "What do you mean?" I stammered.

"She was holding it in her hand and she laughed at me, held it up, showed it to the other guys, ran off laughing, threw it into the water, where it's deep, where they dive and she screamed at me that she hated me and I'd never do that to a girl ever again. So you see," he said bitterly, "your woman was quite safe with me. You had no reason to be worried about her, about me. I couldn't fuck a fly. That's why I killed her, any man would kill a woman who did that to him. I plotted and planned and worked it all out and then I did it."

"But you got the wrong car, the first one."

"I didn't want to look, but I could see there weren't any women in the car. They were both dead, smashed up badly but they were men, they had hats on. Or they had before they went through the windshield. One of them was bald. They had ties and suits on."

"What did you do?"

"Do? I dragged the car into the pond and waited again. The log was still there. It was a big one and a car crashing into it didn't do much. It was still where it needed to be. I hid the truck again and waited. I knew she'd come. Harry wouldn't let me down. And I watched the lights wind along the road, could picture her, just like me, thinking everything was fine, going along just hunky-dory, no worries in the world, that it would last forever, not realizing that just over the hill that cruel split second that separates before from after was lying in wait for her, that life would change suddenly, would alter abruptly for the worse. I was doing to her what she did to me. She deserved it!" He stopped his narration and stood up again, swaying slightly. Then he looked over to the wall behind me and stared at it. The gun hand was drooping I was glad to see, no longer pointed hard at me. He was lost in the past now.

"She was everything there was in my whole life, everything. She was perfect and I couldn't believe my fortune to have found her and that she loved me too. And then she changed it all with a slash, with a slice of her knife. And I got her back for that, I changed things for her! I couldn't look!" He was crying now, streaming with tears. "There was blood everywhere but I couldn't look at her, couldn't bring myself to see her ruined. She had ruined me and looked at me but I could not look at her."

"Did you ever ask her why she did it?"

"She said she didn't cut it off, that she found me like that with it lying close by and she said she wasn't laughing, she was screaming."

"But you didn't believe her."

"No." He was staring back into the past. It was frightening to watch him. "She lied, of course she lied, why would she tell the truth? But she was frightened of me afterwards, wanted nothing to do with me. It changed everything, of course it did. How could it not. If she were alive still I'd kill her again," he said with fury and then he started to cry again. "But I loved her, oh god I loved her so much, she was my life, my entire world. Why, why, why?"

All of us in life sooner or later ask that heart rending why. There's never any answer to it. It's just something that life does to you eventually, sometimes more than once and there was nothing I could say to answer him. I couldn't answer my own why let alone his.

"Sometimes I come into this room and face the wall behind you and try to live in the past. I light candles and sit here and think of her, pretend we are still 18 and she is the love of my life, with the future glitteringly bright ahead of us, oblivious of the dark wall we are about to collide with." He shook his head. "God, it's pitiful isn't it, pretending like that! I would sit, thinking of her, of what she was like, of how I felt about her, how she felt about me, how perfect it was, unbelievably perfect! For moments sometimes it would work and I would be at peace again, happy once more;" He paused and then he started to cry, his whole body shaking. "Oh, god!" he said, grinding it out. "But then," he said, his voice becoming deeper and more snarly now. "Then I turn and face this wall, the one with the door and I see her as she was the bitch and I become angry and snuff out the candles, stupid candles, dumb idiotic candles and look at this wall, at the real Stephanie." His tears had dried now and he looked at me and started waving the gun around again.

"I think I'm going to have to lock you in here for a while, so I can get away."

Well, at least he wasn't going to shoot me. "Jimmy, listen to me! I don't think Stephanie did cut you. I don't think it was her at all." It was all suddenly crystal clear in my mind, the whole nasty truth of it. "Stephanie loved you! You know she did. So there's no way she would do that to you, no way at all, no matter how angry she might have been." I was working it out as I went but I could see it all now, how clever and diabolical Harry had been, not only to get Jimmy to kill Stephanie but to give him the reason for doing so in the first place. "Harry did it, Jimmy! He was jealous of you and Stephanie. He wanted her himself!"

"Harry? Don't be ridiculous! Why would Harry do it? You're lying to me aren't you? Lying! She had it in her hand. She laughed at me. She thought it was funny!"

I knew with certainty now that Stephanie hadn't done it, hadn't laughed at him and that he had killed her just as Harry hoped he would. Harry had a lot to answer for now.

"Lock you in, yes," Jimmy said. "It will take you a while to bash your way out I figure, give me some time to do what I have to. Yes, Mr. Therman, I loved her and I killed her. I would love her again if I could but I would kill her again as well. That's the truth of it."

He'd lost his manic edge now, was calm and determined. I no longer feared he would shoot me out of anger or frustration. He'd decided to run away I could see, to flee the scene, leave it all behind. I had no way it seemed to persuade him that I was no threat to him, that I could do nothing that would survive in a court of law.

"How did Harry do it?" I asked him. "Tell you about her, I mean. How did you find her?"

Jimmy looked at me calmly and shook his head. "Not so smart are you! He sends me messages of course. He sent me one not too long ago, said someone was snooping around. I knew about you before you showed up! Then you waltzed into the Water Rat with that lawyer bouncing her boobs at me, not realizing of course that it was pointless."

"He's been sending me messages too." I said.

Jimmy looked startled.

"He's playing us like puppets!" I said.

"Oh no," Jimmy said. "You're wrong about that. You see he was there, at the beach, at the party. He saw it, he was part of us, he knows what happened to me, he saw her do it, and he told me where she was and what she was planning to do, when she would travel and where."

"He wanted you to kill her, don't you see that! He set you up and then he set her up!"

He shook his head again. "No, he helped me that's all. He knew I wanted to kill her, I told him so. He said what she had done was horrible, terrible, no man could ever forgive a woman that. He was a real friend."

"Don't you see, he manipulated you!" I shouted at him. I was frustrated that Jimmy just couldn't see it, see how clever Harry had been, how evil. "God damn it - he's the one who cut you!"

"No," he said, shaking his head. "I know the truth about her and about him."

"But he told you where she was, what she was doing. Why did he do that?"

"So I could get back at her. She cut off my penis, do you understand, made me not a man, never able to be a man, not with her, not with anybody. How could she do that?"

"Exactly! How could she? The answer is, she didn't. But someone else did, someone who was jealous." I willed him to accept what I was saying, to see it as clearly as I did now, to understand what a horrid, long-term plot Harry had made. Harry his friend, Harry his tormentor. "Harry was jealous," I said. "Jealous of you, angry with her for loving you, that's all. It's a simple, horrible story and you're as much the victim of it as Stephanie was."

"You'll not trick me," he shouted suddenly. "Not you, not now. I know the truth."

"But you loved her man, and she loved you!"

"The world ended that day," he said, "just stopped, went black. There's been no light since then, never, not a single day of it. I have always remembered her, how she was, before that day, the life we were going to live. We might have had children and been grandparents by now and then it all went away, just slipped away, sliced away."

He looked at me and said he knew what he had to do now, now that I had found out the truth, now that I knew his secrets. He would lock me in the room and he would go away. He pointed the gun at me again, went to the door, went through it, and locked it.

After a while I heard the engine of his boat start up and roar away. The door looked pretty solid but the hinges were on the inside of course, so I was able to pry the pins out and move the door that way. It only took me a minute, but by then it was already too late.

21

ANOTHER DEATH AT WEST HAWK

Perhaps if I had known what Jimmy really intended to do, I'd have gone after him sooner. Perhaps, perhaps not. But I'll never know. I really thought he meant what he said, that he was just going to run away somewhere. I should have known that Harry would have figured it all out a lot more accurately than me, had known exactly what Jimmy would do when I confronted him. But it didn't occur to me and in any case I wanted to examine the stuff in this room while I had the chance, before the police came and got their grubby paws on it and it all became secret and out of bounds. So the fact is I stayed there in that room and searched it and when I finally emerged it was all over, he'd done what he'd planned to do and there was nothing I could do about it.

Jimmy said he'd got messages and I wanted to see them. I'd brought my camera for some reason, instinct I suppose, or just lucky happenstance, so I started taking pictures of the items on the wall. He had all her letters and notes, things she'd passed to him at school, cards sent on his birthday, at Christmas, even a diary in which he'd written his secret excitement on first meeting her and how their relationship developed. I skimmed these quickly, taking pictures as rapidly as I could, for it wasn't his love life I was interested in now but his hate life. How had he found her and how had he learned she was going to be travelling east along that highway when she did? Harry had told him, he said but how had he told him and what had he said exactly? There was in fact a collection of notes I soon discovered, pinned in a group. The top one seemed to refer to me. I took its picture and then took the whole collection off the wall, set them on the desk and photographed each of them. Please batteries don't die on me I kept thinking as I worked, not now!

I wasn't in any particular hurry now that Jimmy had left. I knew that I couldn't remove all of the things in this room. There were simply too many and Jimmy might come back eventually for all I knew. But then I thought of the messages and thought to myself, yes, why not. They were the Harry connection and it was that that interested me. The rest were a testimonial first to his love, and then for his anger towards her, his blind hatred. Harry, I knew, had had a critical role to play in that transformation from lover to murderer and I decided that I would take Harry's messages to study. If Jimmy ever wanted them back well he could have them.

The memorabilia on the wall facing me were heartbreaking, silly, touching, ultimately tragic little things, minutiae of love, the little expressions of affection and endearment that build and support and buttress love, and then the other wall showing how they were all swept away suddenly, rendered pointless by that catastrophic beach party, the party at which Harry had seized his chance and savagely changed everything. I had never brushed against evil so clearly as now. Perhaps in my daughter's case there was evil involved but the fact was I had no direct knowledge of it, that evil lived there only as a possibility. Here it was clear, sharply defined. I could touch this evil, see its corrosive influence, its acid embrace.

I gathered up my camera, and the collection of messages and took one last look around the room. I took a picture of the whole wall, the love wall, and then one of the other one, and then stood, hand on the door soaking it all up again with my eyes. Without Harry, I was sure there would have been only a love wall, in fact no need for a secret room at all, just a life lived with love. I took my last look, and left the cottage for the last time.

I came out to discover the full horrid extent of Harry's evil, to discover how savagely he had used me to his own nasty purposes. Divers were already pulling Jimmy's body out of the water there where they do practice dives, in the deep water. Jimmy's boat still floated there, empty. I took in the scene with horror because I knew instantly that this was exactly as Harry had thought it would unfold, and was the reason he had wound me up and pointed me here, to precipitate precisely the outcome that had just come to pass. I had been a stupid, ignorant idiot blindly stumbling along the trail that had been craftily laid for me, obediently responding to every little enticement he had directed at me, hoping against hope to find out something, anything about Cindy, and so willing to do anything Harry wanted me to. In effect, just as Harry had been the real killer of Stephanie, so he was the real killer of Jimmy, and I was a willing if utterly stupid accomplice. How I wished now that I had never risen to the bait in that first email long ago. If only I had listened to Alex' caution. All along she had been suspicious. Why is he doing this, she had wanted to know. What is his motive?

Of course I wasn't the first person to rue the day he didn't listen to his lawyer. I had fallen in love with the adventure of it and so ended up killing a man, or at least driving a man to his death. As well, I realized, I had jumped at the chance of going around, doing things with Alex, not because I wanted to cheat on my wife or anything seedy like that, but because she was an attractive and fascinating young woman. It was all part of the adventure. But damn it, I was old enough to know better, sufficiently cynical to be able to see through myself by now, and I ought to have stopped well before I got to this point.

I thought about all the time I had spent wondering why Harry had chosen me, when that was precisely the wrong question. Harry hadn't done it for Stephanie, he had done it for Jimmy. He hadn't cared if I solved the Stephanie mystery or not – all he wanted was to frighten Jimmy. And he hadn't chosen me for any deep reason at all, it was just that he had some leverage he could use with me, knew my own daughter was missing. He couldn't do it himself for obvious reasons, so it had to be somebody else and I just happened to fit the bill.

Well I could see it all clearly now but that was no excuse. Still there was nothing to be gained by wallowing in self-recrimination. I would have to talk to the police and I would have to give them the collection of messages. They would be angry that I had taken them, but that couldn't be helped. First, though, I had better copy them I decided. I went up to the motel office and asked to use the photocopier.

"Did you hear about Jimmy?" the woman wanted to know."Killed himself. Man at the campground saw it, saw him come up in the boat, stop the engine, take the anchor, wrap the rope about his body and jump in. It's dark down there, black as night I hear."

I shuddered at the image, of him descending dead into the dark embrace of the deep, cold water.

I took the copies I'd made and put them in the car and then went to find Corporal John Simard. They had put the body in a little tent they had erected on the shore and were waiting for forensic specialists to arrive. The sun was beginning to redden as it descended towards the horizon. I shivered and thought suddenly that in another couple of months Jimmy wouldn't have been able to do this, that the water would have been frozen over. It'd waited, been slower off the mark.....

Simard came out of the tent, saw me hanging around and came over. "Happy now Mr. Therman?" he asked angrily.

"This is Harry's fault, not mine," I responded.

"So you say. But let's face it, none of this would have happened without you."

"Harry drove Jimmy to kill Stephanie and then Harry enticed me into investigating what had happened to Stephanie and led me to Jimmy's doorstep and then he frightened Jimmy, told him I was going to have him locked away forever and so he terrified him into killing himself."

"That's quite a theory, Mr. Therman, quite a theory. None of that is going to do Jimmy any good, or bring Stephanie back to life now is it?"

I shook my head. "There are some messages here I took from Jimmy's house. There's a secret room there, that shows everything." I handed him the collection of notes that Harry had sent over the years.

"Jesus Christ, Mr. Therman. You're a one- man wrecking crew, you know that. A god-damn wrecking crew. Why don't you go away from West Hawk and leave us the fuck alone!"

I understood his anger but there was no point directing it at me. "Why don't you direct some of that fury to your boss, Corporal. Don't take it out on me. If I hadn't come here, Stephanie would still be rotting in that scummy pond, her whereabouts and what happened to her unknown."

"Yea, and Jimmy would still be alive!" He looked at me and shook his head. "You're lucky I don't arrest you for tampering with evidence. Just give me the messages and then get the hell out of here!"

"There's one more thing you should know," I told him. "You'll find that Jimmy there has no penis. Someone cut it off long ago. At that beach party. Jimmy thought it was Stephanie who did it. That's why he killed her. But I think it was Harry."

I left him with his mouth hanging open and walked back towards the beach. I stood there on the sand and thought about what must have happened at that deadly party, the one that had sowed such evil seeds. As I had told Simard, I was damn sure it was Harry not Stephanie who had cut off Jimmy's penis. Everyone was drunk or getting there, everyone except perhaps Harry, who waited in the shadows like the spider he was. Some of the boys, Jimmy among them, had got naked and some girls too and they'd fooled around on the sand, the boys fondling the girls, the girls fondling the boys and at some point Harry had come down there in the dark and drunkenness and just swooped in and sliced off his rival's penis, seen his chance and acted on it. And then perhaps Stephanie had come along, annoyed at the sexual high jinks, seen Jimmy, wondered what had happened, seen something, reached down and picked up his penis, then realized what it was and freaked out, gone running screaming away, thrown it into the water, perhaps the same spot where Jimmy had drowned himself. Jimmy had come to to find Stephanie holding it and that had been that. He'd assumed she had done it and nothing could persuade him otherwise, at least not with sweet Harry whispering poison into his ear.

Harry probably told him she was laughing, that she held his prick like a trophy, showed it to the other girls, giggled as she held it and then gleefully threw it into the water where there was no hope it would ever be found, a place he would see every day and know it was down there, rotting, eaten. And then later he had told him of Stephanie's travel plans and urged him to take action, niggled at him how wrong it was for a woman to do that to a man, no real man would let it go, would duck the chance for revenge. And so Stephanie had come driving down that road in the early hours of the morning, wanting to get a good head start for a long journey. Around the curves she had come, happy perhaps, full of the adventure of it, travelling in the dark, setting off for a new phase of her life, alone, but planning to meet a friend half way. And then she had come over that final twist in the road and the rise and down. Too late she had seen the obstacle in the road, the massive tree trunk lying across the road. Going far too fast to be able to stop in time she had smashed into it and that had been that, the end of her life.

After that Harry now had one living victim and one dead victim, well three dead victims if you count the other two men, accidental victims who had just come along at the wrong time. And Harry had gloated for decades knowing what he did, watching Jimmy live his petty, diminished life. Then one day he decided Jimmy had lived long enough, and so he had found me and wound me up and pointed me in Jimmy's direction and I cleverly took care of the rest.

I took the copies of the messages out of my pocket and looked them over again. There were eight of them. I knew they would be useless as a way of bringing Harry to justice. That just wasn't going to happen, I was clear about that. Harry would remain a free man no matter what I did. For one thing, there was nothing to prove that the messages were from Harry in the first place. As well it would be impossible to show that Harry had done the deed to Jimmy. Jimmy's notebooks acknowledged that Jimmy had killed Stephanie.

No, Harry was safe, and I was sure he knew it. I intended to run it all by Alex of course but I was pretty certain that she would confirm that I had no legal recourse at all. But there was one way I could get the truth out I realized suddenly, a way that wouldn't result in Harry behind bars or anything as satisfactory as that, but a way that would cause him some embarrassment at least. That's really why this book exists. Because I was also pretty sure that Harry had written other messages over the years, just as he had written to Jimmy, and to me after he thought of the locomotive thing, calling on his friends, first for the train, then for the car and finally for the messages in the building Alex and I had broken into. And some of his messages I suspected involved dear Betty Kingsford. I have no idea why he wanted to harm her, but perhaps it was just for the sheer hell of it, to keep his hand in, to launch his spite into the environment and watch its ripples poison and destroy.

Yes, I would write a book, I decided, a book for Stephanie and Jimmy and Betty. I looked out over the lake with a bitter taste in my mouth. I had risen so willingly to Harry's bait, never imaging I was serving evil. I took a last look over the water and then got into the Audi, started it up and drove home.

22

FORENSIC EVIDENCE

I had gone to Falcon to drop in on Linda Evans. I don't suppose she was really losing any sleep over it, but I wanted to reassure her that her failures to produce the kind of information she thought she should have been able to supply hadn't stopped me. It was also an excuse to let the Audi stretch its legs I suppose more than anything.

As soon as I arrived I felt that sensation again, of someone watching me. I had parked the car near the beach, wanting to walk it one last time before winter got its icy talons firmly fixed on the place. There were still boats out on the water, going slowly, which probably meant fishing, or maybe getting one last slow melancholy run in before beaching the boats, hauling them out of the water, putting the engine away for the season. It would be May before they saw the water again, just part of the prairie's long-stretch winter, a season as long as all the others combined.

I looked around carefully, nonchalantly but could see nothing. Still I felt it, eyes boring into me, someone observing but remaining hidden. It made the wind coming off the water seem even colder than it was. The beach stretched before me with not a soul on it, the ice cream stand boarded up, the change rooms deserted, the swings and merry-go-round empty. It was hard to image that just a couple of months ago this had been thronged, noisy. Someone watched me from the shadows, the lone figure walking on the sand.

On a sudden, childish impulse I whirled around, stuck my finger up in the air and jerked it upwards a few times.

Take that you son of a gun. Linda would have rolled her eyes and told me to stop it. Alex would have said it was unprofessional, which was absolutely correct, but sometimes it's necessary to give in to impulses like that, or so I rationalized. It was a way of telling whoever it was that I knew he was out there. I may not be able to see him but I could sense him, watching.

I walked back to the car and got in. I had only gone a short distance when there was a blip of a siren and a flash of the light bar behind me. I looked in the mirror and saw the cruiser behind me, signalling me. I pulled over and shortly after Corporal Simard opened the passenger side door and got into the front passenger seat of the Audi.

"How about treating me to a cup of coffee," he said.

"Sure." I put the Audi back in gear and started off again.

"One of these days, civilization is going to come to these parts and a Tim Horton's will be built here or at West Hawk! As if!" Simard said.

I pulled into the restaurant parking lot and turned off the engine.

When we were seated with mugs in front of us, Simard said he wondered if I was interested in seeing Stephanie.

"You serious?'

"If you want to, I can arrange it."

"Do I want to?" I asked him.

"It's not as bad as you might imagine," he told me. "Sure, 40 years is a long time for a body, but in a pond like that there's not much oxygen and without oxygen things don't decay much. It's damn cold most of the time too and that really helps, slows down the things that gobble up flesh. You can recognize her, just, if you don't mind ugly colour, stains, the usual discolouration of the dead. A lot of soft tissue is gone, but there's still skin. The trauma from the accident though is still pretty obvious."

I shuddered and shook my head. "So you know it's her?"

"I don't think you would want to make the identification by looking at her," Simard said. "But her bag was there, with ID and stuff. A lot of it was paper in those days, but it was all in a mass and much of it survived. The lab guys were able to separate the stuff, dry it, look at it. It's her all right. The car hit something big and unyielding. No seat belts, no air bags, well the G forces alone would have killed her. Same thing with the other car."

"It was a log," I told him. "Jimmy told me that. Just over the brow of a hill, so she wouldn't have enough time to react, right across the road. The other guys hit it first and he dragged them out of the way and left it there and then Stephanie came along."

We sat there thinking about it for a while. Then I thought of Stephanie's body and then decided. "No," I told him. "I really appreciate the offer but I really don't want to see her like that. I want to remember her as she must have been." I didn't tell him that it might make me think of my daughter that way too. I knew she was dead but I didn't want to see her or imagine her that way. To me she would always be alive somewhere even if I knew better. "I appreciate the offer though."

"Sure."

We got back into the Audi and I started it up.

"Nice car!" Simard said.

"This was Harry's doing," I told him.

"Harry? My Harry?"

"Yep, the man himself."

"Bit expensive for him I would have thought," Simard said.

"That's how Harry did it all," I told him. "Favours from friends!" I took the lease papers out of the glove compartment and showed him the signature.

"See that? That's Tim Surtowski. Mad about cars when he was in Stephanie's grade. Harry was in that same grade too, did you know that?"

"You're kidding me."

"Nope, he was there. Didn't like his picture being taken, never volunteered for anything, always last to put up his hand in class. Managed to avoid being photographed for the grad pictures, that's what took me so long to get onto him. But his name was there. He couldn't avoid that."

"I'll be damned. He knew Stephanie!"

"And Jimmy too from way back. There's something else too. I started down this trail when he sent me an email offering to let me have a ride on a diesel locomotive. Those things fascinate me, so he hooked me. But I couldn't figure out for the longest while how the hell he managed to arrange that. The engineer told me his name was Arnie and there was an Arnold Nesbitt in the class as well."

"And so the grand conspiracy emerges."

He was laughing at me and I suppose I couldn't blame him.

"One thing you've got to watch for when you're a cop is a string of coincidences. It happens more than you might imagine and it can surely lead you into trouble."

We had reached his car again and I pulled the Audi over and brought it to a stop.

Simard turned to me. "Going to be different around here without you nosing around all the time. Now that the case is solved I mean. The remains will be released for burial or whatever soon. But we won't be charging Harry with anything, but I've changed my mind about inviting you to his farewell thing."

"Afraid I might try to punch him out?"

"Something like that. You know when I saw you with Alex way back when this whole thing started, remember that? You were there to catch a train, well an engine I guess. Anyhow I knew you were up to no good, could tell."

I laughed. "Alex said you would sniff me out."

He reached over and shook my hand. "So long, Mr. Therman. May your future path be untroubled by mysterious emails and benefactors bearing Audis."

"Thanks, John. For all your help."

Simard got out of the car and I drove off giving a wave in the rear view mirror.

23

SAYING GOODBYE

There was a funeral for Stephanie Shawcross and one for Jimmy Case. The other two victims had been taken elsewhere for burial. Stephanie had had a sister, unknown to us all this time, and living not far away in Ontario, which just goes to show that all the research in the world can't necessarily turn up stuff you should know. A few others came to Stephanie's funeral, including Betty Kingsford and Linda Evans. Corporal Simard was there in his dress uniform, looking unbelievably smart and of course there was me, my wife Linda and Alex. It was a bitterly cold day, with snow drifting down from a white sky. Winter was fully in charge now, with no nonsense about summer any more, that was clear. Inside the little church it was cool enough for our breath to show and most of us kept on our coats.

I had planned to say certain things about Stephanie but the unexpected presence of her sister made it impossible for me to say some of those things. Instead I just explained why I had wanted to put her disappearance to rest and how sad I was that it had turned out the way it had. "Stephanie was a beautiful young woman with a generous heart and a zest for life. Sadly, I have no doubt that it was the person she loved who made sure she never got to live the life she had wanted to. As for how love can drive us to kill, well some would say that this is a mystery of the soul. I say it's just what evolution wrought, proof positive that we aren't designed, but forged naturally and imperfectly in the midst of the terror and joy of the real world. We talk about putting the dead to rest but it's not the dead who are restless, but us. Now we can be at rest having put her to rest." I felt a bit embarrassed when I sat down, as if I'd pontificated a bit too much, but funerals sometimes bring that out in people.

Afterwards her sister came up to me and thanked me for finding her. Sara was a trim, self-assured woman with dyed hair, dressed in smartly tailored black. Her eyes were green and intense and I could see she echoed some of Stephanie's reputed attractiveness. "I always knew that Jimmy had killed her," she told me. "I knew about your work, heard about it. I didn't get in touch because, well I had nothing to tell you that would have helped. I was three grades behind her, so I knew about the beach party, was even looking forward to my own, although they were never the same afterwards you know." Her eyes smiled at me but there was nothing soft about her or her manner. "Yes, I always knew inside me that she was dead," she continued. "And I knew that Jimmy must have done it, although there was nothing I could have done to prove that."

I wondered what her real reason was for not coming forward and getting in touch with me. I wanted to shake her for not having done so. She could have told me all about Stephanie's classmates for one thing. Whatever the reason was it wasn't because of modesty, not this woman.

"Jimmy deserved to die. He should have died long ago." she said. "I would rather someone had killed him than his having committed suicide but there it is."

"Jimmy was a very confused young man," I told her. "And something very nasty happened to him."

"Don't be preposterous!" she exclaimed angrily. "He was a murderer, that's all there is to it."

I looked her carefully. Clearly she wasn't interested in nuances or perhaps just not yet. So I didn't tell her about Harry. She must have known about him or of him, if she'd known Stephanie's school chums at all, but there wasn't any point in discussing the spider-like behaviour of the man. She was a bit like a spider herself. She'd known all about me investigating but never once got in touch, turned up out of the blue at the funeral and then refused to consider anything but the most stark, black-and-white interpretation of the events. Sara had done her duty and would now go back home steadfast in her attitudes but none the wiser. I wondered if Stephanie might have turned out anything like her. It was a possibility of course, but from all I had heard about her, I suspected not.

"I'm in charge of her ashes," I told her, "but of course they didn't know about you and since you are here. If you like."

She recoiled. "Certainly not!" she said, then added, "I'm perfectly happy for you to have them."

I didn't tell her I was planning to sprinkle them or part of them at least on the Lake, near where Jimmy had drowned himself. She wouldn't have approved. "Thank you for coming," I said, dismissing her.

"Bit about evolution probably went over their heads," Linda suggested after we were safely back in the car. "Good one for getting it in though."

"I can see them now," I laughed. "Muttering to themselves: always knew he was a Darwinist. Had that look about him!"

"What, the monkey look?" Alex joined in and we all laughed.

Jimmy had a funeral too, just as bitterly cold but without snow and with a bright sun in a blue sky shining down. It was larger and better attended than Stephanie's. After all Stephanie was a bit distant for most of them, too far in the past, but Jimmy was more recent, someone they actually knew. The mourners included the bartender whose name I never did find out, the two biker buddies who had given us a hard time in the Water Rat, some people I recognized from West Hawk, and Betty again. As for Jimmy's family, if he had one, nobody from it was there. Linda Evans also didn't attend, nor Sara and neither did Simard, who probably only went to victims' funerals not those of murderers.

The church was warmer than last time but the atmosphere colder if anything. Here was a man who had murdered the love of his life yet in some ways was as much a victim as Stephanie had been. Harry should be here to see his handiwork, I thought savagely. Then I could have stood up and denounced him, but of course he would never give me that satisfaction.

I'd had the chance to say something, even had a speech prepared but in the end I decided against it. What could I say in a few words that would sum up why Jimmy had killed himself, or what drove him to kill Stephanie? As I sat there in the silence of the church I decided instead to let this story do the talking, explain it, if anything can explain it. As the silence stretched, I thought that it would be nice to imagine a place where Stephanie and Jimmy could be reunited now, at peace with each other, in love again, but of course that was a fairy tale, something we invent to comfort ourselves when it grows dark and cold and we huddle for protection around the fire. Evolution's handiwork again, to forge the mind to invent such solaces. The jury was still out on whether that was a fit adaptation or not.

Outside there was a police car waiting. Behind the wheel was the familiar figure of Corporal Simard. I asked Linda and Alex to wait in the car and got in beside Simard.

"John."

"Mr. Therman."

"Christ! Call me Colin for God's sake. Or am I suspect in something and you have to keep your distance?"

He grinned. "Colin," he said. "Yes, I guess I can do that. I just want you to know I reviewed the stuff in Mr. Case's secret chamber of memories and tried to find some way of involving the Chief, tried hard."

"But you can't."

"Well for one thing, your fingerprints are all over everything, and there was plenty of opportunity for tampering with the evidence. The sad fact is I've a stronger case against you than I do against Harry."

I was silent, just thinking about how clever Harry had been.

"Besides," Simard continued, "It's no crime to write letters, send emails. And Jimmy boy killed himself, that's open and shut."

"Well actually Harry killed him," I pointed out. "But I'm sure he's in no danger of going to jail for it."

"There's nothing to connect Harry to a crime." Simard said.

"To incite murder, make a man kill himself? I'm not so sure about that!"

"Well, no one's going to be charging him, Colin, you know that. You might try if you like, although I suggest you'd be wasting your time. There are things that sometimes you have to let go, you know. Jails would be overflowing if we could convict everyone guilty of some kind of wrong doing. I could charge you for trespassing for example, but you see Jimmy's not here to make a complaint. Are you going to make a complaint about Mr. Cunningham?"

"No, probably not."

"Even if you were, and you were to base it on the papers you found, well you've mucked up the evidence trail. After all, you could have planted those papers yourself for all we know. You see my point?"

"Yes. I suppose I've never seriously imagined that Harry would be prosecuted for anything he's done. He was a spider, waiting and occasionally coming out of his lair and injecting someone with his venom and then scuttling back to wait and watch, to observe the death throes."

"So you say, but he was a good cop. Sure he was strange in some ways I admit, but he was a good policeman. He knew the town, he knew everything that was going on. He could diffuse situations with a word or two, knew who to talk to, what to say. And he was honest. There's not much opportunity for corruption around here, but even so he was scrupulous about stuff like that. Drugs perhaps you might manage to squeeze some money out of the mostly local creeps that grow stuff or smuggle stuff in, but it's small-time stuff. We've made a few big-time busts on the highway thanks to him."

I had criticized Sara for having no patience with shades of grey, but I was guilty of the same crime, having a hard time thinking of Harry in any way other than as a diabolic evil man. That he wasn't evil in everything he did should be no surprise. Monsters, too, can have charm and love their mothers. That he was a good cop may be true but part of the time Harry was also a monster, a patient, evil manipulator.

"Harry was jealous of Jimmy, and he was angry with Stephanie for loving Jimmy and not him. So he smashed that love. And he then drove Jimmy to kill Stephanie and then he wound me up like a puppet and when I started sniffing around Jimmy he frightened him into thinking he would go to jail, spend the rest of his life behind bars and in this way he also drove Jimmy to kill himself. He did it deliberately. He enjoyed it and he's getting off scott-free, just walking away with a smile. Perhaps he was a good cop as you say, but he was also an utterly evil man. Calculating, cunning, clever and evil. I will never think of him in any other way."

"Well, Mr. Therman," John said – I guess he hadn't liked my insistence that good cop Harry was an evil man, and could no longer call me Colin – "whatever you say about him, he admired you, you know, thought you were pretty good. I have to say I agree with him. But you have good instincts, that's clear and I can see why you say what you do about him."

He reached over and we shook hands. "Pleasure meeting you Mr. Therman," he said. Anytime you're around, drop in."

I didn't tell him I had no intention of spending any more time in West Hawk, that I'd had quite enough of the place for the time being.

"You've been very helpful and I really appreciate it," I told him sincerely.

"Well," he said. "Got to be going. Bad guys to catch, damsels to rescue and all that. But there's one more thing. Harry asked me to give you this. Said he was sorry he couldn't come to the funeral but that you would understand."

He handed me a small brown envelope. I opened it and found three sheets of paper. One was a picture of a mangled piece of wreckage, with some twisted tubes, sitting on what looked like ice. The second sheet of paper was stapled to the photograph. It was a short message:

This should start your detective juices flowing for your next assignment. Don't sweat it too much for the moment, as there will be plenty more later. But what is important is that there is, I believe, a link between your daughter and this object. You will think me crazy when you discover what the object is, and find it absurd to suggest a link, impossible, bizzare beyond belief, but I urge you to accept the idea as a possibility at least. Even if you don't accept it, go with the idea, because if my hunch is right, it will reward you. Until later...

Harry

The third sheet was a riddle.

Where stops the Christmas train?
Old things stored where?
Some to do with grain.
Others cannot move from there!
Computers no, before their time.
Check the keys, not for a lock.
With these as is there'd be no rhyme,
Yet meaning will unblock.

I showed the papers to Simard. "You see! This is the kind of thing he does. Manipulates, throws out tantalizing clues, just like those he sent me before."

"Are you going to be able to resist these messages any more than you could the others?"

"I don't know, John, I really don't know."

"Well, Harry did mention you might be a bit fed up with all this mystery stuff, but he told me to tell you need to be patient, to go at things methodically."

What else had I done, I wondered, except go at things methodically! "Hah!" I said. "Maybe if I hadn't been so bloody methodical Jimmy would be still alive. And it doesn't seem to have brought me any further towards solving the mystery of what happened to Cindy, despite his miserly little clues in today's message, this supposed link between her and some piece of meaningless rubbish somewhere. I'll kill him if he's just pretending to know something about her, if he's been stringing me along all this time. It's very important to me. Do you know anything about that?"

He shook his head. A moment or two went by and then he turned to me and said, "I'll say two things about Harry. One, if he said he knows something about your daughter, he really does. He wouldn't fool around with something like that. Maybe he doesn't know as much as you would like, but I'm sure he knows something anyway. And second, if he hasn't told you yet, it means delay won't hurt her." He stopped and looked at me. "That's not necessarily good news I know but....".

He was right of course. If Cindy was dead, delay certainly wouldn't hurt her any more. But then again it could just mean she was safe and not in any danger in which case a further delay wouldn't hurt either.

"Somehow I don't think Harry is through with you yet, Mr. Therman," he added. I had a horrible feeling he was right. I nodded, and thanked him again.

"So long, Mr. Therman, " Simard said. "And good luck!"

I got out of the car and watched him drive off. I looked at it as it receded into the distance and shook my head. God damn you Harry!

I walked back to the Audi and got into the driver's seat. "Harry's left me some more clues," I told them.

"Colin, if you go after these ones, you're a raving idiot! You'd be absolutely idiotic, the biggest dolt that ever walked the earth. It would be proof positive that your brain has turned to mush and that there's absolutely nothing between your ears except some little perverted fascination with rhymes. Dodo brain, that's what I'll call you if you don't just tear the pages up and forget about them."

Linda was looking on with her mouth open. "Alex? Could I put you on retainer by any chance? You know, official reamer out of husbands after really dumb things said or done?"

"Too much work," Alex said. "It would be a full-time job!"

"You see how cleverly he's worked trains into it again," I commented." But you don't have to worry. It's just his parting shot, his having the last word, that's all it is. It's not going to lead on to a new quest. Nothing like that." It was a lie of course because I knew as sure as I was alive that it was going to lead to something else. The picture was just the beginning. Harry wasn't finished with me – Simard was right about that.

"You're sure that's the end of it, are you?" Alex asked.

"Look," I said. "I found the girl, so quit your carping."

"You found the girl? All by your little lonesome? My aren't you the clever one!"

"Sure I had some help," I said, "but all along, Alex, now come on admit it, all along you were: don't do this and don't do that. I had to struggle the whole time with you."

"Jesus, Colin, what are you talking about! I was the brains right from the start. And who held the flashlight, steadied the ladder and waited helplessly as you crashed around in that building that night? Don't interrupt! And, who was it who put her body on the line so to speak, you know the reptile brain appeal of cleavage to get Jimmy to open up? You would have got nowhere without me and you know it!"

I laughed suddenly, provoking two hostile stares. "Look at us," I said. "Harry has got us quarrelling!"

We sat and smiled, realizing as I had just done, that the messages might have been intended as more than just messages. Bastard, I thought to myself.

"Ok, so to celebrate our team, and the great work that none of us could have done on our own, I'm treating us all to Jennifer's," I said. And I did.

24

SOLVING THE FINAL RIDDLE

I **wasn't sure why** Harry was still playing his games, with poems and riddles, not to mention that weird picture of wreckage. The poem wasn't too hard to figure out. The reference to the Christmas train? That was Whitemouth, a pretty easy answer for anyone who liked trains like me and knew the area. Every year it comes, the CP Christmas train, stopping at special locations for a concert to collect food and money for the needy. Right across the country it goes. I've seen it on nights that are unbelievably cold, arctic in their intensity, the brightly decorated train a wonder in the dark. But where in Whitemouth?

Whitemouth is a pleasant little town on the banks of the Whitemouth River, and bisected by the CP mainline, which runs right beside the main street. It was first settled in about 1880 and at one time even boasted Manitoba's first woman doctor. The highway reached it in 1929 and was paved in 1936. Today the town is mostly a service centre for surrounding farmers and contains the High School that Stephanie Shawcross and Jimmy Case and yes Harry Cunningham attended and where Betty Kingsford taught. It also has a museum consisting of a rather strange collection of old farm equipment, a railroad caboose and a couple of buildings.

I figured this was what Harry meant in his message but I didn't understand the bit about keys yet. Was there a piano there I wondered, and even if there were, how could that unlock anything? And the bit about computers indicated it was something before computers but related to them in a way. What came before computers? Adding machines did, but that couldn't be it. I didn't know the answer but wasn't unduly worried, realizing that I'd probably figure it out when I came across whatever it was that was in the museum that Harry was thinking about. But getting into the museum was going to be difficult. The problem is that it's purely a volunteer organization and there's precious little call for visiting museums outside the tourist season, and the off-season around here lasts most of the year. I had two choices: wait until summer again or try to roust someone into giving me a special tour. I opted for the latter. It took me the better part of a week, passed from person to person, to find the right individual who could arrange for me to tour the museum.

It was early November by the time I got inside the two buildings that were part of the exhibits there. One was an old house, the building I had thought the most likely to contain whatever it was that Harry had arranged for me, but it proved disappointing, simply a few rooms with old furniture, a glimpse at the somewhat rudimentary furnishings typical of a place around the time the town was settled. The initially less interesting building was a barn-like structure of no interest in itself. Downstairs were china, old books, posters, and so forth. Upstairs was a collection of old typewriters. As soon as I saw them, well of course I realized they were what had brought me here. I counted 17 of them, 9 on one side of the table and 8 on the other. Machines with keys, that's what they were, and something wrong with some of them, I suspected, letters substituted for other letters. What the hell was Harry up to now, I wondered.

After he'd finished turning on all the baseboard heaters, the young man in attendance told me that the typewriters had been collected by a local man who had donated them to the Museum as a stipulation of his will. He had rescued them from being thrown out over a number of years he told me. "There's a pamphlet somewhere I'm sure," he said. "It lists the makes and their dates." He went off to find it. I pulled up a chair and sat down in front of one of the machines and put a sheet of paper in it, then struck the keys, going through the alphabet letter after letter: abcdefghijklmnopqrstuvwxyz. Well nothing wrong with that one. The second machine produced this: sbcdefhijklmopqratuvwxyz. This time the a key produced an s when it struck the paper in the machine, and the s key returned the favour, producing an a. One or two of the machines had no ribbons, so couldn't be tested, but I assumed that Harry had taken that into account. How had he set this up I wondered? It must have been a lot of bother, surely.

I continued around the table, testing the machines by typing out the alphabet and eventually found that seven of them had letter substitutions.

By then the attendant had returned, having failed to find the brochure. "Someone must have stuck it away somewhere," he said.

I showed him how the machines had been altered. "The police chief from Falcon ever come here?" I asked him. "Mr. Harry Cunningham?"

His mouth dropped open. "How did you know! He came a month ago," he said. "Told me he needed to check out the machines. I thought it was a crime he was trying to solve. I didn't know he was fooling around with the machines. But he left something, said to show it to whoever mentioned his name in connection with the typewriters."

"Oh Harry likes his games all right!" I told the young man as he handed me an envelope containing a sheet of paper with the following written on it:

Δρσε θε. Ψηρεφσν, θε φστ Ι χσλλ τθπ Χθλρ νθω? Τθπ ησφρ
δθνρ ωρλλ σνδ Ι χθνγεσψπλσψρ τθπ. Βτ νθω τθπ ωιλλ βρ σνγετ
ωιψη φρ, σνδ χθναιδρε φρ οπιψρ ρφιλ. Ι χσν□ψ υεθφιδρ τθπ ωιψ
η σ χθνϖρααιθν, Ι□φ απερ τθπ φπαψ εεσλιζρ ψησψ, βπψ Ι χσν
υρεησυα ασψιαϖτ αθφρ θϖ φθπε χπειθαψψ □

Μιφφτ ησδ ψθ δθ νθψηινγ ψθ ωιν Αψρυησνιρ, νθψηινγ σ
ψ σλλ. Βπψ Ι λθφρδ ηρε ψθθ, σνδ Ι ψειρδ αθ ησεδ ψθ ωιν ηρε.
Σϖψρε σλλ Ι ωσα σ βρψψρε φσν. Σνδ Μιφφτ ωσα ωρσκρε ψ
ησν αηρ ερσλιζρδ, ησδ σ λσζτ αψερσκ ιν ηιφ ψησψ ωθπλδ η
σφρ ηρε δθων. Βπψ Αψρυησνιρ διδν□ψ ωσνψ φρ. Αθ, ιν ψηρ
ψιφρ ηθνθεδ ωστ θϖ ψηινγα, Ι φσδρ απερ ψησψ ιϖ χθπλδν□
ψ ησφρ ηρε, ωρλλ ψηρν νριψηρε χθπλδ Μιφφτ.

Μιφφτ ηασ ψθαλδ τθπ Ι□φ απερ ωησψ ησυυρνρδ τθ ηιφ. Η
ρ ψθπγηψ ιψ θσα Αψρυησνιρ θϖ χθθεαρ, σα ιϖ αηρ χθπλδ δθ α
θφρψηινγ λικρ ψησψ! Ηρ ωσα αθ γπλλιβλρ, βρλιρφρδ ρφρετψηι
νγ Ι ψθλδ ηιφ.

Ι ωσα χθνψρνψ ωιψη ηθω ψηινγα ψπενρδ θπψ. Μιφφτ ωσα
ωσλκινγ ωθπνδρδ σνδ Αψρυησνιρ ωσσα δρσδ, Βπτ ψηρν ιψ χσ
φρ ψιφρ ϖθε φρ ψθ λρσφρ Ωραψ Ησωκ σνδ ςσλχθν. Ι χθπλδρν□
ψ λρσφρ ωιψη πνϖινιαηρδ βπααινραα. Αθ Ι ϖθπνδ τθπ σνδ υθι
ντρδ τθπ ιν ηια διερχψιθν. Μιφφτ κιλλρδ Αψρυησνιρ σνδ ψηρν
ηρ κιλλρδ ηιφαρλϖ, ψησνκα τθ τθπ. Ψησψ ια ϖιψψψινγ αθφρη
θω, σ νρσψ χθνχλπαιθν ψθ ψηρ βπααινραα.

Υρεησυα φθπ ϖρρλ παρδ, αλλιρδ αθμρηθω βτ τθπε πνωιψψ
ινγ υσεψ ιν ψηια υλστ θϖ φινρ. Βπψ εμρμβρε ψηια: ψηρ βιγγρα
ψ φιχψιμ ιν ψηια δεσμσ ια φρ, ψηρ βθτ αηρ αηθπλδ ησφρ μσεει
ρδ βπψ νρφρε ωθπλδ. Σνδ ψηρ θπψχθφρ θϖ ψηιρ ασδ αψθετ ωσ
α ινρφιψσβλρ, ωιψη θε ωιψηθπψ τθπ. Πμυο νρξψ ψιφρ,
    Ησεετ
    ps. There are two ways of doing this, a hard way and an easier
way.

A bit verbose for Harry, I thought. And what was I supposed to do with it? The letter substitutions weren't going to help me with this gobbledygook, that was for sure. It looked vaguely Cyrillic, Greek. And two ways of unscrambling it presumably – what did he mean by that? I thought to myself that there was clearly something wrong with Harry besides his penchant for getting other people to do his dirty work. The encrypted message and business with the typewriters seemed over-elaborate and unnecessary now that I was through with Stephanie. Why did he want to dress up what he wanted to tell me in these silly games, or did he think somehow that this was how he could keep me interested? Didn't he realize that hinting he knew something about Cindy was quite enough for me? Maybe he wasn't as sure of himself as he wanted me to think he was. I shook my head. I knew nothing about what made Harry tick, that was the truth of the matter. I'd only seen his sinister side, his weird side, but Simard had told me he was a good cop, effective with people and honest.

I turned to leave but something made me hesitate, a sense that Harry had one more message for me, wasn't quite finished with his silly nonsense. Acting on a hunch, I lifted each machine up one by one and sure enough, under the tenth one was a small brown envelope. It was sealed and had my name on it. I picked it up and put it in the pocket of my parka.

I thanked the attendant for his help and drove home. It had started to snow. I'd not thought to put a snow brush in the Audi yet so had to use my sleeve to brush snow off the windows. The wind was driving the snow hard across the road in places, producing near white-out conditions. The Audi was sure footed but I kept the speed down.

When I got home I looked at the message Harry had left for me but just shook my head. I didn't have a clue how to proceed. Fortunately I've got smart friends, so I scanned the message and sent it to Arthur with a request that he see what he could make of it. Almost immediately he called me.

"It's in symbol font," he said. "If there was a good way to get it into machine readable form it would save you a lot of work, but OCR's not accurate enough. You're just going to have to retype it in an English font. There's a Wikipedia article that shows you how to do that. I'll send the URL by email. But there's still something funny about it – it doesn't come out in anything that makes sense."

I laughed. "Well it was written by Harry, so of course it doesn't!" I responded. "But what does he mean by the easy way, do you think?"

"He probably meant OCR – optical character recognition, but it's just not good enough, that's the truth of the matter, not for something that looks as if it is still encrypted. You wouldn't be able to know if you had it right or not and that's fatal."

I had a vague idea of what he was talking about, but didn't see much point in pressing him for clarity at that point, so I thanked him and rang off. The email arrived a moment later and I got to work on the keyboard. I can only say it was tedious, boring and tiresome and there was only one thing to be thankful for - that the message wasn't even longer than it was! The result of my painstaking keyboarding exercise was this:

Drse Je. Yhrejsn, qe jst I csll tqp Cqlin nqw? Tqp hsfr dqnr wrll snd I cqngesyplsyr tqp. Bt nqw tqp will br snget wiyh jr, snd cqnaidre jr opiyr rfil. I csn'y ueqfidr tqp wiyh s cqnvraaiqn, I'j aper tqp jpay eeslizr yhsy, bpy I csn urehsua asyiavt aqjr qv fqpe cpeiqayy.

Mijjt hsd yq dq nqyhing yq win Ayruhsnir, nqyhing sy sll. Bpy I lqfrd hre yqq, snd I yeird aq hsed yq win hre. Svyre sll I wsa s bryyre jsn. Snd Mijjt wsa wrskre yhsn ahr erslizrd, hsd s lszt ayersk in hij yhsy wqpld hsfr hre dqwn. Bpy Ayruhsnir didn'y wsny jr. Aq, in yhr yijr hqnqed wst qv yhinga, I jsdr aper yhsy iv cqpldn'y hsfr hre, wrll yhrn nriyhre cqpld Mijjt.

Mijjt has yqald tqp I'j aper whsy hsuurnrd tq hij. Hr yqpghy iy qsa Ayruhsnir qv cqpear, sa iv ahr cqpld dq aqjryhing likr yhsy! Hr wsa aq gplliblr, brlirfrd rfretyhing I yqld hij.

I wsa cqnyrny wiyh hqw yhinga ypenrd qpy. Mijjt wsa wslking wqpndrd snd Ayruhsnir wssa drsd, Bpt yhrn iy csjr yijr vqe jr yq lrsfr Wray Hswk snd Vslcqn. I cqpldrn'y lrsfr wiyh pnviniahrd bpaainraa. Aq I vqpnd tqp snd uqintrd tqp in hia diercyiqn. Mijjt killrd Ayruhsnir snd yhrn hr killrd hijarlv, yhsnka tq tqp. Yhsy ia viyying aqjrhqw, s nrsy cqnclpaiqn yq yhr bpaainraa.

Urehsua fqp vrrl pard, allird aqmrhqw bt tqpe pnwiyying usey in yhia ulst qv jinr. Bpy emrmbre yhia: yhr biggray ficyim in yhia desms ia jr, yhr bqt ahr ahqpld hsfr mseeird bpy nrfre wqpld. Snd yhr qpycqjr qv yhir asd ayqet wsa inrfiysblr, wiyh qe wiyhqpy tqp. Pmuo nrxy yijr,

Hseet

As my friend said, it was still not readable but now I could see how the typewriters in the Whitemouth Museum could help me. I took the alphabets I'd typed on the old machines and made the following letter substitution map:

Original Letter	Substituted letter
A	S
E	R
F	V
J	M
M	J
O	Q
P	U
Q	O
R	E
S	A
T	Y
U	P
V	F
Y	T

Then I went back and painstakingly retyped Harry's email, this time substituting the letters in the original text according to the chart I'd made.

Dear Mr. Therman, or may I call you Colin now? You have done well and I congratulate you. By now you will be angry with me, and consider me quite evil. I can't provide you with a confession, I'm sure you must realize that, but I can perhaps satisfy some of your curiosity.

Jimmy had to do nothing to win Stephanie, nothing at all. But I loved her too, and I tried so hard to win her. After all, I was a better man. And Jimmy was weaker than she realized, had a lazy streak in him that would have let her down. But Stephanie didn't want me. So, in the time-honoured way of things, I made sure that if I couldn't have her, well then neither could Jimmy.

Jimmy has told you I'm sure what happened to him. He thought it was Stephanie of course, as if she could do something like that! He was so gullible, believed everything I told him.

I was content with how things turned out. Jimmy was walking wounded and Stephanie was dead. But then it came time for me to leave West Hawk and Falcon. I couldn't leave with unfinished business. So I found you and pointed you in his direction. Jimmy killed Stephanie and then he killed himself, thanks to you. That is fitting somehow, a neat conclusion to the business.

Perhaps you feel used, sullied somehow by your unwitting part in this play of mine. But remember this: the biggest victim in this drama is me, the boy she should have married but never would. And the outcome of this sad story was inevitable, with or without you.

Until next time,
Harry

I stared at the screen where I'd typed the unscrambled message. I got up from my computer chair and cursed. I wanted to scream, to grab Harry by the throat and throttle him. What poison oozed from his words, what bilious self-justification! There was nothing in the message that I could use against him. The most damaging sentence was his statement that he had made sure nobody could have Stephanie, but that could be interpreted in many ways, was hardly enough to nail his hide to the wall in a court of law. And Harry could just as easily pretend it was all just a game, a game that spiralled out of control perhaps but a game. I'd seen it as such initially, a grand adventure, not realizing I was doing the work of evil, spreading his rot over everything I touched, hounding Jimmy to his grave. Alex had warned me not to make it personal and I truly had thought it wasn't. I could see how stupid that idea was, because my own daughter had been an unseen presence all the time, her ghost egging me on at every step. The other hateful thing was that he had mentioned Cindy, by using that number on his first email, but he'd given me nothing more about her until right at the end and with a clear indication that it was going to be a long while before he actually got around to telling me anything useful about her. It was just another cruel way of using me, giving me the hope that I might learn something about my daughter, only to let me down in the end and then finish with that reminder once again that maybe just maybe he did actually know something about what had happened to her.

I sent Alex the unscrambled message by email then took out the envelope I'd taken from under one of the old typewriters. I turned it over in my hands. Did I want to open it or not? Clearly, Harry was still at it, still playing games with me. He knew I'd go to the Museum, known I simply couldn't resist and so of course he'd left me yet another message or riddle. When would it end? What did he want me to do now? I hadn't told Alex or Linda about the envelope and I wasn't sure I was going to. For the moment, I wasn't sure what I was going to do, so I folded the envelope and put it in my pocket.

25

SCATTERING STEPHANIE'S ASHES

I had one more function to perform before I could put this whole thing behind me. So on a relatively mild morning in November I drove for the last time in the Audi to West Hawk. The weather had warmed up somewhat and the snow had mostly melted off the road, leaving a few treacherous patches of ice and some pockets of snow still. The road was deserted, with not another vehicle the entire trip, just me, the road and the sunny day.

The marina had closed for the season but after some hard arm-twisting the man who ran it had agreed to make a boat available for me that day. I parked above Crescent Beach, the snow not yet deep enough to prevent me. It looked nothing like it had in the summer, the sand deserted and cold, the water grey and uninviting. Nothing moved out there except the waves.

I'd asked for a boat I could row, not wanting to disturb the moment with the noise of an engine. I pulled against the oars out to where the divers go. I thought about Stephanie and how she had loved life, how she had come driving down the road that day, unaware of the fate that awaited her, the evil lurking around the corner and over the hill. I had found her grave, discovered her killer and, as Harry said, hounded him to his death. I took the small urn and unscrewed the top and then emptied half the contents onto the water, watching some of the grey dust whirl away and some of it settle on the surface of the water. I don't believe in heaven, or hell for that matter, but at that moment I wished there was a heaven for Stephanie and Jimmy and a different place for Harry.

I rowed back to the dock, thanked the attendant for coming out on this cold day, gave him a generous tip and got back into the Audi. I looked one last time at the lake andn the sand and drove away.

I had one more call to make. The pond where Jimmy had dragged her car wasn't an ideal place for a grave, but it was where she had lain for 40 years and it really wasn't all that bad. You couldn't see it now, but in the spring the trees would come into leaf and new saplings would grow where they had been cut down to get the machinery in here. Birds would nest, swallows perhaps flit across the surface of the pond. Dragonflies would hatch and the summer would come, and then the winter and so the seasons would pass. And it was away from the traffic, the rushing hordes of tourists, none of whom would ever set foot here. I opened the urn once more and scattered the rest of her ashes onto the water. Goodbye Stephanie I said aloud. I thought to myself that perhaps someday someone somewhere would do something similar for my daughter. As I thought that I had a sudden feeling that Cindy was with me, standing beside me, that I could reach out and touch her. I wanted desperately to hang on to the feeling, not daring to move, but the sensation, the physical sense of her lasted only for a few seconds, then faded away. And then I started to cry. I wept for my daughter, I wept for Stephanie and I wept even for Jimmy. And as I cried, I took the envelope that Harry had left for me out of my pocket and moved my hands to start to tear it up and then suddenly stopped. I wanted so badly to destroy it, to scatter the pieces, I really did. I wanted to stop playing Harry's games, to get off the treadmill he had me on, to be free of him forever. But of

I couldn't. Not while there was still hope of finding out what he knew about Cindy, if indeed he knew anything at all.

Perhaps there was nothing in the envelope, and it would turn out to be a last cruel joke from Harry, but I couldn't risk it, and so I opened it.

Dear Colin. I believe Cindy was kidnapped, mistaken for someone else whose parents her kidnappers wanted to intimidate. There is some evidence that Russians were involved. I'm sorry but that is all I can say for the moment. I'm going away now for a year or so and cannot deal with this while I'm away. When I return, I will have another task for you, this one related to your daughter, although you will be skeptical at first that there is any connection. After that, I promise you I will tell you all I know about your daughter. It will not solve the puzzle of her disappearance but will, I hope, put you in a position where you may be able to do so.
    Until then,
    Harry

I could hardly believe what I was reading! Kidnapping? Russian involvement? In Pinawa! That could only mean it was tied in somehow to the nuclear program at Whiteshell.

I thought again about what John Simard had said – that Harry wouldn't endanger Cindy by delaying telling me critical information. Again, that could be bad or good news. If he knew Cindy was dead, wouldn't he just tell me? Or was it just too valuable as leverage until I had done whatever this next task he mentioned was?

In a way I now had more information than I really wanted, enough to start snooping around, but undoubtedly not enough to solve the mystery or Harry would certainly not have told me what he did. I cursed the man again. Why did he torment me like this? He'd watched Jimmy for 40 years, gloating all the time, so torturing me was hardly beyond him!

Still, I had something to go on. There can't have been that many young women who went to Pinawa Collegiate at the same time as Cindy. I should be able to make a short list and then try to figure out whose parents might be of interest to the Russians.

I walked back to the car, got in and started the engine. Harry was out there still and I vowed that if I ever caught up with him I would do something to get back at him. I had no idea what but I would find something, I was sure of that. I had set out expecting an adventure but had encountered evil instead. That was the way of the world sometimes, I suppose. My daughter, too, had probably met evil somewhere, somehow. I didn't think Harry had had anything to do with it, but I had a hunch he really did know something about it and that he really wasn't finished with me.

I shivered suddenly. It was time to go. I put the Audi in gear and moved back onto the road and drove for home.

Epilogue

In late January of the following year I wrote a letter to the Whitemouth school board. I told them that a miscarriage of justice had taken place many years ago and that they were in a position to do something about it. I explained to them the sad history of Stephanie Shawcross and Jimmy Case and how Harry Cunningham was undoubtedly responsible for both of their deaths, one 40 years ago, the other just last year. Harry was the Chief of Police of Falcon Lake detachment and has now disappeared, I explained and it was undoubtedly he who had spread the false rumours about improprieties between Betty Kingsford and her students. I told them that I had come to know Betty quite well, had discovered and benefited from her incredibly detailed memories of every class she ever taught and that it was amply evident that she had been a dedicated and inspired teacher, the kind money simply can't buy. At the time the school board acted shamefully, as did her union, in failing to protect her. Everybody just wanted the fuss to die down. Nobody was interested in finding out the truth. Betty was dispensable. And so she was pensioned off, fobbed off with a trifling payment and told to leave. It was that or be sacked for cause. She had no chance of finding another teaching job after that.

I told them that I didn't expect them to turn back the clock; nobody could do that, but some gesture of appreciation after all these years, some indication that she was respected and admired still would be a simple way of undoing some of the damage done many years ago. It was high time to neutralize some of Harry's harm.

I received no reply until early June when an invitation to attend the Graduation ceremonies at Whitemouth arrived. There was no letter or note with it explaining why I had been invited, but when I read the venue I noticed, as a final item among the list of presentations and awards, the Betty Kingsford Exemplary Teacher Award. There was a hand-written note beside it that read, "We shall be awarding the first in this new series of awards to Betty Kingsford herself. Perhaps you'd like to say a few words?"

And I thought to myself: perhaps I would.

Postscript.

This is a work of fiction, and while most of the locations are real, they are certainly not always exactly as described in this book. As for the characters and the events, they are purely the product of my imagination and thus entirely fictitious.

Over the years Jennifers in Seven Sisters has gone through many changes. Currently, it is operating as a take-out diner in the summer only, but still provides the same good food and economical prices as always. The building it used to occupy is now an Italian restaurant.

The strange yellow brick building Colin and Alex broke into in this story no longer exists. I discovered this when I went to photograph it again for the cover of this book, only to find that it had been torn down. And as for the Water Rat, well if it does exist, it's even harder to find than it was for Colin and Alex!

The story of Colin Therman's search for his missing daughter, Cindy, continues in three more books: The Morning Light Conspiracy, Book 2 of Finding Cindy; The Murder House, Book 3 of Finding Cindy; and Finding Cindy, the newly published final book in the saga.

If you'd like to write to me you can send snail mail to The Write Luke, PO Box 684, Pinawa, MB, R0E1L0. My email address is: michaelowenluke@gmail.com

www.ingramcontent.com/pod-product-compliance
Lightning Source LLC
Chambersburg PA
CBHW021309250626
47155CB00002B/457